LOVE

Rekindled

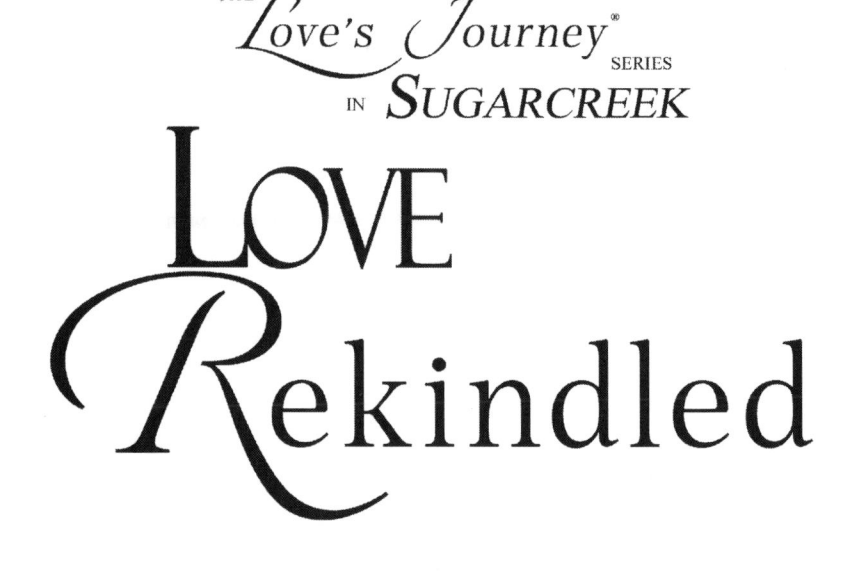

THE *Love's Journey*® SERIES
IN *SUGARCREEK*

LOVE *Rekindled*

BY SERENA B. MILLER

LJ EMORY
PUBLISHING

LJ EMORY PUBLISHING

Find more books by Serena B. Miller at *SerenaBMiller.com*
Find her on Facebook, *FB.com/AuthorSerenaMiller*
Follow her on Twitter, *@SerenaBMiller*

The town depicted in this book is a real place, but all characters are fictional. Any resemblances to actual people or events are purely coincidental. Serena B. Miller is not a medical professional nor legal advisor. Any references to medical or legal advice and procedures is purely for entertainment purposes.

Scripture references are from the Holy Bible, King James Version (KJV). The Holy Bible, New International Version®, NIV®. Copyright © 1973, 1978, 1984 by Biblica, Inc.™ Used by permission of Zondervan.

Most foreign words have been taken from *Pennsylvania Deitsh Dictionary: A Dictionary for the Language Spoken by the Amish and Used in the Pennsylvania Deitsh New Testament* by Thomas Beachy, © 1999, published by Carlisle Press.

Front cover photo by Doyle Yoder and DYP inc.
  DYPinc.com - Used by permission.
Author photos by Angie Griffith and KMK Photography
  KMKphotography.com - Used by permission.

Cover & Interior design by CJ Technics

Published by L. J. Emory Publishing
Love's Journey is a registered trademark of L. J. Emory Publishing.
First L. J. Emory Publishing trade paperback edition July 2018

For information about special discounts for bulk purchases, please contact L. J. Emory Publishing, sales@ljemorypublishing.com

Printed in the United States of America

10 9 8 7 6 5 4 3 2 1
ISBN 978-1-940283-37-1
ISBN 978-1-940283-38-8 (Large Print)
ISBN 978-1-940283-39-5 (ebook)

To Steven

God sets the lonely in families,
Psalm 68:6a

Acknowledgements

....

I am blessed with friends who help keep my facts and plots on track.
Thank you from the bottom of my heart to:
Katie Weaver—Amish midwife
Aaron Ellis, MD
Stephanie Miller, RN
Kristie Cordle, RN
Lisa Rothwell, Esq.
Rick Brown, Esq.

My brilliant brainstorming group:
Shelly Bloomfield Ph.D, Connie Laux, and Emilie Richards

And my amazingly supportive family:
Derek, Julie, Hannah, and Johnathan
Caleb, Meaghan, Clara, and Cecily Rose
Jacob and Michaela Miller

Chapter One

....

December 25

Keturah Hochstetler's eyes grew heavy as her buggy swayed down the graveled township road. It was two o'clock in the morning and she was tired to the bone. The dark December sky drizzled rain against the buggy's thin roof and she shivered inside her second-best coat. Even the extra warmth of the soft, black shawl her daughter-in-law had given her could not counter the chilly wind.

The Sugarcreek area was filled with beauty, but it got quite frigid in the winter. She wished she had thought to put a woolen lap blanket in the buggy before leaving home. Heated bricks to put at her feet would have been welcome as well, but the drive was not far. She would be home soon.

Although she was cold on the outside, she felt the warmth of contentment within her heart. She smiled as she remembered the details of the birth. It had gone well. That's all that mattered. At sixty-seven she had less stamina than in her twenties, but bringing babies safely into the world was her greatest joy and a holy profession. The miracle of birth consistently gave her strength.

The buggy gave a lurch as its wheels hit a bump and jarred her wide awake again. The uneven tracks that had been carved into the road by hundreds of iron-shod buggy wheels made for a bumpy ride. Because of that, the Englisch vehicles tended to avoid these back dirt roads around Sugarcreek and she was grateful.

The birth she had attended today was especially gratifying. It had been a long labor. First babies were often reluctant to come out into the world, but the young mother had done well. The baby, a healthy little boy, had such strong lungs that his cries had set the porch dogs to howling in sympathy. She and the baby's grandmother laughed together at the baby boy's indignation over having to leave his cozy spot beneath his mother's heart. Had he waited a few hours longer to make his appearance, he could have been a Christmas baby.

The older women in the extended family, wise in the ways of babies and new mothers, would take over now. They would make certain that the young mother got plenty of nourishing bone broth and other good foods. They would rock the baby so the mother could sleep and recuperate. Things were as they should be in that house, and her responsibility was over for now. She was free to think about her own family and the Christmas celebration they would have today.

She had prepared as much of the food ahead as possible. Her daughters-in-law would bring the rest. Soon their home would be filled with love and laughter. There would be one small wooden toy each for the little ones who would be coming to their home in a few hours. Her husband, Ivan, had made the toys in his wood shop and he was as eager as a child himself, waiting for Christmas morning to see the grandchildren discover their presents. It had been a mild winter so far, but snow was finally predicted and Ivan was still holding on to the hope that by evening he could take the whole family for a sleigh ride.

She could hardly wait to give her husband the gift she had bought for him. The handle of his old straight razor had broken last year. Instead of buying a new one, he had taped it back together and continued to use it to trim the beard away from his mouth and face. It worked fine, he said.

No need to spend money on a new blade.

Then last week they were visiting Lehman's store, and she noticed him lingering over the new straight razors in the display case. He walked away without making a purchase. She could understand why. The razors were shockingly expensive.

Ivan had few wants. It was not often that she had the pleasure of finding the perfect gift for him. While Ivan was engaged in conversation with a clerk about a broken piece he needed to replace on their outdoor hand pump, she managed to slip back to the razor display. With some of her midwife money, she rushed to purchase the best straight razor Lehman's carried. It was made in France and had a lovely bone handle. It cost over two hundred dollars, but it was such good quality she felt it was worth the expense for something he would use daily. It was now hidden away in the bottom of her birthing bag; the one place she knew Ivan would never look. He was going to be so surprised!

The light from the lantern on the back of her buggy swung back and forth, and the sound of the rain and the rhythmic beat of Brownie's hoofs flinging dirt against the undercarriage combined to create a sort of hypnotic lullaby. Only two more miles to go before she could climb into her warm, cozy bed.

Her head nodded and the reins grew slack in her hands. It was not the first time her good horse had taken her home while she dozed.

The sound of a vehicle startled her wide-awake again. Somewhere up ahead a car was coming and the car was very loud. She didn't know much about motor vehicles, but she knew the sound of a bad muffler.

Careful not to slip into the ditch, she guided Brownie to the far right side of the road, making certain to leave enough room for the Englisch vehicle to get past them. Also, up ahead was a sharp curve. She slowed Brownie down so they could stay back, far out of the way until the car got around it.

It sounded like the driver was going too fast for these rain-slicked roads, but what did she know? She was used to driving at the top speed of ten miles per hour.

The sound of a crash startled her.

"Whoa!" She pulled back on the reins, bringing Brownie to a complete stop so she could listen. A car horn was blaring on and on, but the sound of a bad muffler had stopped.

She was neither a doctor nor a nurse but, during her years as a midwife and as the mother of sons who were not always careful, she had learned a great deal about the human body and what to do to stop bleeding or deal with broken bones. She even knew CPR. The fire department in Sugarcreek had sponsored a free class she had faithfully attended.

Hesitating only long enough to draw a deep breath before yelling "Giddyup!" she slapped the reins on Brownie's rump. The old horse was so startled he broke into a gallop.

Chapter Two

....

Ivan Hochstetler was a happy man as he stoked the fire in their black cook stove. The stove and this kitchen was second only to his own good wife in being the heart of the home.

He loved the coziness of long winter days. He and Keturah had been enjoying the hundreds of jars of produce she and their two daughters-in-law had put up during the hot days of August, back when it seemed like the good earth couldn't produce vegetables and fruit fast enough. The richness of the soil they had built up over the years made quite a difference in the robust vegetables the garden gave them.

They were also enjoying the homemade sausages they had canned on their family's butchering day, and they often dug into their bin of fresh, crisp apples and cabbages tucked away beneath insulating straw in the cellar.

Deep winter was a time of rest for the earth and he loved watching the snow replenish his fields with minerals. It was a time of rest for his plow horses, as well. Come spring, he would be careful to allow them to build up their muscles, before giving them harder tasks. It was also a time of rest for a farmer and his family. At least it was a time of rest compared to the twelve- and sixteen-hour days he put in during the other months. When it was planting season or harvest, there weren't enough hours in the day to accomplish everything he needed to do. He was grateful that their youngest son, Noah, was still at home to help.

He and Keturah were hospitable people. Winter was a good time to invite friends and family over in the evenings to enjoy a good visit and much laughter along with giant bowls of popcorn and apple cider.

Yes, Ivan loved winter. He had been storing up farming magazines, seed catalogues, and good books—enough to get him through to spring. He loved to read, but winter was the only time he allowed himself to indulge. He was especially enjoying the small stack of old Zane Grey paperbacks he had picked up at a garage sale last fall. In fact, it was Zane Grey's fault that he was awake right now. That last book had kept him up far into the night. It was one of his many weaknesses; he loved a good story.

He glanced at the clock on the kitchen wall and saw that it was well past one o'clock in the morning. The Yoder girl must be having a difficult birth, poor little thing. Keturah had been gone for nearly eighteen hours.

He listened to the rain on the tin roof of the farmhouse and hoped that the baby was here by now and that his wife had chosen to spend the night with the new mother. Keturah did that sometimes if she was too exhausted to make the drive home, or if there were no other women in the family to take over after the baby arrived. Of course, in their Amish community that sort of thing was rare. In fact, the only time he could remember there not being other women ready to help was when a young mother's sister and mother were delayed by a creek too swollen with flood water to cross.

He was proud of Keturah. Sometimes maybe a little too proud. He tried not to let it show. *Hochmut* was something their people discouraged and with good reason. God did not approve of pride.

And yet, how could a man not be proud of a wife such as Keturah? Even after forty-eight years of marriage, she was still lovely in his eyes, and so smart! Over the years, his wife had read every medical book she could get her hands on. She might not have as broad a knowledge as an Englisch doctor in all things medical, but he would put her knowledge of pregnancy and childbirth up against anyone's.

The rain began to pick up, which was a worry to him. He hoped she didn't try to come back home in this weather, but she might. After all, it was Christmas and their sons' families would be there early.

He heard the creak of floorboards overhead. Noah was also up. Probably awakened by the sound of rain on their tin roof. It was always so much louder upstairs.

Noah padded down the stairs in his stocking feet and pajama bottoms, rubbing sleep out of his eyes. "Is *Maam* home yet?"

"Not yet."

"She has been gone a long time. You don't suppose she is outside in this weather, do you?"

"I was wondering the same. Your mother is not always as careful with her health as she should be."

"Mom is tough as nails, *Daett*, and you know it."

"True, but she is such a little thing."

"Whose baby is it this time?"

"The Yoder's middle girl," Ivan said. "Stephen's Martha."

Noah, unmarried but wise in the way of birth from being a midwife's son, brought a jar of instant coffee from the pantry, poured water into the cast-iron kettle, and set it on the stove to boil. "That will be Martha's first baby. We might not see *Maam* again for a while."

***

As she turned the curve, Keturah saw that an old, blue car had collided head-on with the large oak tree that stood in the middle of the bend in the road. The oak tree was old and massive. It had easily withstood the crash. The car was not as fortunate. The windshield was partially knocked out and the car's front end was crumpled. The horn continued to blare.

Brownie pranced nervously as she tried to calm him. As soon as he was steady, she grabbed her flashlight, stepped out of the buggy, and carefully approached the wreck in the rain.

Playing her flashlight over the car, she saw that blood was splattered all over the windshield. Her knees grew weak at the sight, but she mustered her courage and crept closer.

There appeared to be no one in the car except the driver who was slumped, limply, against the door. The driver's face, which was pressed against the window, was a young woman with short, blonde hair, wearing multiple earrings that sparkled against the light from the flashlight.

She wondered why this girl had chosen to disobey the Englisch law. If she had been wearing a seatbelt, she would not have been thrown against the windshield.

"Hello." Keturah knocked on the driver's side window. "Do you need help?"

The girl stirred, opened her eyes, and looked at her blankly.

Keturah tried the door, but it was locked.

"Can you unlock it?"

The girl fumbled with the door, managed to open it, and then toppled out. Keturah caught her before she could hit the ground. Her heart dropped when she saw the girl's hugely-rounded belly. Unless she missed her guess—and she rarely did—the girl was about eight months pregnant. The seatbelt had probably felt uncomfortable against her swollen stomach.

There appeared to be a large gash in the right side of her head. It was hard to tell because of all the blood. She hoped it was not as bad as it appeared.

The girl was agitated and grappled at Keturah's coat. "Don't let him take my baby," she said. "Please..."

She lost consciousness and fell back against the ground.

Keturah hunted for a pulse in the girl's wrist then, growing more frantic, she pressed her fingers against the girl's neck right below her ear.

There was no pulse.

Chapter Three

She had never had to use her firehouse CPR training before, and had hoped she would never need it, but Keturah was grateful for it now as she placed the palms of her cold hands on the girl's sternum and began to push rhythmically as the rain soaked the girl's pink t-shirt.

Two minutes later, she still could not find a pulse. A surge of panic hit. In all her reading about childbirth, she knew that a fetus could only survive for about seven minutes in a dead mother's womb without brain damage or death.

"Come on, come on." Keturah said, as she resumed chest compressions. "Please breathe."

If nothing else, she knew she was forcing the mother's blood to carry the residual oxygen that was still in her lungs to help the baby. There was a chance that the small amount of oxygen might keep it alive a little longer.

The cold drizzle that had accompanied her here began to turn nastier. A wind blew up, showering her and the girl with wet, dead leaves. She prayed for strength and endurance in her fight to keep the mother and baby alive. Her coat and clothing became soaked with rain. The car horn blared on and on. It was nerve wracking, but she was grateful. It might be her only hope of help. She prayed that the sound might cause a neighbor to investigate.

There was a strong smell that clung to the girl's clothes—a food smell.

It reminded her of a niece who had once been employed frying dough-nuts at a bakery. The smell had been so strong, the family complained.

The rain had washed much of the blood away from the girl's face and hair, making it possible for Keturah to see the wound clearer. She nearly recoiled from the severity of it. Unless God sent a miracle, this girl was never going to breathe on her own again.

Now the burning question remained—what about the baby? The precious seven minutes were quickly running out.

Although she possessed much knowledge about the herbs and tinctures that midwives had passed down over the centuries, it did not prevent her from embracing newer technologies. A small Doppler fetal monitoring device was back in her birthing bag in the buggy. It would make it possible for her to check and see if the baby still lived.

She had fervently prayed for God to send help but, as each second ticked away, it had become apparent that the only help He had seen fit to send to this pregnant girl and her child was herself, a tired Amish mid-wife. Her aging knees cried out in pain as she rose and ran to the buggy where she kept her bag filled with supplies.

The rain increased as she slipped on the wet leaves and fell in her hurry to get the birthing bag. As her left knee hit the ground, she cried out from the sharp pain, but immediately scrambled back up and limped to the buggy where she unhooked the battery-operated lantern hang-ing on the back. It would give her better light than the small flashlight she carried. Then she grabbed her birthing bag and rushed back to the mother.

Squatting, she sat the lantern down near the girl. Then she reached into her bag for the tube of ultrasound gel, shoved the denim jacket aside, pushed the girl's pink t-shirt up and smeared some gel on her belly. Then she fumbled for her Doppler monitor and searched for the baby's heartbeat.

There. Right there. She could hear it. The baby lived, and the heart was relatively strong. The irony was not lost on her that she was allowed to own such a technically advanced instrument, but did not have permission to carry a cell phone.

If there was one thing the Amish leadership took seriously—and they took many things seriously—it was trying to be a good example for the young. She understood their church leaders' fear that owning cell phones would be too much of a temptation to their young people. She had heard that many evil things could be accessed on those picture phones, unspeakable things. But oh, what she wouldn't give for a way to call 911 right now.

The thought struck that perhaps this Englisch girl might have a phone. Practically all the young ones she had seen walking down the streets of Sugarcreek had such devices in their hand. Quickly, she searched the girl's pockets. Nothing there. She glanced inside the car. There was nothing there either that she could see, not even a purse.

***

It was half past two in the morning and Ivan could not sleep. He paced the floor of the kitchen, poked at the fire, made himself a cup of tea from the water Noah had put on to boil, then he neglected to drink it. Something did not feel right. He was getting more nervous and upset by the minute. He glanced out the window a dozen times but there was nothing to see.

As the husband of a midwife, he was used to Keturah keeping odd hours. It was part of the sacrifice of being a midwife's family. After tending a difficult birth, she sometimes slept during the day when other wives would be up doing chores. She often came home in the middle of the night or at dawn. The inconveniences were worth it to him because he believed in the importance of his wife's work.

He went out the backdoor to the woodshed and brought in a large armload for the wood box behind the stove, all the time chastising himself for being concerned, but he couldn't help it. He could not shake the feeling that something was amiss. To make matters worse, the wind had kicked up and the rain was intensifying. Ivan knew he should have more faith, but the bad feeling would not go away.

If Keturah were here, she would probably tell him that his problem tonight was reading too many Zane Grey novels. The thought made him smile, but it did not ease his worry.

Noah had gone back to bed, but once again Ivan heard his youngest son stirring upstairs, and then heard his footsteps coming down again. This time Noah was wearing his work shoes.

"I'm not going to be able to sleep until I know *Maam* is okay," the young man said. "Do you mind if I call the Yoders and check on her?"

"They probably won't even hear the telephone in this kind of weather. It is a long way down their lane to their phone shanty."

"That is true, but I have knowledge that the youngest Yoder sister has a cell phone in her possession."

"In spite of the bishop's ban against it?"

"Beth has not yet made her confession, *Daett*," Noah reminded him. "She also owns a car."

Ivan's eyebrows shot up over that revelation. He had always thought the youngest Yoder girl a model of modest Amish womanhood. He hoped she wasn't enjoying her 'running around' time too much. On the other hand, sometimes the wildest Amish teens became the most sober members of their church. Not always, of course, but Ivan had learned not to judge the youngies too harshly.

"I have not seen an automobile parked at the Yoder's farm."

"Her father does not approve and does not want our people seeing it parked in their yard. She pays to keep it in an Englisch neighbor's barn."

"Ach. Her poor father! He must be very worried about her. I am grateful to have only had boys to raise. You have her telephone number?"

"She gave it to me recently." Noah's normally ruddy complexion grew slightly deeper. "I will call her right now if you want me to."

"Please. It would be good to get some sleep tonight," Ivan said. "The family will be here for Christmas in a few hours."

Noah threw on his heavy barn coat, grabbed a flashlight, and walked out to the phone shanty while Ivan watched through the window. The boy had a good heart and had been baptized into the Amish church when he was barely eighteen. Now, he was twenty-six, handsome and strong and, as of yet, none of the young women in the nearby Amish settlements had caught his eye. Now he was interested in a girl who was apparently going through a rebellious stage. A car *and* a cell phone! She probably owned a radio as well and listened to modern music. A dangerous thing.

This was most definitely something to pray about. If she chose not to put away her worldly desires and join the church, things could get bad. If Noah chose to marry her even though he had already joined the church, their people would expect Ivan and Keturah as well as the entire Yoder family to shun the young couple. He could not imagine shunning his youngest son. This could become quite a mess.

Thinking about such a future caused the joy he had felt earlier to evaporate as he watched the wind strip the final leaves from the trees in front of their house. In a few moments, he saw Noah leave their phone shanty and come running toward the house.

"Beth says that *Maam* left over an hour ago!" Noah shouted as he plunged into the kitchen.

It was less than a half-hour buggy ride to their house from the Yoder's.

The two men stared at each other. No words were necessary. Ivan grabbed his coat and both rushed out the door.

Chapter Four

Dr. Michael Reynolds stared at a document lying on his kitchen table. It had never occurred to him that a mere piece of paper could make his stomach cramp, but this one did.

Doc Mike, as the people from Holmes County were beginning to call him, was fit, strong, barely thirty, and could eat cold pizza at midnight and still sleep like a baby. But looking at this document made his stomach churn so badly it was all he could do not to throw up.

It was from Cassie, his wife, who apparently had decided that she would not be moving here to be with him—even though he'd just landed a job he'd dreamed of most of his life, getting to care for farm animals and people's pets in his beloved hometown of Sugarcreek, Ohio.

"I am a corporate lawyer," she reminded him as he packed his bags. "Unless you haven't noticed, Sugarcreek isn't exactly overrun with corporations. Seriously, Michael, you know how hard I've worked to achieve my position at Blackwell, Hart & Cooper. How can you expect me to move to an area where a large percentage of the population thinks it's a sin to litigate?"

"How can you expect me to give up a chance of a lifetime?" he said. "I've admired Doc Taylor my whole life. He's the reason I chose to become a veterinarian in the first place. I will not turn down his wife's offer to take over his practice now that he's gone. The farmers relied on him, and now they need me."

Cassie was curled up on their cream-colored living-room couch with legal papers strewn all about her. Her long, auburn hair was piled on top of her head with a clasp. She was wearing her midnight-blue gown that had probably cost more than one of his Amish friends' prize steers. She was a head-turner in every way, whether dressed for court or padding around the apartment barefoot in her silk nightgown.

Her beauty had made him do a double-take the first time he saw her when they were in college, but her beauty was only part of the reason he had worked so hard to convince her to marry him. She was also the smartest woman he had ever met, and the most disciplined. He had done a competent job working at a local suburban animal clinic, but her rise in the corporate world had been breathtaking.

"There are other vets in the world," Cassie had said. "I'm sure there are tons who would jump at the chance to take over for Dr. Taylor."

"Of course there are." He could still feel the anger that had risen inside him at the mere thought of anyone else taking over old Doc's practice. "But how many vets are fluent in Pennsylvania Deutsch? The fact that I can communicate in their mother tongue will make a huge difference in dealing with the Amish farmers."

"They also speak English," Cassie said. "The fact that you know their other language is no reason for me to give up everything I've fought for. You *know* how hard I've worked. Other lawyers would kill to be in my position."

He had finished packing, gave her a peck on the cheek, and walked out the door without another word.

It was a gamble for him to take on Dr. Taylor's veterinary practice against her wishes, but he didn't feel like he had a choice. Not if he was going to be true to himself. This was the life he wanted. He had wanted it for her too. Living in Sugarcreek would be good for her. He was sure of it. He was also convinced that she would eventually swallow her pride and figure out a way to follow him here.

That's what wives were supposed to do. Follow their husbands. Right?

Even he realized how unreasonable and out-of-date that sort of thinking was but, seriously, it just made good sense to make the move. He owned a lovely old farmhouse in Sugarcreek that his grandfather had left to him. The young Amish couple who had been renting it had recently moved out, so the timing was perfect. This offer from Doc Taylor's widow couldn't have come at a better time. He had been saddened by the news that his mentor had passed away, but ecstatic that Mrs. Taylor had chosen him to take over her husband's work. It would be such a good life for him and Cassie in Sugarcreek. A wonderful life for them.

She had begged to differ.

Cassie was as stubborn as a mule and apparently too proud to make the first move toward a reconciliation. It had been two harsh months of silence between them. Each waiting for the other to capitulate.

Well, it wasn't going to be him who gave in this time. It felt too good to get out of that high rise apartment she had chosen. He hadn't realized how much he truly hated living in the city until he had sunk his roots back into Sugarcreek. He chose to dig in his heels and wait long enough for Cassie to come to her senses.

Instead, she had begun divorce proceedings.

He lay the papers on the kitchen table, furious with her for having forced his hand. Could a marriage truly be destroyed by geography alone? Apparently so.

His grandfather's old wind-up clock in the living room struck twice. Two o'clock! He should have been asleep hours ago.

He grabbed a pen. Better get this thing signed and get the thing in the mailbox. Better get it over with so he could go to sleep. The rest of the day was going to be rough if he didn't get at least a little shut-eye before dawn. A vet had to be awake and ready to go to work early in the morning if he were to keep the respect of this rural community. Dairy farmers, especially, had little sympathy for a veterinarian who slept in when they were up and about their jobs long before dawn.

Chapter Five

....

Keturah quickly began the compressions again, regretting the few precious seconds she had wasted searching for the girl's cell phone.

The CPR instructor who trained her had taught them how to do mouth-to-mouth resuscitation but warned that it was no longer advised. Especially if one was working on a stranger. It had to do with the possibility of contracting life-threatening diseases.

With the seven-minute clock ticking down in her head, Keturah decided to ignore the instructor's warnings. That baby needed oxygen! She bent over the girl, pinched her nose shut, and began to force her own breath into the girl's lungs while she prayed that someone would hear that car horn and come to their rescue.

Once again, she stopped and listened for the baby's heartbeat. It was there, but it was growing fainter.

"*Du net schtauva, li,*" she whispered. "Please don't die, baby."

Sick to her stomach with fear and worry, Keturah made one of the hardest decisions of her life. She held her hands out palms up, and allowed the rain to cleanse them of blood and gel before she reached into her birthing bag for the sturdy surgical scissors she used to cut umbilical cords. They were such a clumsy tool to use for a C-section but it was all she had.

Then she remembered Ivan's gift! She dug deep into the bottom of the bag and pulled out the slim box that held the bone-handled blade.

The well-honed straight razor was as sharp as any doctor's scalpel.

"I am so sorry," Keturah said to the young mother who could no longer hear her. "But I have to do this."

Biting her lip with concentration, she pulled the too-small coat away from the young mother's stomach, lifted the pink t-shirt, and tried to shield the girl's abdomen from the rain with her own body as she opened the razor. From somewhere deep within her, she found the grit to do the unthinkable. With steady hands, she drew the blade across the dead girl's skin.

"Lord, please help," she said, as she exposed the thin membrane in which the baby lay.

Chapter Six

Michael's hand hovered over the line beside the red X. The letter that had come with the divorce papers stated that Cassie did not want to keep anything that belonged to him. There would be no litigation over community property. He was welcome to whatever furniture or household items they had purchased together that he wanted.

There were no children to fight for; no beloved pets for which they needed to work out visitation. Their lives had been so sterile there wasn't so much as a goldfish or potted plant to discuss. He had his money. She had hers. He had his IRAs. She had hers along with her 401Ks. No fuss. No muss. If she had her way, a simple document and a trip to see a judge would sever their relationship as neatly as if it had never existed.

In a weird way, it made sense. Cassie made certain that their apartment had absolutely no clutter. She was brutal about cutting out unnecessary items. He did not know why, except she'd once mentioned that her mother was a sloppy housekeeper and it had bothered her. She did not want to be like her mom.

So Cassie had created a determinedly minimalistic lifestyle. They did not have keepsakes or family heirlooms lying about. Unwanted clothing did not linger in the back of their closets. She said it was the only way she could manage to live and still put in the hours she needed to succeed at her law firm.

Friends were also something that seemed to fall into the category of "clutter." They had never indulged in the habit of inviting other people to their home to share a meal. There was no sitting around with pie and coffee, talking and laughing with people they cared about, and who cared about them.

They were young professionals who had careers to build. That sort of thing could come later, Cassie said. When they were better established. Michael was about as well-established as he wanted to be at the suburban animal clinic where he worked alongside two other veterinarians. He would have enjoyed having friends over. Eating popcorn and watching a movie with another couple—even if that other couple had kids. Cassie said that, for now, she just did not have the time.

It occurred to him for the first time that perhaps the reason he had felt so strongly about moving back to Sugarcreek had less to do with the desire to take over Dr. Taylor's practice than it did with the fact that he was so *lonely*.

As he thought about the past five years, he realized that the more responsibility Cassie was being given at work the more ruthless she became about a clutter-free life.

Apparently, her determination to live a minimalist lifestyle was part of why she was so willing to end their marriage. Having a husband had become inconvenient; superfluous.

As he stared at the legal papers, he was surprised to discover that he would have preferred the wrangling and fighting in which other couples seemed to engage when they split up. At least it would have felt more… more what? Human? This felt so soulless. So bloodless.

Laying down the pen, he took a swig of Pepto Bismol and grimaced as he swallowed the sweet, pink stuff. The document could wait until morning. He would sign it then. Maybe. On the other hand, perhaps he'd wait a few days. Make Cassie sweat a little before giving in to her demand. Force her to pay attention to what she was doing. Force her to pay attention to *him*!

On the other hand, maybe she was just calling his bluff. Maybe she didn't really want a divorce. Maybe she did still love him. Perhaps she even missed him. It would be just like her to do something like that. Ask for a divorce to shock him into coming back.

Well, maybe he needed to call her bluff as well.

The thought struck that perhaps they should have gone through the premarital counseling their minister had insisted on. There had been that short period of time while they were dating, when they had made a stab at going to church.

The old preacher had an annoying policy of requiring six sessions of premarital counseling before he would perform a couple's marriage ceremony. He wouldn't budge on it. The counseling also involved reading certain books together, and filling out pages of questionnaires.

The minister was in his seventies. His requirements had felt old-fashioned and irritating. They were young and in love and closing in on graduate degrees. The idea of spending that much time talking about their marriage felt like a waste of precious time—especially since they knew exactly what they were doing.

Michael shook his head at their naivety. They were convinced that they were way too smart to make the same mistakes that other, lesser, couples made.

They chose to forego a traditional wedding. Cassie had never really wanted one anyway. Instead of a wedding, they went to the courthouse. Fifteen minutes flat and they were husband and wife. Such a great saving of time!

He remembered how they had gone to their after-wedding dinner at McDonalds and laughed about how surprised the old preacher would be when they showed up at church wearing their wedding bands.

Except that never quite happened. Skipping church turned out to be a great saving of time as well.

Unfortunately, practicing law on the professional level she had chosen to do had changed Cassie. It had made her harder and even more disciplined.

He wandered around the house, hurt and angry and unable to settle down. Even so, he was grateful no farmer had called. It would be miserable to have to make a barn call tonight. The wind had begun to howl as it whipped around the corners of his home.

While pacing the floor in his bare feet and pajamas, he heard hoof beats. Looking out the window, he could just make out two horses galloping past his house. One was about the shape and size of his next-door neighbor's. He was fairly certain that was Ivan's horse, and beside him... yes, that was definitely Noah on his new prize mare.

He glanced at his watch. Two-thirty in the morning. What were those two doing out in this kind of weather? Ivan and Noah were careful with their animals. They did not run their horses like that for fun. Something must be bad wrong and, if so, he needed to be ready to help. That was the way it was between him and the Hochstetlers and it always had been. He ran upstairs to throw on some clothes.

Chapter Seven

Ivan and Noah had barely gone a mile before they heard a car horn blaring in the distance. Ivan urged his horse to go even faster. When he and Noah rounded the curve, his heart nearly stopped as he saw the crooked headlights from a wrecked car. Keturah's buggy was sitting nearby, wreathed in shadows, but apparently intact.

The increasing rain made visibility difficult but, as they drew nearer, he could see a lantern burning, illuminating a woman's figure huddled on the ground. She was bending low over something that he couldn't see, but suddenly he heard the pitiful wailing of a newborn baby.

"Keturah!" he shouted as he jumped off his horse and ran toward her. "Are you all right?"

As long as he lived, he would never forget the face she turned toward him. He had never seen such intense grief on his beloved's face.

"I had to do it," Keturah said. "I had to. I could not let the baby die, and there was no one here to help."

It was then that his stunned eyes took in the rest of the scene. A young woman was lying motionless in the rain, her t-shirt stained with blood. In Keturah's arms was a newborn baby. She was bent over, trying to shield it from the rain.

"I tried to keep her alive." Keturah had wrapped the baby in the long, white, birthing apron she had still been wearing. She rocked back and forth now with the newborn in her arms. "I tried so hard to keep the mother alive, but the baby's heartbeat was getting weaker."

Rain continued to soak her black bonnet, her hair, her coat. Rain had turned the area around her into a puddle of ugly mud. Rain dripped from the brim of his hat as he tried to wrap his mind around the horror his wife had just gone through. Had Keturah actually done life-and-death surgery in the dark of night, on this backcountry road, alone?

"I'll stay here and guard the woman's body," Noah said. He did something to the car to make the horn stop blaring. "You take Maam and the babe home. Then call someone to come."

Ivan thanked God for the gift of his son's strength and good sense. Alone, he might have continued to stand there in the rain several more seconds, gaping at the terrible scene before him.

"I will call the Sugarcreek police," Ivan said, "once I get your mother and the baby safely home."

"Help me," Keturah held out one hand. "I can't get up. I've been kneeling here for too long. My knees have locked up."

Ivan took the baby from her hands and cradled it while Noah simply gathered his mother into his strong arms and carried her to the buggy. Ivan saw that her warm black shawl lay on the ground where it had fallen near her. He quickly wrapped the wet shawl around the cocoon Keturah had made around the baby with her apron. The precious little thing continued to cry with all her might, her tiny chin quivering.

"Oh, little one," Ivan soothed. "You are safe. We have you now. There is no reason to cry."

No reason to cry at all... except that they had to leave its mother lying in the mud. Sometimes, life could be unbearably sad.

With Noah's hand on his elbow steadying him, he mounted the step into the buggy with the baby in one arm.

Once Ivan was seated, he naturally started to hand the baby to Keturah, then he realized she was shivering too badly to safely hang on to it. He pulled her against him, hoping the heat from his body might help. Then he cradled the small bundle firmly with one hand and grasped the reins in the other. With the apron and shawl wrapped tightly around it, with rain no longer hitting its little face, the baby's cries began to subside.

"Someone will come to you soon, son," Ivan shouted over his shoulder as they hurried away. "And may *God* be with that poor dead mother and this child."

Chapter Eight

Keturah continued to shiver. If Ivan had done what he wished, he would have made Brownie run all the way back home, but he could not allow that. With this dirt road getting muddier and muddier, the best he could safely manage was a hard trot without the risk of sliding into a ditch. Still, it was hard to go slow when all he wanted to do was get his wife and this newborn infant home to their warm kitchen. Keturah had a tendency to catch colds and, when she did, they often settled in her chest for a long time. He did not want her to have to deal with pneumonia on top of the trauma she had already been through tonight.

"Did the woman wreck her car trying to avoid you?" He was fearful what the answer would be. If his mother had crashed trying to miss Keturah's buggy, there could be repercussions from the Englisch community as well as the woman's family.

Keturah pressed closer against his side. He wished he could put his arm around her, but his hands were both already full. He glanced down at the baby and saw that the tiny thing was already sucking its little fist.

"No," she said, her teeth chattering. "Before."

Ah, Keturah had not caused the wreck. That was one blessed thing. There were locals who were greatly annoyed by the slow-moving Amish buggies and wanted them banned.

"God's will," he said.

"Yes." She gripped the collar of her wet coat closer together and hunched against the cold. "God's will."

If at all possible, it was Ivan's habit to come see to the horse's needs whenever Keturah came home. After a birthing, she would often be drained of energy and would need to go straight to bed. Ivan would unhitch the buggy and make certain that Brownie was rewarded with extra oats, an apple or two, and a good long drink. Even at night, Ivan had trained himself to come wide awake the second he heard the buggy's wheels on their graveled driveway.

This time, he left poor Brownie to stand in the rain as he took his wife and the infant into the house. He had momentarily considered stopping by the phone shanty at the end of the driveway first to make that emergency phone call but, with Keturah shivering beside him, he knew that would be unwise. His highest priority was to get her and the baby warm and out of the weather. The dead mother would not be helped by his haste, and Noah would not be harmed by a few extra minutes of standing watch.

He thanked God for so many things as he helped Keturah down from the buggy. He gave thanks for a well-trained, gentle-spirited horse that would not run off if he left it a few minutes to get his wife settled. He gave thanks for this courageous woman who had just performed an operation that many strong men would not have had the stomach to do. He thanked God for his three good sons who would drop everything to come and help if he or their mother needed them, and he gave thanks for the warm kitchen and the soft rocking chair in front of the stove into which he quickly settled his wife who was trembling almost uncontrollably.

"I must make that phone call," he said. "I will be quick."

He was not sure Keturah was strong enough right now to safely hold the baby on her lap. He did not want to set it on the floor to wail at her feet until he got back. There was nothing he could think to do except continue to cradle it against his chest while he ran to the phone shanty.

Halfway to the phone shanty, Ivan saw Michael, their good neighbor, running toward him through the rain.

"What's wrong," Michael said. "What's happened?"

Ivan had seldom ever been happier to see anyone in his life.

"Here." Ivan handed Michael the baby. "She is less than an hour old, so take her inside. I must go call 911. Noah is out there alone."

"Something's happened to Noah?"

"Take the baby back into the house," Ivan said. "I'll explain…"

He did not finish the sentence because Michael was already running toward the house. He breathed a sigh of relief. Keturah and the baby would be in excellent hands with Michael looking out for them.

Ivan entered his phone shanty and dialed the number. As he waited to be connected to help, he gave thanks for one more thing, the great gift of having Michael as their neighbor again. It was no exaggeration to say that he and Keturah had practically raised the boy.

They were so happy when Michael chose to come back, move into his grandfather's house next door, and take over Doc Taylor's practice. It was wonderful to have him so close, although it did seem odd that, after two months, his wife had not yet joined him. Nor, to Ivan's knowledge, had Michael gone to Columbus to see her. He could not see how that could be good. He felt as helpless as any father who suspected one of his children might be silently suffering.

The list of things to pray about was getting very long, Ivan thought, as the 911 operator answered.

Chapter Nine

Rachel was not thrilled that she had to work the nightshift, but Kim Whitfield had a cold, and the other two officers wanted to celebrate Christmas with their families on Christmas Eve, leaving her to do patrol and Ed to take care of the office. She and her husband, Joe, preferred to open gifts on Christmas morning, so she volunteered. When she had left for work, Joe and her seven-year-old stepson, Bobby, were cozied up with cocoa and popcorn watching *A Charlie Brown Christmas*.

With any luck, they would fall asleep after the movie and stay asleep until she got off work at seven in the morning. Joe had promised to keep him from tearing into his gifts before she got home. Bobby was a bit of a handful. She did not envy Joe having that job.

It generally wasn't too hard to keep Sugarcreek safe. To her knowledge, the worst thing that had ever happened in the town was when her father—also a cop—had been shot and killed while trying to stop a bank robbery. Apart from that, patrolling tended to be an occasional DUI. Sometimes, she would pull over a buggy if it was meandering a little too suspiciously down the road. Teenagers were still teenagers even if they were Amish.

She was proud of the fact that, from a recent report that measured the livability of a town, Sugarcreek had received an A+ for their low crime rate. This was something for which she would like to take credit, but she knew it was much easier to be a cop if one worked in an area that was predominately made up of hard-working, family-focused, Amish and Mennonite people.

Cleveland had been her home for a few years until she responded to a desperate domestic violence call that went bad and she ended up in the hospital. She knew exactly how lucky she was to have this job. Still, every so often, she longed for slightly grittier police work than what she was doing now. Something that would require a bit more of her training. After all, she had finished at the top of her class at the police academy.

One of the many nice things about being a cop in Sugarcreek, however, was having the freedom to check on her three Amish aunts anytime she wanted to. They ran a small Bed and Breakfast only a mile outside of town called the Sugar Haus Inn, and were getting on in age. There was Bertha, the oldest, then Lydia, and sweet Anna, their younger sister who had Down Syndrome. All three were still quite viable, although Anna had to be careful about her heart condition.

She could not imagine herself living without them in her life. They were the ones who had picked up the pieces after her father was killed. They had raised her with gentleness and compassion and she would be grateful to them forever—even if they were still upset she'd chosen to become a cop like her father instead of joining the church.

Often, while on patrol, she drove past their inn just to reassure herself that all was well. Sometimes, she'd stop in for a few minutes for a cup of coffee and a piece of one of Lydia's pies or cakes. All somehow felt well with the world when she visited her father's Amish sisters.

Tonight, she did not expect to see any lights on—it was well after midnight after all—but there was the glow of a propane lamp downstairs in the kitchen that was never left on unless someone was up. She pulled in to make certain everything was all right.

When she entered the kitchen, not only was everything all right, she felt like she'd walked into cookie heaven. Aunt Lydia was outdoing herself again. There was every size, shape, and color of Christmas cookie imaginable spread out cooling on snowy-white dish towels lying on the kitchen table.

"Hi, Aunt Lydia," she said. "You're up late."

Lydia smiled a welcome. "And *you* look like something the cat dragged in."

"It's raining hard out there." Rachel removed her hat and coat and shook them out before laying them on a kitchen chair. "What's going on?"

"We have guests," Lydia said. "A family from Miami with three little children. They are celebrating their Christmas here early in the morning before they drive back. I thought having some cookies to take with them would be a nice surprise."

"Why are they celebrating here?" Rachel said. "Why not their own home?"

"The children wanted to see snow for Christmas, so the parents decided to bring them."

"There's not a lot of time left for it to start snowing before Christmas morning. I'm afraid they're going to leave disappointed."

Lydia used her favorite, old, green-handled spatula to remove small gingerbread men off the last cookie sheet.

"Yes. They are already disappointed. It was an unwelcome surprise that we do not have a Christmas tree. They said they had no idea we didn't decorate for Christmas. They complained that they had nowhere nice to place the children's presents. They offered to go purchase a tree for us, but Bertha said no."

"Where did they put them?"

"Stacked in a corner of the front room. The stack is very high. I think it cannot be good to teach children to expect so many gifts."

"I agree," Rachel said, feeling a little guilty over the gifts waiting for

Bobby to open in a few hours.

Lydia rinsed the cooled cookie sheet in the sink, dried it with a dish towel, put it away, then folded the dishtowel and placed it neatly on the counter. The only thing left to show that Lydia had been baking was the cookies. The kitchen was always pristine when Lydia finished. It was a skill Rachel admired but had never managed to duplicate.

"That family's Christmas is not your responsibility, Lydia."

Lydia ignored that. Rachel could tell that there was something else bothering her.

"Yesterday, after they arrived, the children kept talking about Santa Claus. It confused Anna. She did not know what they were talking about. She had never heard of Santa Claus. Instead, I heard her trying to explain that Christmas was about a baby in a manger named Jesus. The parents intervened. They were quite offended. They told her to please stop talking to their children about her religious beliefs."

"They did *what*? Criticizing Anna is like kicking a puppy. Is she okay?"

Lydia sprinkled red crystalized sugar on a candy-cane shaped cookie. "She went to her room and didn't come out all evening. I checked on her several times and she had gotten her shoebox of seashells out. She was sorting and counting them out loud. You know how she does that whenever she needs comforting."

"I thought she'd given her seashells to Bobby."

"She has new ones. Doc Peggy and Carl brought them back from Sanibel Island last month. They collected them on their honeymoon just for her."

"How nice of them. But why are you making Christmas cookies for these rude guests?" Rachel glanced at her watch. "At nearly three o'clock in the morning?"

"It is not the children's fault that their parents are *dummkoffs*!" Lydia glanced up in surprise that such a thing had come out of her mouth. She was not one to ever call people names. "I'm sorry. I should not have said that. It was wrong."

"No, Lydia. You were right the first time. They hurt Anna's feelings," Rachel said. "In my book, that definitely makes them dummies."

Lydia sighed. "I will never understand the Englisch."

It was a never-ending struggle between the two cultures. For so many years, the Amish had lived relatively unmolested in their tight-knit rural church communities. Then, as Englisch society became more disjointed and chaotic, many people felt themselves drawn to the Amish way of life. They seemed to equate horses and buggies and lack of electricity with peace and simplicity. They came to the Tuscarawas area in droves, enchanted with what they saw as the quaintness of the Amish culture without ever understanding the sacrifice and discipline such a lifestyle required.

The reality of Amish life, however, was almost always more complicated and difficult than the fiction that disgruntled Englisch spun for themselves. The lack of a Christmas tree, for instance. No plain-living Amish household would ever think of dragging a pine tree into their home and decorating it. Santa Claus was definitely not part of their lives. As far as chastising sweet Anna for talking about Jesus in her own home—well, some people were just... *dummkoffs.*

As she watched Lydia's arthritic fingers decorate the delicate sugar cookies so carefully, she felt a fierce protectiveness toward her. Her aunt was one of those people who, in Rachel's opinion, was too good for this world. She had a beautiful, loving, soul. Having no children or grandchildren of her own to make cookies for, she was here losing sleep trying to make a surprise treat for the children of these rude Englisch guests.

Rachel often wondered what life would have been like for her widowed aunt, Lydia, if she had not miscarried every pregnancy. Not that

Lydia ever complained. She accepted her lot in life and made the best of things no matter what. Rachel often wondered if Lydia somehow tried to bake the pain away, one pie crust and cookie at a time.

They had grown even closer since her own miscarriage last year. Lydia had truly understood her grief and helped bring her through it.

"Well, I just wanted to see why the light was on." Rachel rose from the table, rinsed her coffee cup in the sink, and set it in the drainer. "Now that I know you are okay, I'll head on out. You probably better get some sleep now though."

"I'm almost finished. I have enjoyed getting to bake the cookies for a change instead of pies for the restaurant. I'm grateful Joe and Darren decided to close Joe's Home Plate down over Christmas." Lydia pulled a large plastic container out of a bottom cupboard and began to layer the finished cookies within. "You and your family will still be coming to share our noon meal?"

"Of course. Darren is coming too, if you don't mind."

"Ah, good," Lydia said. "Joe's brother should feel free to come as well. We will have a wonderful good time."

Rachel was putting on her coat when her radio squawked. She listened, answered, then jammed her hat on her head and swung on her heavy coat.

"I don't know how you can understand that thing," Lydia complained. "What did it say?"

"There's been a wreck on a township road near here," Rachel said. "A woman's been killed. I have to go."

"I will pray." Lydia handed her a small, plastic container of freshly-baked cookies. "Be careful, Rachel."

Rachel was as careful as she could be, but it was growing colder and the roads were icing up from the cold and rain. As she rounded the corner where the wreck was supposed to be, she felt her tires slipping a bit.

The first thing she saw was the body of a young woman stretched out upon the side of the road. Rachel ran to her in the rain, knelt and felt for a pulse. There was none. The sight was a gruesome one. The woman's head was badly damaged and the lower front of her t-shirt looked like it was bloody, although it was hard to tell with all the rain.

Rachel drew on nitrile gloves, carefully lifted the t-shirt up, and winced at what she saw. In the middle of the woman's abdomen was a gaping wound.

"Maam took the babe," a man's voice spoke out of the darkness. "She had to. There was no one here to help her."

The scene was so macabre that Rachel automatically pulled her gun and stood upright, pointing both it and the flashlight at the area from which the voice had come. What she saw in the flashlight glare was a wet and miserable-looking young Amish man holding the reins of two horses. She played the flashlight over his face and did not recognize him. His head jerked back from the sudden light and he shielded his eyes with his hand.

"Do I know you?" Rachel asked.

"I'm Noah Hochstetler," he said. "My maam is Keturah. She is a midwife."

"You have grown up since I last saw you," Rachel said. "Keturah was here?"

"Ja. Daett left me to keep watch until someone came."

"Where's the baby? Did it survive?"

He wiped the rain from his face with one of his hands. "It was alive. Maam and Daett took it home with them to care for."

As he explained, she holstered her gun, then bent over and pulled the t-shirt back over the wound. It felt indecent not to do so. She was so young, probably barely out of her teens, and Rachel had never seen her before. What was an outsider doing on one of Sugarcreek's backroads on

Christmas Eve in this sort of weather?

In the far distance, she could hear the wail of an ambulance. She strode to her squad car and came back with a large, black, umbrella.

"Can you come here and help me, Noah?" she asked. "I need to take a few pictures before the squad gets here."

Clearly reluctant, but determined to be helpful, Noah held the strong light of the flashlight on the young woman's face and body, and the umbrella over Rachel and her camera phone, while she snapped pictures from various angles. She also took several of the wreck. The pictures would be far from ideal, but better than nothing.

By the time she was finished, the siren of the Swiss Valley Joint Ambulance Service was growing closer.

"Go ahead and get your horses out of here," Rachel said. "The siren might frighten them and there's already been one accident tonight. I don't want you getting hurt too. You've done enough. Thanks."

Noah did not argue. He leapt bareback onto the nearest horse then, wheeling around and clicking his tongue, he headed home at a trot, leading his father's horse behind him.

Rachel understood why he was glad to leave. It could not have been easy for an Amish farm boy to keep watch over a gruesome scene like this in the dark, but how much more awful it must have been for his mother! Keturah was not young, yet she had performed a C-section alone in the rain.

What a miserable Christmas morning this was turning out to be for the Hochstetler family! But receiving this terrible news tonight would be even worse for this girl's family. Rachel hoped that she would not have to be the one to tell them.

While waiting for the ambulance to arrive, she ducked into her squad car and turned up the heater full blast. Then, with her headlights illuminating the back of the old Buick through the rain, she called to check the number on the license tags. Within seconds the information came back. The car belonged to a Mabel Evans, an eighty-two-year-old woman who lived in Cleveland.

The girl lying on the ground in the rain was definitely not an eighty-two-year-old woman. A relative? Maybe a granddaughter? Rachel doubted the car was stolen. A pregnant woman did not exactly match the normal profile of a car thief.

It was obvious what had caused the wreck. The girl had been driving faster in the rain than was safe. When the curve came up, the car slid about six feet in the mud before it hit the tree. The impact had been hard enough to crumple in the front end.

She got out of her squad car and played her flashlight over the interior. Except for the glass pebbles from the broken windshield, the vehicle was immaculate. There wasn't even a fast-food wrapper tossed onto the floor. Reaching into the still-open driver's door, she popped the trunk so she could inspect it as well. Nothing back there except the spare tire and a jack.

This was highly unusual. She had seen everything from milkshakes to small pets slammed against the windshield after an impact, but there was nothing in this vehicle of a personal nature. Not even a purse. Had it been anyone but Noah watching over the girl's body and vehicle, she would have suspected that the purse had been stolen before anyone else could arrive, but she knew Noah was as honest as the rest of his family.

Rachel wasn't a big fan of purses and often just slipped a small wallet and her cell phone into her jeans pockets. If the girl was anything like her perhaps she, also, carried her ID in her pockets.

She was preparing to go through the girl's pockets when the ambulance arrived, interrupting her search for identification.

"Who is she?" the driver asked.

"I don't know yet. I'll need to search her pockets before you leave. It would be helpful if you could lift her up first."

She stood back while the two male emergency technicians placed the girl's body onto the gurney. Then they waited while she went through her pockets. Nothing.

"I guess we'll have to identify her as a Jane Doe," Rachel said. "At least for now. You can go ahead and take her."

Rachel was perplexed. No one traveled that light. Then she saw a small bulge in one of the ankle socks the girl wore.

"Hold on a minute," she said.

She pulled down the sock and there was a small roll of five twenties. Not much, but enough for gas and food, assuming the girl wasn't planning on going far. She checked the other sock and found nothing.

"Okay," she said. "I'm finished here."

While the men loaded the body, she pulled a plastic baggie out of her coat pocket and bagged, dated, and labeled the money before handing it over to the EMTs. The money needed to travel with the girl, to be handed to her nearest of kin when they came to identify the body. She hoped there would be someone besides an eighty-two-year-old woman in the family to help them identify.

Chapter Ten

....

Keturah hoped that it would not take Ivan long to make the phone call. The heat from the wood stove was comforting, but she was so exhausted she wasn't sure how much longer she could hold her head up.

She gave thanks again that her husband and Noah had come for her when they did. She wasn't sure she could have made it home alone with the little one. Slowly, she unbuttoned her rain-soaked outer coat, shrugged it off and dropped it in a pile on the floor beside her chair. At that moment, her beloved Michael came bursting into the house. "Maam, are you all right?"

She was grateful to see that he was securely holding the baby in his arms. Who better to see to the tiny infant than her Michael? So tender he had always been, even with the smallest baby rabbit.

"I will be fine," she said. "You see to the baby. That little one has had quite a harsh journey, she has."

He scanned Keturah's mud and blood-stained clothing with concerned eyes. "It looks like you have had a harsh journey, yourself."

She glanced down and brushed at her muddy dress.

"Tonight has not been easy," she admitted. Her dress was badly stained from the birth and from kneeling on the ground, but she felt too weak yet to do anything about it. She lifted off her wet, wilted, black bonnet and laid it on top of her coat piled on the floor. Tomorrow she would worry about her ruined clothes. Not tonight.

"It was too dark out on the road to see clearly," she said. "Is she all right?"

He reached over his head and turned up the gas jet light that hung from the ceiling. The kitchen was suddenly illuminated with a harsh, bright light. Then he laid the baby, still wrapped in Keturah's white apron and black shawl, on the kitchen table.

"Let's see who you are, little one." He gently unwrapped the newborn.

"Her heartbeat was growing very faint before I took her," Keturah said. "She was most definitely in distress. Is there any sign of Meconium stain?"

"No," Michael said, checking. "None."

Keturah breathed a sigh of relief. Meconium was a bowel movement that a baby sometimes had in the womb. Often it meant that the baby had been in some sort of distress. If it ingested the sticky substance, it could cause serious problems with the baby's lungs. Because the bond between pregnant mother and fetus was so strong, it was Keturah's opinion that what a baby felt, sensed, and heard while in utero was greatly underestimated.

"Where is your birthing bag?" Michael said. "I need a stethoscope."

"Ivan carried it in. I think he dropped it beside the door."

Michael glanced around, located the blue diaper bag in which she carried her midwife supplies, and unearthed the stethoscope. He blew on it to warm it. Keturah watched as he listened intently to the baby's lungs and heart while the baby kicked and fretted.

Then he pulled a receiving blanket from the birthing bag and hooked it to the handheld weighing device Keturah also carried. He dangled the baby a few inches above the table just long enough to read her weight on the scale. "Five pounds, eight ounces."

"I think she was about three weeks early," Keturah said. "So, that's not bad."

"I'm no pediatrician," Michael said, putting the stethoscope away. "But considering all she went through, she looks and sounds very healthy to me. If she were a baby goat or a puppy I could officially give her a clean bill of health."

Michael's joke made her smile.

"I did manage to hold the cord above her long enough to give her the extra umbilical blood before I clamped it off," Keturah said. "I knew she needed every bit of extra help I could give her."

"Good thinking."

Even though the room was warm, being uncovered made the baby kick and mewl. Her little arms flailed and each time a fist touched her cheek she turned toward it like a kitten searching for its mother's milk.

The thought that there was no mother to nurse this infant, no one to give it the healing power of colostrum that carried within it the benefit of the mother's immune system, made Keturah ache inside.

She wanted to believe that this precious little girl had a loving family somewhere who would care for her, but the girl's plea right before she died was a great worry. How could Keturah keep "him" from getting this fragile little newborn when she didn't know who "him" was?

"They are sending an ambulance for the mother," Ivan said, returning. "And the police will be here soon to talk with you about what happened." He pulled a quilt off the couch and draped it around her shoulders. "May I bring you something hot to drink to help warm you?"

"No." Keturah shook her head. "I do not need something to drink, but please help Michael care for the baby. It should be bathed and dressed. I have diapers and clean receiving blankets in the bottom drawer of our bedroom."

"I'll go get them." Ivan went to collect the supplies she kept at the ready in case a young mother might be unprepared or too poor to afford what they needed. There was often great poverty, especially within the

Swartzentruber Amish, who sometimes needed help. Not so much among the Old Order Amish, which was the sect to which she and Ivan belonged.

"I left my plastic baby tub at the Yoders'," Keturah told Ivan. "I planned to get it when I went over there tomorrow evening to check on that mother."

"Tomorrow has already become today," Ivan said. "Shall I go fetch it?"

"No," she said. "The large turkey baker will work just as well."

"Turkey baker?" Michael said.

"When our babies were small, we could not afford the luxury of a little bathtub made specifically for babies," Ivan chuckled, remembering. "But for our wedding we had received an extra-large pot for baking a turkey. When our first child was born, Keturah padded that oval pot with a towel, filled it with warm water and bathed our Reuben in it. He did not mind being bathed in a cooking pot. It has been quite the useful possession." Ivan grinned. "Every so often we actually use it for what it was meant for—baking a large Thanksgiving turkey."

Keturah did not worry about allowing the two men to care for the newborn while she tried to get some strength back. Michael had a medical background, and Ivan had always been good with babies.

As they prepared the baby's bath, Keturah heard them fall easily into speaking to one another in Pennsylvania Deutsch. Michael had been very young when they realized he had picked up their language. He had been spending a great deal of time at their house because his father had just died and his mother had moved in with Michael's grandfather and had gone to work to support them. Keturah felt great compassion for her grieving neighbor and offered to care for little Michael during the long hours his mother had to be gone. The little boy had picked up their language surprisingly fast.

"The babe is going to enjoy this." Ivan drew warm water from the faucet at the kitchen sink into a large kettle, then poured it into the blue-spackled turkey pan. "Just watch. Newborns love their bath."

"I didn't realize," Michael said. "I've no experience bathing human babies. The mothers I serve tend to take care of that, themselves, with their tongues."

She watched the two men doing the delicate work and felt her heart swell with gratitude and love for them. She remembered the day that Ivan had been getting the horse and buggy ready to go to the store, and he asked her if there was anything she needed. Michael had looked up from the building blocks with which he was playing, and asked Ivan to please purchase some candy to give to his mother. It was going to be her birthday the next day and he was worried about not having a gift for her. He had been four.

When Ivan agreed to get the candy, Michael stood up and solemnly handed him a penny from the pocket of his little jeans. She remembered how Ivan had gotten down on one knee in front of him and asked what kind of chocolate his mother liked. Michael informed him that his mother liked peanut M&M's best.

Keturah had always loved Ivan's way with children. Her husband told the little boy he thought that was a fine idea, and a penny would be just the right amount to cover the cost. He had been quite solemn about it, as though he and the child were working out a serious business deal. Michael had been so proud and happy to give his gift to his mother later when she came to get him.

They had been careful from that point on to never say anything in their mother tongue that Michael could not hear. That was how smart that child was. He'd picked up their language without them even once trying to teach him.

Ivan began to lay out the necessary bathing things from her birthing bag, including a small bottle of baby soap.

"Do you have a thermometer in there?" Michael asked her. "I'd like to take it before we bathe her."

"Side pocket."

"Thanks."

Even though the room was warm, she still felt a little chilled. She moved her chair closer to the stove.

"Be careful. You're starting to steam," Michael pointed out.

She glanced down at her lap and saw that steam was, indeed, rising from her dress. Quickly, she scooted back.

"Temp is ninety-seven point three," Michael said. "So it is in the normal range. I can handle this, Ivan, why don't you take Keturah upstairs and help her change into some dry clothes."

"No," she said. "I am fine. Please tend to the infant first."

Keturah had always been grateful that she got to help raise Michael. Three children of her own was simply not enough. Not nearly enough. She would have gladly given birth to more had the doctor not explained that there were problems and it would be too dangerous.

She had grieved at giving up her dream of a large family, but the idea of Ivan remarrying and another woman getting to care for her children was enough to make Keturah decide that there would only be her three sons. She had secretly been in a place of silent grief when Michael came along. He was a gift to her hungry heart. A gift from God whom she had begged for the ability to raise just one more child. Just one. He had given her Michael who became, in every way but birth, her fourth son.

As Michael slipped the baby into the warm bath that Ivan had prepared, he began to talk to the infant. Not baby-talk. She wasn't certain Michael had ever spoken baby-talk. Not even when he was a baby. He talked to the newborn as though it could understand every word.

"It isn't going to be easy, little one. You lost your mommy even before you got to know her. But there are some people coming who can tell us who you belong to. Maybe you have a daddy who is worried about you and will take good care of you."

After what the mother had said to her, Keturah doubted that.

"Such a sweet babe," she said. "I wish we could keep her."

"We are old, Keturah," Ivan brought a thick bath towel from the bathroom and laid it on the table. "She will grow out of being tiny and sleepy, and soon we would be running around after a toddler. Do you remember what it is like to chase a toddler from morning until night? We are not as fast as we used to be. We would lose her."

Keturah heard the sound of hoofs outside.

"Noah is back." Ivan opened the door and shouted out into the rain. "Please care for Brownie too, son."

Keturah heard her youngest son's voice agreeing to do so.

Michael was carefully bathing the baby when they heard a car pull into the driveway. Keturah saw the flashing blue lights and knew that the police had arrived. Even though she had done nothing wrong, this made her nervous. Her people tried to stay as far away as possible from those who enforced the *Englisch* laws.

Even though she was feeling a bit stronger, Keturah remained seated in her rocking chair as her husband opened the door to a very wet female police officer standing on their porch. The officer looked strange to Keturah, a grown woman all dressed up like a man. She was young, thin, and tall. Her hair was pulled back in a ponytail, and she wore the blue uniform of the Sugarcreek Police. She also wore a wide leather belt beneath her coat with various-shaped leather pockets sewn onto it. One pocket held a hand gun.

Keturah was used to her boys having hunting rifles. They were hunters and brought home enough meat each year to fill the two freezers that they rented at one of their Englisch neighbor's barns. They had always eaten a great deal of venison in their family. It was cheap and nourishing, and kept at least two animals from eating her garden. The deer were increasing in number at an alarming rate. They had even come up into her yard and chomped off the tops of all her lovely tulips last spring.

Yes, she was familiar with hunting rifles, but a handgun was a whole different thing. It was meant for one thing only—to shoot people. It was frightening to her to have such an alien presence in her cozy kitchen now, even though she knew in her heart that this policewoman was not there to do her harm.

"Hello. I'm Officer Mattias. Are you the Hochstetlers? Ivan and Keturah?"

To Keturah's surprise, the policewoman addressed them in Deutsch. Also, she pronounced the "ch" deep in the back of her throat the correct way. Not with the soft "k" sound like most Englisch pronounced it.

"*Ja*," Ivan said. "We are. You must come in out of the rain and cold."

The policewoman came inside as Ivan closed the door. She removed her hat, placed it beneath her arm, and shook out her hair. Then she glanced at the baby being bathed in the makeshift bathtub. "The baby is okay?"

Ivan nodded. "By the grace of God, it looks as though she is quite well."

"That is good to know. I just came from the scene of the wreck. The ambulance has taken the mother's body. It is good to meet you Keturah. I've heard of you but I don't think we've formally met. You are the midwife who did the emergency C-section?"

Keturah's fingers worried with the quilt Ivan had placed around her shoulders. "I—I had no choice."

Rachel came over, squatted down beside the rocker, and looked her in the eyes. "Many people would not have made that choice. It took courage to save the baby's life."

"I was not able to save the mother."

"You did what you could."

Suddenly, the policewoman did not seem so alien anymore.

Just as suddenly, the baby began to cry again. Keturah looked behind the police officer and saw that Michael had just lifted her from her warm bath water and laid her on the soft towel Ivan had laid out.

"She does not like being wet and cold," Keturah said. "Wrap her quickly in the receiving blanket. Make it tight."

"Here," Ivan said. "I will show you. I learned to do this with our babes."

With Ivan's help, the two men managed to dry the baby off, diaper her with one of the newborn disposable diapers Keturah always kept in her midwife bag, and wrap her tightly in the receiving blanket.

"Here she is." Michael held the baby up. "Sweet and clean, but not at all happy."

"Bring her here." Keturah held out her arms and he brought the tiny bundle to her. She held the baby closely against her chest and began to rock. The cries ceased, and the baby dropped off to sleep, exhausted from her ordeal. Unless Keturah missed her guess, the babe would sleep deeply now for a while.

"And you are?" The policewoman, who had stood patiently until the baby was content and quiet, turned to Michael.

"I'm Dr. Michael Reynolds. A neighbor."

"You're the vet who took old Doc Taylor's place?"

"I am."

"I remember you," Rachel said. "You were a few grades below me in school, but I remember you coming to my aunts' farm with Doc Taylor a couple of times. I think you helped him patch up our milk cow after she got hung up on a barbed-wire fence. You would have been about ten."

"You were Rachel Troyer back then. I apologize for not recognizing you."

"No need. At that time, my aunts were still trying to raise me to be Amish. I would have been wearing a long dress and kapp."

"You are Bertha Troyer's niece?" Keturah asked. "The one who went away to the police academy?"

"I am."

"I have known Bertha for many years. She is a good woman."

"A very good woman," Rachel agreed.

"But very bossy and opinionated sometimes, I think," Keturah said. "She has not been pleased with your choice of profession."

Rachel smiled. "Yes, that's my Aunt Bertha."

"I remember one of your aunts gave me a sack of fresh-baked ginger-bread cookies that day," Michael said. "Things like that stick in a small boy's mind."

"That would be Aunt Lydia. She still sends people away with fresh cookies. By the way, I've been hearing good things about you from the area farmers. They were worried when Doc Taylor died, but seem very happy with your work."

"I'm relieved to hear that," he said.

Keturah felt a rush of pride at Rachel's words. Of course people were happy with Michael. Who wouldn't be?

Rachel leaned over the rocking chair and gazed down at the baby sleeping so soundly in her arms. "Welcome to Sugarcreek, little girl. You've had quite a night of it, haven't you?"

"She's a healthy little thing from what I've been able to see," Michael said. "I assume you'll want to take her to the hospital now to be checked out?"

"I don't know quite what to do. The roads are terrible and I don't have access to an appropriate car seat right now. With it being Christmas, I don't think there's a store open where I could even purchase one in the middle of the night," Rachel said. "In the meantime, I'm going to have to ask you a lot of questions, Keturah. Are you up to it? I know this night has been rough on you."

Keturah felt a chill at the idea of being questioned by a police officer; even one as nice as this. She shivered involuntarily and Ivan noticed.

"My wife is not young, and her clothes are soaked," Ivan said. "We've all been too occupied with the baby to care for her properly. Could your questions wait until she can change into dry clothes?"

Keturah had been so focused on the care of the baby, she'd nearly forgotten that she was soaked to the skin. Now that he mentioned it, she realized that she was most definitely miserable.

"Of course, I'll wait," the policewoman said. "Would you like for me to hold the baby while you change?"

Chapter Eleven

....

The baby began to fuss again the moment Rachel lifted her from Keturah's arms. While Ivan helped his wife to their bedroom, Michael emptied the baby's bath water and repacked Keturah's midwife bag. As he tidied up, he noticed that the Sugarcreek cop was humming an Amish lullaby as she walked the floor with the baby.

"Is that *Schloof, Bobbeli, Schloof* you are humming?"

"*Sleep, Baby, Sleep*? Yes it is." Rachel didn't stop pacing. "You recognized it?"

"It's the lullaby Keturah used to sing to me when I was little and she was babysitting me. She would use it to try to get me to take a nap. I always fought sleep as a child. Too many interesting things to do."

"Aunt Lydia always sang it to me when I was little and staying the night with her and my other two aunts. She would sit on the bed, stroke my forehead, and sing until I fell asleep."

"So the lullaby worked for you?" Michael said.

"It did. Much against my will, if I remember correctly."

"Do you still know the words?"

"Of course," she said. "Don't you?"

"It's been years since I heard it. I think the first verse is: *Sleep, baby, sleep. Your father tends the sheep. Your mother shakes the dreamland tree, and from it falls sweet dreams for thee.*" He shook his head. "That's all I can remember. What's the rest?"

"*Sleep, baby, sleep. Our stars guard the sheep.*" Rachel sang the second verse, softly, as she walked with the baby. "*The little lamb is on the green, with snowy fleece so soft and clean.*"

She continued with the third verse. "*Dream, baby, dream. The robin sings in the tree. The stars, the robin and the sheep, they guard and keep you in your sleep. Dream, baby, dream.*"

"Is it working yet?" Michael whispered.

"I think so," Rachel said softly, as she glanced down at the little face. "Yes, it seems to have done the trick."

"You must have drawn the short straw to be on duty tonight." Michael picked up Keturah's wet coat and bonnet and hung them on the wall pegs near the back door.

Rachel lowered herself into Keturah's chair and began to rock.

"There are only five of us on the force." She tucked the receiving blanket more securely around the baby. "We try to take turns on major holidays."

With the baby being cared for by Rachel, Michael brought in an armload of firewood, filled the stove, punched up the embers, refilled the teakettle with water, and put it on to boil.

"You certainly know your way around this kitchen," Rachel observed.

"I grew up next door. Keturah and Ivan have been like second parents. They cared for me while my mother worked to support us."

"That's why you can speak their language so well."

"I was so young, I don't even remember learning it."

"Me, too." Rachel began to hum the lullaby again as she rocked the baby.

It was easy to see that this Sugarcreek cop was thoroughly enjoying this very non-police moment, so he left her to it.

He used a soapy dishcloth to wash off the kitchen table, then dried it with a fresh towel, the way he'd seen Keturah do hundreds of times after family meals. He was always comforted by being in this particular kitchen. It wasn't just the childhood memories. It was the warmth of the wood stove, the soft hiss of the gas lights, and the enduring smell of herbs that Keturah dried each year to use for medicines.

When he finished his tasks, he pulled a kitchen chair away from the table, turned it around, and straddled it. The baby was thoroughly asleep now and there were things he wanted to ask Rachel before she left.

"How long do you think it will take to find the baby's relatives?"

"I hope not long," Rachel said. "But there is a lot about this situation that makes no sense to me."

"Like what?"

"The license said the car was from Cleveland. Why would a girl that age from Cleveland be doing on a dirt, backroad here? Why in the middle of the night? And on Christmas morning at that."

"Maybe she was coming here to visit family and got lost."

"I hope that's the case, but I doubt it. There would have been at least some stab at bringing a gift, or food. There was nothing in that car. Nothing at all."

"Any clue who she might be?"

"Not yet. Neither the police chief nor I recognized her. He is at the crash site right now making arrangements to have the car towed, and making another search for a purse or a wallet. All I found was a small roll of cash she'd hidden in her sock. It's strange for there to be no ID on her at all."

"No cell phone?"

"None that anyone has found so far," Rachel said. "Which is a little odd because pretty much everyone uses a cell these days, except for the more conservative Amish."

"Unfortunately, that describes Keturah's church. If she'd had a cell phone, she could have called me for help," Michael said. "I was only a few minutes away and I could have been there almost immediately. Who knows? There might even have been a chance of saving the girl's life if we had gotten her to the hospital in time."

"Are you surprised that your neighbor managed to do surgery in the middle of a rainstorm?"

"Not at all. Keturah may be small, but sometimes I think her spine is made of steel. Also, she has an enormous amount of medical knowledge. With the exception of her Bible, I've never seen her with any kind of reading material in her hands that wasn't medically based. It's Ivan who reads *The Budget* newspaper cover to cover and collects as many Zane Grey novels as he can find."

The door opened, and Noah walked in with a tall, middle-aged man wearing a Sugarcreek cop uniform.

"Hi, Ed," Rachel said. "Do you two know each other?"

"Ed used to be my little league coach," Michael said.

"I'd heard you were back home," Ed said. "I'm sure the Hochstetlers are happy about that."

"Not nearly as happy as I am." Michael caught a glimpse of Noah's face. The young man did not look well. He was shivering with cold and his face was ashen. It was also obvious that he had been crying. Michael had wondered why Noah hadn't come in yet. Unless he missed his guess, his friend had been out in the barn, crying his heart out while caring for the three horses that had been run hard tonight.

"Is Maam and the baby okay?" Noah asked.

"They will be," Michael said. "The baby has had her bath, and I'm pretty sure Keturah is also taking one right now."

"Good." Without another word, and ignoring Rachel and Ed, Noah headed straight toward the stairway. They heard his heavy boots drop onto the floor above their heads, then the bed springs creaked. Michael knew him well and could envision Noah crawling deep beneath the quilts. He was a stoic, quiet man who knew how to work hard, but emotional things took a toll on him.

"Did you find anything, Ed?" Rachel asked.

"The only thing I found was this." The police chief handed her a newspaper clipping inside a plastic baggie. "It was wedged between the two front seats."

Rachel held the baggie with one hand while still cradling the sleeping baby with the other. She glanced at the clipping and handed it back. It was an article that had been written up in the Cleveland Plain Dealer about the opening of her husband's restaurant, and it also covered how she had nearly died trying to save their son and a little friend from kidnappers just days before.

"Why would she be carrying around an article about Joe's restaurant?"

"You didn't look close enough." Ed handed it back.

"Michael, could you turn the light up again?" Rachel asked.

He did, and she peered closer. "The address of Joe's Home Plate is underlined… and the restaurant's phone number is penciled in the margin."

"You have any ideas about this?" Ed asked.

"Not a clue," Rachel said. "Did you get hold of the woman who owns the car?"

"No," Ed said. "I called, but there was no answer and no answering machine to leave a message."

"So what now?" Rachel asked.

"I'll call the Cleveland precinct nearest that address and ask them to send a couple uniforms over to see if they can find out anything. Until we hear something back from them, I guess what we need to do is call social services and take the baby to the hospital."

Michael saw Rachel's grip on the baby tighten. He decided to intervene.

"Normally I would agree with you," he said. "But most hospitals are understaffed during the Christmas holidays. Foster care is always iffy, especially with a newborn. I don't know anything about the legalities involved, Ed, but from a practical standpoint that baby is probably better off staying right here with me and the Hochstetlers than anyplace else, for now. Besides, the weather is awful. I would hate to see the newborn taken back out into the cold."

"He's right," Keturah said, with some authority, as she and Ivan walked back into the room. "The first twenty-four hours of a newborn's life is critical. This one has been through a great trauma. She needs to be held close today, not left to lay alone in a hospital nursery."

"Hi, Ivan." Ed nodded. "Hello, Keturah. I hear you saved a life tonight."

"The Lord was with me," Keturah said. "How is your new granddaughter?"

"Sophie and Teresa are doing well," Ed said. "I appreciate you being there for them."

Michael was relieved to see that Keturah was almost back to her old self. There was color in her cheeks and she was no longer shivering. She had put on a fresh, dark brown dress, and her hair was neatly combed back beneath a pristine white kapp. Although her hair was gray, she still had the dark eyes of her youth, and they snapped at the police chief now at the mere thought of taking that baby away from her care.

"Our whole family will be here soon," Keturah said. "Including our middle son, John, and our daughter-in-law, Agnes. They have a two-month-old daughter."

She said this as though it held great weight. Michael could see that

Ed didn't catch the import of her words. Instead, he stood looking at her blankly.

Michael explained. "I think Keturah is telling us that Agnes could have enough breast milk to feed the new baby, and that she'll be here shortly."

The chief colored at the mention of breast milk.

"Yes." Keturah said. "Agnes is a very healthy young woman. She will be able to feed another baby. I sewed extra thick nursing pads for her just last week."

Michael was used to Keturah's matter-of-fact attitude about such subjects. He had grown up listening to it, but he was amused to see that Ed's face had grown beet red.

"What do you think, Rachel?" The police chief quickly changed the subject. "Should we leave the baby here until we can locate the family? It's not exactly protocol."

"I think we're lucky to have Keturah and Agnes willing to care for her," Rachel said. "It would be difficult to find formula for her tonight."

"It's starting to snow!" Ivan pointed to the window where thick snowflakes had begun to fall.

"The temperature is dropping." Ed glanced at the Lehman's thermometer right outside the kitchen window. "The wet roads were getting icy as I was driving over here. D & S Towing is going to be busy tonight. Coming, Rachel? I think we're going to need you."

She stood, kissed the baby on her downy head, and handed her back to Keturah.

As Ed and Rachel walked back to their squad cars, the snow continued to fall, and the wind had, indeed, gotten colder.

"What a night!" Ed said.

"I agree."

"Can you think of any connection you or Joe could have had with that young mother? Maybe something in the past. Her having that newspaper clipping with her is about the only clue we have."

"It's very odd," Rachel said. "But I have a good memory for faces. I'm fairly certain I've never seen her before."

"Do you suppose it could be someone Joe knows?"

"I have no idea. Joe knows a lot of people, but I can't think of anyone from Cleveland he knows well enough for her to try to track him down. Most of his former friends are from the time he spent in L.A."

"I figured," Ed said. "But it's the only thing we have to go on except talking to the old lady who owns the car, and maybe getting a match from her fingerprints. What I can't figure out is why she was on that particular road. It isn't exactly a shortcut to the restaurant if that was where she was headed."

"Me either, but it was dark. It was late. She was probably tired. Made a wrong turn, maybe?" Rachel pulled open the door of her squad car. "Let me know the minute you hear anything."

"Sure will." Ed had something else on his mind. "One more thing, Rachel. You know I've always liked Joe, but when I think of a young pregnant girl trying to make her way to his restaurant—well, I'm just going to say it—do you suppose there's any way she might have had some connection to him? Things like that happen, and Joe is a good-looking man, and a former famous baseball player…"

Rachel stood very still as the snow fell heavily on her hair and coat. Ed thought there might be a chance that Joe could have been unfaithful to her? Just because a pregnant girl was carrying a newspaper clipping of his restaurant?

No way. On the other hand…

"Joe isn't the only owner of the restaurant," she said. "His brother, Darren, is also part owner. He was mentioned in the article too."

"Might not hurt to ask them," Ed said. "Maybe one of them were friends with her boyfriend or something. I know it sounds far-fetched, but that clipping is the only thing we have to go on for now."

A voice crackled over the radio, giving a location.

"Bad wreck over on 93," Ed said. "Meet you there."

Chapter Twelve

When Cassie Pinson-Reynolds let herself into her lovely, fourth floor apartment, she was not happy. As she sank into her cream-colored couch and removed the high heels from her aching feet, the fact that she was not happy puzzled her. She clocked a breathtaking hourly wage as a corporate lawyer, could well afford this gorgeous apartment in a trendy section of downtown Columbus, and her closet was stocked with expensive clothes and shoes.

When she was younger, she would have assumed that, when one got to this point in one's professional life, happiness would be guaranteed.

But tonight there was no denying the fact that she was unhappy.

It was all Michael's fault, of course.

It isn't money alone that brings happiness, Cassie. It's the people in your life and what you can do for them with it that brings happiness.

There it was again, her husband's irritating voice in her head. She hated it when he started spouting the platitudes he'd learned from his Amish friends. It was a voice that she hoped would go away once he became her ex-husband. She hoped he was not going to be difficult about this divorce. He must see the inevitability of their split up. Their basic needs were just too different.

No doubt that was the thing spoiling her happiness. She needed for him to sign the divorce papers so that she could get this whole first marriage mistake behind her. Cassie did not like having loose ends in her life, and Michael had become just that.

Marrying Michael, who was the most decent man she'd ever met, was the only thing that had ever made her waver in her determination to make it to the top of her profession. She had fallen in love with him way back while they were still in undergraduate school, back when he was seriously debating whether to become a medical doctor or a veterinarian.

To her, it was a no-brainer. Become a doctor, of course. Preferably the kind that made a lot of money.

He chose to become a veterinarian.

She should have bailed right then, but she convinced herself that being married to someone with a nice, normal practice that involved taking care of fluffy old ladies cats and dogs wouldn't be so bad. By the time she discovered that his real dream was to work with farm animals, she was already married to him.

She had been relatively happy as long as he was working for that animal clinic in Upper Arlington. He was a handsome man with blond, good looks. With her auburn hair and slim figure, she knew they made a striking couple. It was nice getting to introduce her good-looking husband to her business associates as Dr. Reynolds.

They really did have it all. Including that farmhouse over in Tuscarawas County that had belonged to his grandfather. Living in Amish country was all the rage right now, and property values had skyrocketed in recent years. It would only make sense for him to sell it and invest the money and she told him so.

Michael wouldn't do it though. He had too much nostalgia for the place. She hadn't fought him on hanging onto it. Especially since it seemed like property values would continue to rise in that area.

They had everything a young couple could ask for, and they could have had even more once she made partner at her law firm—which she was determined to do.

All it had taken for her dreams to crumble was one short call from Doc Taylor's widow offering Michael the practice that the old veterinarian had built up over a lifetime in Sugarcreek. Her husband didn't even take time to consider it or talk it over with her. He was so thrilled with the fact that the widow had chosen to call *him* that he had agreed to do it on the spot. It had been shocking how quickly he gave notice at the clinic where he worked. Even more shocking how quickly he began to pack, barely listening to her well-reasoned arguments as she tried to talk some sense into him. The man acted as though living in this apartment with her had been some sort of nightmare from which he couldn't wait to escape.

Leaving her for another woman was something she could have understood. She'd be furious, of course, but it would have made some sense to her. It happened so frequently to couples, it was almost expected. But it was humiliating to lose one's husband to… livestock.

"This is my dream, Cassie. It has been my dream ever since I was a little boy following Doc Taylor on his rounds. I've done it your way for five years," he'd said. "Besides, you work so many hours, I barely ever see you."

"That's *billable* hours, Michael," she'd said. "I'm not exactly twiddling my thumbs over at Blackwell, Hart & Cooper. I work hard! I'm climbing the ladder faster than any female attorney ever has done there. I'm trying to make a better life for us."

"If you really want a better life for us, then turn in your resignation and come with me. We don't have to wait for a better life. We can have one in Sugarcreek without you having to work so hard. I love you, Cassie. I want to be with you, but I'm not staying here. Not any longer."

And that was how her marriage had ended. Not with an affair, or from abuse, or financial wrangling. They didn't even have any irreconcilable differences, except this one thing. He wanted to practice his profession in a rural area, and she most certainly did not. It might not seem like that much of a problem to many people, but to her it was an unsolvable problem. The only way they could stay together was if one of them was profoundly unhappy.

She was determined it would not be her.

So here she was, with a husband who planned on spending the rest of his life mucking around in people's farmyards and pastures. He even seemed to be under the impression that he could make a decent living doing this. Her guess was that about half the time he would forget to charge anything for his services. That was the type of man he was. Compassionate to a fault.

Except toward her. Apparently her great need to build a career she could be proud of in law did not compute with him.

Sugarcreek was over a hundred miles away. Considering what they both did for a living, a compromise was not an option. She did work a lot of hours. He was right about that. Ninety hours per week was not unusual. Sometimes there was a small crisis. If so, Blackwell, Hart & Cooper expected her to be ready to drop everything at a moment's notice and come in to the office. As a country vet, Michael would have a few random days off, but he still needed to be available around the clock. Sick cows did not observe office hours.

In Michael's eyes, she knew she was the one most able to pick up and move. He seemed to think she could just hang out a shingle on Sugarcreek's Main Street and start taking on cases.

It wasn't that simple. She knew how hard small-town lawyers had to scramble to make a living. The fact that she'd landed this job straight out of college was a small miracle, even though she did have a stellar resume. She was impressing the daylights out of them with her smarts and hard work. Making partner someday really was a possibility. If only Michael was willing to wait.

Glancing at her watch, she realized that she had spent a full fifteen minutes staring into space, thinking about Michael. That was not acceptable. As usual, she had brought at least four hours' worth of work home with her tonight, and it was already eight o'clock.

After a quick shower to sluice the grime of the city off, she carefully rebandaged the small incision from the biopsy her doctor had insisted on doing the week before. She wasn't particularly worried about it. There had been two other biopsies in her past—both benign. She had a tendency toward fibroid cysts. The doctor had suggested she cut down on caffeine. That was a laugh. With her job load, that was not going to happen any time soon.

Now dressed in her favorite silk dressing gown, and with her wet hair still wrapped in a thick towel of Egyptian cotton, she nuked a frozen low-calorie dinner and sat at the dining-room table eating while she worked.

Two hours later, for a brief moment, she allowed herself to glance out the window at the night sky and wonder what Michael was doing. On her way home, the city had been packed with last-minute shoppers and was aglow with Christmas lights. She, on the other hand, was spending Christmas Eve in the company of a stack of legal papers and an empty, microwaveable, plastic container.

Not a big deal, she told herself. Christmas was just a date on the calendar.

She put a fresh pod in the Keurig coffee machine, carried the cup back to the table and dove back into her work. It took focus and determination to climb the ladder at Blackwell, Hart & Cooper. Michael wasn't the only one with childhood memories and dreams. She had memories and dreams too. Memories she would never tell him, and dreams that she had every intention of achieving with or without him.

Michael's dream was to be a hero to the farmers around the village of Sugarcreek.

Her dream was simpler. To make enough money that no one could ever call her "trailer trash" again.

Chapter Thirteen

With no farm-animal crisis happening, and with no reason to go home except to stare at those blasted divorce papers, Michael was grateful when Keturah invited him to stay on for the Christmas brunch their family would be enjoying.

"You need to eat with us." Keturah lifted a pan of homemade buttermilk biscuits out of the oven. She had taken a quick nap after Rachel left, and now appeared re-energized. "There will be so much food, we won't know what to do with all of it."

"I'd love to," he tucked the baby's receiving blanket in a bit tighter as he sat in the kitchen rocking chair, enjoying the sight of Keturah and Ivan rushing around getting ready for the rest of their family to arrive. His stomach rumbled and he realized he'd had nothing to eat since lunch the day before… except for the Pepto Bismol. "What are we having?"

"It will be a simple meal this year," Keturah said. "Agnes and John are bringing the sausage gravy. They have an abundance of tasty meat after butchering one of their hogs last week. Her family uses a different recipe for sausage than I do. She's from the Gallipolis settlement, you know. They do things a little differently there. It's very good sausage. I think I might like it better than my own recipe."

"Seems like forever since we had supper," Ivan said. "It was an awfully long night."

"That is true." Keturah paused and stared out the window for a moment, as though momentarily reliving the horror of the night before. "I'm so grateful that it is daylight again."

Then she took a deep breath, and busied herself with putting the biscuits into a cloth-lined basket that he'd seen her slip an oven-warmed ceramic disk into the bottom. She covered the steaming biscuits with a blue-checked dish towel.

"Betty and Reuben are bringing a big bowl of applesauce and five loaves of that good sourdough bread she makes," Keturah continued. "They had a bumper crop of apples this year from those four old trees beside their barn. We canned over a hundred quarts of applesauce together back in September. Good thing too. Their Benjamin loves applesauce, and so does little Aaron."

The baby began to cry again, the full-out wail of a newborn. Michael stood up and tried walking with her, but she could not be comforted. Then suddenly, the crying stopped. Michael glanced down at her.

"Come look at this!" Michael said. "She's already found her thumb."

Keturah dropped what she was doing and came to look. "*Ach*, she must have been sucking that little thumb even in the womb. This is going to be a good baby, she's already learned to comfort herself."

"Do you suppose she's hungry?" Michael asked.

"Of course she is," Keturah said. "Plus, she has that instinctual need to suck. She will be okay. Agnes will be here soon, then her little belly will get filled."

"Is there any chance that Agnes will mind nursing her?" Michael asked.

"I don't think so," Keturah said. "She's fostered babies before. No one loves an infant more than our Agnes. It is very lucky for you that she is lactating."

"Me?" Michael was confused. "What does Agnes lactating have to do with me?"

"Because otherwise, I would be sending you out in this nasty weather to find some formula. Instead, you get to sit and rock a newborn here in this warm kitchen." Keturah grinned. "You will have to thank Agnes when she gets here for saving you so much trouble."

"I don't think I will do that," Michael said. "But I will be relieved to let Agnes take over."

"Our Noah was a thumb sucker," Ivan said. "At least that's what I remember."

"He was," Keturah said. "And the easiest one of the three. By the way, did you remember to put plenty of last night's milking into the refrigerator to cool for this morning?"

"Ja," Ivan said. "No worries there. Our grandchildren will have more than enough."

"Good. I churned last week and made plenty of butter. That Jersey cow you bought this fall gives such good rich cream!"

"Aren't Betty and Reuben also bringing the eggs?" Ivan asked.

"Oh yes. I've saved enough bacon grease to fry them in once they get here. Agnes and Reuben's little Clara is bringing two raisin pies she helped her mother make. She's only four, but Agnes says she did almost all of it herself. Remember to tell her how good they are. Children must be encouraged in their work. Another year, and she shouldn't have to have her mother's help at all."

Keturah was talking more than usual. Since she was not a woman given to chatter. Michael knew a lot of it was from nervousness. She was still trying to find her equilibrium. He knew her well, and could see that she was determined not to let the night's trauma show in her behavior. She didn't want to act upset and ruin Christmas day for her family. Talking about homey things like food and grandchildren was comforting to her.

Earlier, he had wished Christmas wasn't today. He was afraid that the chaos and extra work created by married sons, wives, and grandchildren, would be too hard on her. There would be virtually no time for her to rest and recuperate, but perhaps it was just as well. Her family would be a healthy distraction.

It was such a pleasant kitchen to be in and it flowed naturally into a large living room. The Amish had embraced the open-floor concept long before the Englisch world had discovered it. Needing space to seat two hundred people for church had made an open-floor plan a necessity in those houses that did not have a workshop or basement big enough to fit everyone.

The wood stove, the now-brewing coffee on the back burner, the aroma of the fresh biscuits, and the sight of freshly-fallen snow outside the window all blended together to absorb some of the sting that had been caused by the divorce papers.

He often worried about Cassie. She worked such terribly long hours. It was rare for her not to work until one or two o'clock in the morning. She lived on four or five hours sleep per night and plenty of high-priced cups of caffeine. On Saturdays and Sundays, they sometimes tried to go out for a leisurely breakfast, but he could always tell she was distracted. Anxious to get back to her work. It was a little ego-deflating to know that his wife was having to put forth an effort to spend time with him.

His job at the small animal clinic in the suburbs was pleasant enough, but he felt ungrounded there, as though he were spending his life going through the motions, floating, waiting for something to change.

Waiting to not be lonely anymore.

He had often felt like he was just putting in time until he could go home, but home was never their apartment complex. Home was, and always had been, Sugarcreek.

Chapter Fourteen

Cassie was stretched out on her sofa, trying to enjoy watching the flames of the gas fireplace she so seldom bothered with lighting. She was having to work very hard at relaxing tonight. It was early Christmas morning after all, and was supposed to be the happiest day of the year.

Of course, it was the most depressing day of the year for many, but she was absolutely determined not to allow herself to be depressed. There was Christmas music playing on her surround-sound system, but it didn't seem to help. There was no lighted Christmas tree in her house, of course, even the fake ones tended to shed and she didn't need the bother. Besides, if she cared to look out her window, she could watch the glow from the city's Christmas lights and the snow blanketing the city.

Her entire Christmas celebration had consisted of flipping through a fashion magazine while enjoying a rare bubble bath. Neither had been relaxing. For breakfast, she had toasted a bagel and splurged by spreading real cream cheese on it. That was about as far as her creativity went in trying to enjoy the first day off she'd taken in months.

It surprised her that Michael had not called last night, not even to wish her a Merry Christmas or yell at her about the divorce papers. It astonished her that he had managed not to have any contact with her since he'd left. Not that anything he could have said would make her change her mind, of course... but it was odd. In their relationship, he was the one who always wanted to talk things out, and always the first to capitulate when they had a disagreement.

He was probably stuffing himself on homemade Christmas foods with his friends in Sugarcreek. Probably hanging out with those Amish neighbors to whom he was so attached. Singing songs. Playing board games. Over the years, she'd heard so much about the marvelous times he'd had with his Amish neighbors that she had grown tired of it. Obviously he was more attached to them than he was to her or he wouldn't have left. For an only child, he certainly seemed to have a large family!

"*Come with me,*" he had pleaded. "*I can support both of us if we move into my grandparent's house in Sugarcreek. No rent or mortgage to worry about. Doc Taylor had a fine practice. You won't have to work so hard. You can do anything you want to do.*"

Right. Whatever.

She had seen first-hand what happened to women who allowed themselves to depend on a man to support them, and it wasn't pretty. She'd watched her mother spend her life waiting for some man to come rescue her. There had been several her mother had gushed over, saying they were her "Prince Charming."

Even as a young girl, Cassie got sick of hearing it. She started privately thinking of them as her mother's "Prince Deadbeats."

Still, it would be nice if Michael would call. After all, it *was* Christmas and she hoped they could at least stay friends.

She knew he was hurt by the divorce papers, but it was the only way she could think of to bring him to his senses. What she was trying to accomplish with her life was important. He had to come to terms with that. Some people seemed to think money wasn't everything. Michael was among them. But, in her opinion, people who thought that way were either naïve or stupid. Money *was* everything. Those who did not believe so had never experienced trying to survive without it.

The coming day stretched out before her, long and empty. With nothing to do and no one to be with, she opened her briefcase and got back to work.

Chapter Fifteen

There were no formal Christmas decorations in the Hochstetler kitchen, no tree and no ornaments. No brightly-wrapped boxes of presents. One thing they did have were all the Christmas cards the Hochstetlers had received this season. Ivan had strung a cord from one end of the room to the other up against the far wall of the front room. Since they had myriads of friends and family, it was heavy with bright-colored Christmas cards.

Then there were the four wooden toys Ivan had made for the grandchildren. Each one had a small, red ribbon tied on it that made it possible to be hung on the pegs that Ivan had placed low enough many years ago for his own young children to hang their hats and coats on without help.

Michael had noticed that the Amish were puzzled by the Englisch need to shower gifts on their children. There were so many things to enjoy other than presents. Was not being together and eating a good meal enough of a celebration? Especially since there would be board games, singing, or walks together in the woods? If there was fresh snow, there might also be sleigh riding, or snow ice cream and popcorn. If it was cold enough, there might also be ice skating on someone's farm pond. The day would be filled with joking and much laughter. Many stories would be told and enjoyed.

From what Michael had experienced, the Amish were only solemn when in church or around Englisch people with whom they were unfamiliar. When they were together for a get-together like this, they could be some of the funniest and best storytellers he had ever known.

Michael had also noticed that every Amish woman he knew loved pretty dishes. It was one of the few things in an Amish household that did not have to be plain. Over the years, he had watched Keturah slowly collect a set of green and white Currier and Ives Colonial Homestead Royal China from various garage sales and thrift stores. Even he had learned the name and to keep an eye out for it. Every now and then, a member of her family would present her with a stray cup, or dinner plate they'd discovered somewhere. This discovery was always a cause for celebration and they all kept an eye out for Keturah's favorite pattern. She now had enough to set a festive table for Christmas, which was exactly what she was doing.

Finished, she stood back and admired her table. The green dinnerware looked lovely on the snowy white tablecloth. Ivan had brought in an armload of holly from the woods, which Keturah arranged in a large, wooden bowl. She had also placed two fat, red candles on either side.

"It's lovely, Keturah," Michael said.

"I think the children will be pleased."

The baby had gone back to sleep. Now that the kitchen was lit with morning light, her downy hair looked like spun gold. She was like a tiny angel lying in his arms. The baby roused, opened its eyes, and looked up at him with wide-eyed wonder.

"Was the baby's mother a blonde?" he asked.

"I don't remember," Keturah said. "It was so dark outside. By the time I placed the lantern beside her on the ground, I was in too much of a hurry to try to save the baby to pay attention to the mother's hair color."

Then she shook her head and her voice lowered. "That's not quite the truth, Michael. I didn't want to look at her any more than I had to. It was the only way I could do… what I had to do."

Ivan was grinding coffee beans at the counter in an old-fashioned coffee mill. The delicious aroma filled the air. The coffee mill was made of wood and iron and looked like it had been in their family for generations. Michael remembered being fascinated by it as a child.

"You did the right thing, Keturah." Ivan carefully pulled out the little wooden drawer made for catching the freshly-ground coffee fell. He measured it out by tablespoons into the blue, enameled coffee pot. "I am pleased to be married to a woman with the skill and heart to save the life of this little one."

Keturah said nothing in return, but Michael saw her face light up with pleasure. The Amish did not shower one another with praise. He'd never even heard Ivan or Keturah say that they loved each other, but Ivan had just now come as close as an Amish husband could to telling his wife that he was proud of her—and Keturah had needed that reassurance.

"I am so grateful you found that sleigh and purchased it," Keturah gently praised him in return. "If it remains cold today, we should have enough snow to take the horses out and give the grandchildren rides. It will be a good activity for the whole family."

"I've been thinking about where to go," Ivan said. "I think I will take them through that trail that goes through our woods and then across that back pasture. While we eat, I will put some bricks into the oven to warm so our feet won't get too cold."

"That will be a good thing," Keturah said. "A sleigh ride on Christmas day will be something they will never forget."

Michael heard the sound of the two oldest Hochstetler sons and their families trotting up the driveway. The jingling of their harnesses sounded almost like bells. As the men took care of the horses and buggies, the women ushered the children in. Ivan stood in the middle of the room with a big grin on his face, waiting for the children to discover their toys.

At first the three older children, four-year-old Clara, eight-year-old Benjamin, and six-year-old Aaron, were hesitant when they saw the hand-carved toys hanging from the pegs. Two-month-old Rosie, of course, was too little to notice hers.

"Go ahead," Ivan said to the older ones. "You can play with them. I made them for you."

In awe, the children lifted the little toys from the pegs, put their hats and coats in their place, and began to choose. There was a cat, a horse, a dog, and a little lamb. Clara immediately chose the lamb for her baby sister and brought it to her. Benjamin chose the horse. Aaron was partial to the dog. That left the cat for Clara, who was quite happy with her gift. Michael had watched Ivan putting much love and joy into carving those farm-animal figurines. They were primitive, because Ivan wasn't a great carver, but Amish children didn't get gifts often and the little toys seemed to be greatly appreciated.

Then the two daughters-in-law saw the baby.

"Michael!" Betty teased, as she brushed snow off her coat. "Is that a baby I see in your arms? Is there something you have not told us? Or did you find it lying in a manger?"

"There is probably a great deal I have not told you," Michael said. "But Keturah delivered the baby early this morning."

"And where is the baby's mother?" Betty's head swiveled as she looked around the kitchen.

He waited for Keturah to explain, but she didn't. It was Ivan who told the story, very carefully, leaving out the details for the sake of the children. As he did so, Betty quietly helped the children remove their boots, and Agnes handed little Rosie off to Keturah.

"Let me see this *kinder*," Agnes pulled the receiving blanket away from the baby's face and took a good look at the newborn who was sucking on her fist again. "Has she eaten?"

"No, but she is only a few hours old." Keturah jostled her own fat grandbaby, Rosie, who was growing restless. "I knew you were coming, do you mind...?"

"Of course I don't mind. Come here, little one." Agnes lifted the baby from his arms and carried her to an armchair at the far end of the adjacent living room, then she turned her back on those who were in the kitchen and began to nurse the new baby.

Michael heard men's voices, and a great deal of stamping snow off booted feet directly outside the door. John and Reuben brought a long gust of cold air into the kitchen with them after taking care of their horses.

"It's coming down fast out there," Reuben said. "If it continues, and if we eat very slowly, there might be enough accumulation of snow for that sleigh ride you've been talking about, Daett."

"And where is Noah," John asked.

Ivan investigated the stove's firebox and placed more wood inside. "He's still abed."

"And you are allowing it?" The other two brothers hooted with laughter.

"You never let us sleep in this late!" Reuben pointed out. "Didn't you make him help you with the milking this morning?"

"No, I did the milking," Ivan said, quietly. "Your brother had a rough night last night. We all did. Your mother especially."

"What happened, Maam?" Reuben put his arm around his mother's shoulders.

"She delivered a baby out on the road last night," Betty said, as she lifted the lid off a large cast-iron Dutch oven she'd brought in and placed on the stove. "She performed a C-section during the night, that's what your mother did!"

"Where's Agnes?" John asked.

"She's nursing the baby," Keturah said. "Here, Clara. I saved a job for you. You may put the napkins at each place. Fold them first, like this."

The little girl had to stand on her tiptoes to place the napkins at each plate, but she did so carefully, and studiously. Michael knew that Keturah had intentionally saved that job to make the child feel like she was a useful part of the bustle in the kitchen.

As John went to check on his wife, Michael excused himself for a few minutes to go back to his house. Another dairy farmer's wife had given him a fruitcake yesterday. He had deliberately not sampled the cake yet because he knew it would make a fine contribution to the Hochstetler's meal and bringing it would keep him from making himself sick on it. He had always been too fond of a good fruitcake.

It was going to be a messy, chaotic, busy morning, with a great deal of talking and laughing. At least one child would knock over their glass of milk, and the baby would be passed around and made much over.

His big old house felt especially empty today, and he could hardly wait to get out of there. When he'd been a small child, it had felt much the same. His father gone, his mother sad and exhausted when she came home from work, and his grandfather elderly and distant. At least next door he had people who cared about him. A place where he would not have to be lonely.

Getting to go next door into the bustle of other children playing, and the sheer joy of Keturah's kitchen had felt like the difference between coming out of the dark and going into the light.

As he walked through the snow, carrying the brightly-colored fruitcake tin to the Hochstetlers, he wondered what Cassie was doing this Christmas day. She didn't have any family; at least none with whom she was close enough to visit for Christmas. The childhood she'd described to him, with her parents dying in a car crash, then living with a bachelor uncle until she went away to college, had always sounded rather sterile. He didn't even know what family traditions she might have grown up with as a kid. Cassie never wanted to talk about anything from her past. He always figured it was because losing her parents as a teenager had been too traumatic, so he never pried.

Chapter Sixteen

By the time Rachel got home, she was aching for sleep, but seven-year-old Bobby was buzzing around the house, waiting for her to arrive.

"Santa came!" he shouted, as she came through the back door. He grabbed her hand and started tugging her into the living room. "Come see."

"Let me take my coat off first," she laughed, brushing snow off her shoulders and shaking it out of her hair. "You go on in and I'll be right there."

"Okay, but hurry!" He ran toward the living room. "I have lots of presents to unwrap!"

"Welcome home." Her husband, Joe, gave her a quick kiss, and helped her take off her police jacket.

"It's good to be home," she said. "The roads are awful and there were three wrecks to deal with, or I would have been here sooner. Why don't people have enough sense to stay home when the roads are iced over?"

"When are you going to give up and figure out that people don't have any sense? Except maybe for me and you—and sometimes I'm not so sure about us. I was worried about you," Joe said. "I hope you're not hungry. I'm afraid Bobby is going to explode if we don't get in there soon."

"Did you have a rough morning holding him back?" She unbuckled her utility belt and laid it on a high shelf.

"Do you even have to ask? Bobby has been up since five."

"Oh dear."

"I let him dig into his stocking. That helped a little."

"Hurry up, Rachel." Bobby poked his head into the kitchen, "Santa brought me a lot more presents this year than he did last year."

"I'm not surprised." She shot a glance at Joe. "Santa must have had a better year than last."

"Santa did have a rather hard year last Christmas," Joe said.

"How do you know?" Bobby asked, a worried look on his face. "Did Santa tell you?"

"No, son," Joe said. "I read about it in the newspaper."

"Why?" Bobby said. "What happened? Why did Santa have a hard year?"

Rachel had experienced this sort of thing before with Bobby. The little boy had such a tender heart, he often took comments they made more seriously than they intended.

Joe looked a little desperate as he searched his brain for an answer. "I think the elves went on strike for better wages or something."

"Oh." The pull of presents was too strong for Bobby to inquire any further. He ran back into the living room.

"The elves went on strike?" Rachel whispered. "That's a new one, Joe."

"What did you want me to say?" he whispered back. "Was I supposed to tell him that the reason he has presents this year is because Daddy and Uncle Darren's restaurant is finally making some money?"

"Hi Rachel," Darren waved from where he sat cross-legged on the floor next to the tree. "I've been trying to protect the presents. Bobby is of the opinion that shaking a box to guess what's inside doesn't count as opening it. I'm afraid some of them are getting a little worse for wear."

Rachel sank onto the couch, rejoicing in the fact that she had a healthy, happy little stepson whose only problem was deciding which present to open first. It was a nice counterbalance to what she'd dealt with earlier—the sight of that poor mother's body after the wreck. She tried to wipe away the memory, at least temporarily, so that she could enjoy this moment, but the mystery of who the Christmas baby belonged to stayed in the back of her mind.

"Okay?" Bobby held a red box in his hand, decorated with a gold ribbon.

"Sure," Rachel said. He might as well open that package first. It contained only a bathrobe and matching pajamas. Bobby needed them, because he was growing like a weed, but they weren't the most exciting present under the tree.

"Don't we need some Christmas music?" Darren said.

"Absolutely." Joe jumped up from the couch. "I'll take care of it."

As Frank Sinatra's voice wafted through the air, Rachel began to relax. It had been a hard year as Joe and his brother tried to make a go of their sports restaurant. They had named it Joe's Home Plate, based on Joe's former career as a professional baseball player.

Their gamble had paid off and, as it did, she'd seen something inside Darren change. Instead of being the neer-do-well brother who always had a hand out to his more successful brother, Darren had found his niche—and that niche was working beside Joe. For the first time since childhood, their relationship was solid, and both of them seemed more content than she'd ever seen.

Now, if only Darren could find a good wife to settle down with! Rachel would welcome having a sister-in-law.

"Thank you for the robe and pajamas, Rachel," Bobby said, dutifully.

"I imagine there are some toys in there too, buddy," Rachel said.

"Yay!" Bobby dove beneath the tree for another package.

Later, after all the presents had been opened, and Darren and Joe were helping Bobby set up a train set, Rachel set out Lydia's Christmas cookies and four mugs of cocoa that she had put on a tray.

"What kind of Christmases did you have when you were little, Rachel?" Darren asked, as he fit two pieces of train track together.

"Traditional; a lot like this, before my mother and father died," Rachel said. "Mom was Englisch and Dad didn't mind her making a fuss. In fact, I think he enjoyed it. Everything changed after I went to live with my Amish aunts. No tree, no decorations, no Frank Sinatra. One or two gifts, maybe, after we'd had breakfast. Then later, we'd climb into the buggy and drive to some relative's house, where there would be more relatives, and more food."

"Not terribly exciting then?"

"No, but it was cozy and we definitely ate well. That's one thing you can always count on when you are getting together with Amish people—eating really well."

"So, what's the plans for the rest of the day?"

"After we get the train set up, we'll go over to visit Rachel's aunts." Joe chuckled. "Where I think it is safe to assume that we can plan on eating well?"

"Always a safe assumption with Aunt Lydia around," Rachel said. "We are having brunch there. They are expecting us about ten o'clock."

"Brunch?" Joe asked. "Your aunts actually used the word 'brunch'?"

"I know, it doesn't sound like a word an elderly Amish woman would use, but that's what Lydia said. I think the idea of 'brunch' is starting to catch on in the Amish community. Afterward, I will have to go back to work. I need to help Ed track down the relatives of a Jane Doe we got last night."

Both Darren and Joe stopped what they were doing, looked at her, and spoke at once. "A Jane Doe?"

"Yes." Using careful words for Bobby's sake, she briefly told them about her night.

"Because of a newspaper clipping Ed found in the car about the restaurant's opening night, Ed thinks she might have been headed to Joe's Home Plate." She took out her cell phone and brought up the least gruesome picture she could find. "I hate to do this to you, she died of a head injury so it isn't pretty, but do either of you remember ever seeing this woman?"

Joe took the cell phone. He shook his head. "I don't know her, but what a pitiful photo."

"I've never seen her, either," Darren said, after he'd studied it. He handed her the cell phone. "I would not want your job, Rachel."

"Sometimes I'd rather not have my job, either," she said. "But we have a newborn baby in limbo right now. I need to find some relatives to take her in, and soon."

Chapter Seventeen

Rachel's biggest challenge this morning, besides staying awake, was making herself shelve the problem of the mystery baby long enough to enjoy being with her family. She itched to begin working on the case, but that would not be fair to her aunts or to Joe and Bobby.

It was always a struggle not to bring her police work home with her, but her worries about their Jane Doe shouldn't be anyone else's problem. Especially not on Christmas day.

As she approached her aunts' Sugar Haus Inn, she stopped for a moment in front of the door, took a deep breath, mentally tried to erase all concerns, smiled wide and opened the door.

"Boo!" Anna had been hiding beside the door, waiting on her.

Rachel jumped, gasped, and placed her hand on her chest. "Goodness, Anna! You scared me!"

This time, Anna really had succeeded in startling her. Rachel had not been expecting Anna to choose this moment to play her favorite little trick on her.

Anna beamed, thrilled with her success. Quickly, she slammed the door in Joe's surprised face so she could do it all over again. She opened the door to his knock.

"Boo!"

Joe feigned great surprise, as did Bobby and Darren. This was Anna's one and only joke and everyone who knew her and saw her delight in it always went along with it.

"Look, Anna!" Bobby said, holding up a new book. "Look what Mommy got me!"

Rachel loved it when Bobby called her Mommy. She hadn't pressed the issue, and he still wavered. Sometimes she was Rachel, and sometimes she was Mommy. It might be wishful thinking, but she thought the 'Mommys' were beginning to outnumber the 'Rachels.'

She had given Bobby permission to bring one of his gifts with him. The one he chose was perfect to share with Anna. It involved photos of every kind of seashell imaginable. Even though it was not a child's book, it was so fascinating she knew Bobby would enjoy it.

Bobby and Anna were great friends. Anna immediately went to her favorite spot on the front room couch, and held out her arms. Rachel pulled Bobby's hat and coat off just in time for him to go barreling over to show Anna his prize.

Yes, Anna and Bobby were great friends—just like Anna and Rachel had been when she was a child. Anna's gentle, childlike mind made her a favorite with all the young relatives. Her sense of perpetual wonder made sharing small treasures especially gratifying.

Bobby crawled up beside her and they began to marvel over the photos in the book.

"I have this one," Anna pointed to a picture in the book, excitedly. "And this one."

"What a good choice you made for your son," Bertha commented. "So much wiser than those electronic gizmos every Englisch child carries around these days."

"Thank you, Bertha." Rachel chose not to mention the fact that Santa had put one of those gizmos under the tree for Bobby as well. In fact, she thought it best not to mention Santa at all. Or the gizmo.

Lydia entered the living room, wiping her hands on her apron.

"Brunch is ready."

"Did your *dummkoffs* leave?" Rachel asked.

"They did," Lydia said. "About an hour ago."

"*Dummkoffs?*" Bertha asked.

Lydia blushed. "I was not as kind last night as I should have been when Rachel dropped by. I said some ugly things about the guests who left this morning."

"I think maybe you were overly tired from the cookies you stayed up so late making for them?" Rachel said.

"Probably," Lydia confessed. "I was very tired."

"Are you talking about those beautiful cookies our guests refused to take with them this morning because you had not used organic flour?" Bertha asked.

"Yes," Lydia said. "Those guests."

"Hmmph! Let us enjoy our morning together and not speak of them again."

Rachel couldn't resist. "You mean they were not strangers who were 'angels unaware'?"

"*Nein,*" Bertha said. "Definitely not angels. Imagine someone having the nerve not to appreciate Lydia's cookies when she'd been up half the night baking! Now, we will have our own Christmas and never speak of those *Englisch* people again."

Although it was not the Amish way to shower one another with an abundance of gifts at Christmas, Rachel and Anna had a tradition. She gave Anna a gift of scented bubble bath every year. Anna, in turn, gave Rachel a carefully selected box of scented bath salts. They had done this for years. Anna happily used up her bubble bath ever year. Rachel, on the other hand, rarely took the time to luxuriate in a tub. She much preferred a quick shower, which caused her bath salts to generally go unused. Down through the years, she had amassed quite a collection.

Throwing them or giving them away was inconceivable because Anna had gone to great pains to select just the right one each year, which made them precious to her. And so, an abundance of bath salts had become part of the décor of her bathroom.

To Bertha and Lydia, she gave a subscription to Mary Jane's Farm, which was a relatively new magazine that some of her younger Amish friends were beginning to discover. It was packed with gardening, crafts, and cooking advice.

Darren gave the aunts some flower seeds; a gift Rachel had suggested. The aunts had bought one present only, but it was meant for the whole family. It was a new sled for Bobby that he was expected to share.

And that was all that was exchanged. A new sled for their family. Some bath salts, flower seeds, and a magazine subscription.

Many Englisch would consider such a Christmas to be Spartan in the extreme. But Rachel and her aunts were well-satisfied, as was Bobby who immediately went sleigh riding with his dad and uncle the minute the last gift was opened.

The Amish, as a people, were not against the giving of gifts. In fact, Rachel's aunts were such giving people, it sometimes seemed that they were forever making or giving her something throughout the entire year. Some gifts were small, but some were large.

For instance, Rachel and Joe's bed was resplendent in a wedding-ring quilt that Bertha and Lydia had pieced and quilted over one long winter. Since Joe preferred a king-sized bed, this had been a huge undertaking. Rachel seldom visited her aunts without walking away with a sack of windfall apples from the small orchard in their backyard, or a loaf of Lydia's bread, or some small treasure Anna decided Rachel desperately needed.

Anna's gifts tended toward pretty rocks, brightly-colored bird feathers, and bouquets of wild flowers. Of course, Anna, herself, was gift enough. Her love for everyone she came into contact with permeated the Sugar Haus Inn. Aunt Bertha's gifts tended to be in the nature of wisdom and advice.

When Joe, Darren, and Bobby went to try out the sled, Anna wanted to be part of the outdoor fun too, so Rachel helped her put on her heavier coat, made certain she had a warm head covering, woolen scarf, boots, and gloves before she went out.

By the time Rachel came back to the kitchen, the table had already been cleared, and the sink readied for dish washing with hot, soapy water and clean drying cloths laid out and ready.

"You are not yourself this morning," Bertha said. "Although I cannot decide if it is worry or simply fatigue."

"It's a little of both," Rachel said. "Last night was tough."

"Then tell us what happened after you left us last night," Bertha said. "Lydia was afraid that the police radio squawking meant trouble. We will talk while you help me wash dishes and you will tell me all about it." She pointed toward the chair they kept in the kitchen. "Lydia, you sit down. You've done enough this morning."

"*Danke,*" Lydia said. "It will be good to give my feet a rest."

With Bobby safely out of earshot, Rachel plunged her hands into the hot water and told Bertha and Lydia about the wreck, the baby, and Keturah Hochstetler's part in it all while she washed dishes. Bertha listened while she dried and put the dishes back into the cupboards. Lydia, whose hands were rarely still even when she was supposed to be resting, was working on some knitting.

"Keturah is a strong one," Bertha said, with great admiration when Rachel had finished the story. "That was not an easy thing for her to do. No one could better care for the babe than Keturah and her daughter-in-law."

"Yes, but unless we find the family soon, I'm afraid the baby will have to be put in foster care anyway."

"Foster care is not a good place?" Lydia inquired.

"Sometimes it is, but not always," Rachel admitted.

"Ach, then. It is an easy decision," Lydia said. "Leave the babe with the Hochstetlers for now. She will be loved and fed and well taken care of. No one loves a baby more than Keturah."

"It won't be legal to leave her there for long. Social services will need to get involved."

"Then you need to find that family and soon," Bertha said, as though that was the end of the conversation.

"It might not be easy," Rachel said. "And there might not be any family member able or willing to take the baby."

"Then I will pray about it." Bertha gave a quick nod as a punctuation to the statement. "And God will sort it out."

Chapter Eighteen

....

"Any word on Sugarcreek's mystery woman?" Rachel asked, as she entered the small police station after dropping Joe, Darren, and a very cranky Bobby off at their house. The combination of playing outdoors for two hours in the snow, combined with too many of Lydia's sugar cookies, had him at the point of tears. Her guess was that a nice long Christmas nap was in his immediate future, and possibly Joe's as well. She wouldn't mind one herself, but she knew she wouldn't be able to sleep a wink today with that sweet baby in limbo.

"Not yet," Ed said. "I heard back from the two Cleveland cops who stopped by the house connected to the license plates this morning, but no one was home."

"Were they wearing uniforms?"

"Probably," Ed said. "I doubt the precinct would send plain-clothed detectives just to see if an old woman was home."

"Would you mind if I drove up there, poked around a little and maybe asked some neighbors what they know? There's a chance the car's owner is having Christmas with relatives. A neighbor might know that. They might even know who she's visiting."

"You aren't on duty today."

"I don't care. I'll be happy to do this on my own time."

"You realize you don't have any jurisdiction."

"Of course, but I'm not going there to arrest anyone. I care about

103

this case and I'm anxious to solve it. That baby needs its family."

"Then go knock yourself out," Ed said.

"I don't suppose you've heard anything back from the coroner."

"I know it's been a long day for us but today is still Christmas for normal people. What do you think?"

"I think that's a no."

"You would be right."

"Any word on the fingerprints?" Rachel said.

"Again, it's Christmas day. When I called the lab, they said they are working with a skeleton staff and it might take a while. I hate to say it, but that poor girl picked a very inconvenient time to die."

"Has there been any reports filed of a missing car?"

"Plenty, but none of them were for a blue '92 Buick."

"What about a young woman who's gone missing?"

"No one who matches the description."

The phone rang and Ed answered it. Rachel waited to see if it was something that might involve her.

"I understand," Ed said into the phone. "Yes, we'll help look for him. Yes, I do understand, my father suffered from dementia too. Yes, I know that it's very cold out. Was he wearing a coat? Good. I'll be right there."

"What's going on, Ed?" she asked.

The police chief was already buckling on his utility belt, and grabbing his coat.

"Ray Jones over in Ragersville wandered off during his family's Christmas this morning, and they still haven't found him. I need to take care of this. I'll leave you to follow up on the Jane Doe mystery." He put on his hat. "I don't think there will be any danger involved in your trip, but be careful up there."

"Always," she said.

As Ed drove off to help find Ray, she decided to stop by the

Hochstetlers before she headed up to Cleveland.

When she arrived, the baby was resting comfortably in a small, handmade cradle made of cherry wood. Agnes sat nearby on the couch with two-month-old Rosie on her lap. Rosie wore a small, white, kapp just like her sister's and mother's and a simple blue dress. Her little feet were bare, even though it was winter, but the wood stove was putting out so much heat that Clara was also barefoot as she hovered over the cradle.

As Rachel approached, little Clara put a finger up to her lips to warn that the baby was asleep. It was a surprise to see that the baby was wearing a tiny, white, kapp exactly like the others. Anyone seeing her for the first time would assume she was an Amish baby.

"How is everything going?" Rachel kept her voice soft so as not to disturb the sleeping baby.

"Oh, we are doing fine. It's going to be hard to let this sweet baby go," Agnes said. "We will happily keep her if no one else wants her."

"I don't think it's that easy," Rachel said. "Social Services will have to get involved if we can't find the baby's relatives. I'm headed to Cleveland today to see if I can trace down someone who is a relative and can take charge of her."

"I hope they are good people," Agnes said.

"I do too," Rachel agreed. "Are you staying here?"

"Keturah thought it might be best for now. We weren't sure if I would be allowed to take the baby home with me. We do not live far away, but we do live over the Holmes County line instead of Tuscarawas. I did not know if it would make a difference to the county government."

"I don't either, but if you don't mind it probably is better for you to stay here at least for today. Where is Keturah?"

"Keturah is helping out on another birthing call," Agnes said. "It might be a while before she comes back. I'm so glad you came. I think there is something you need to know."

"Like what?"

"My mother-in-law did not tell you everything that happened yesterday morning."

"Why not?" Rachel asked.

"I'm not sure she remembered it with everything that was going on this morning," Agnes said.

"And what was it?" Rachel hoped for even a small clue she could follow up on.

"The mother was still conscious for a moment after Keturah helped her out of the wrecked vehicle. Before she died, she told Keturah not to let him have her baby."

"Not to let *who* have the baby?"

"That's what we don't know," Agnes said. "She just said 'him.' We think the mother might have been trying to run away from whoever 'him' is."

"Thanks for telling me, Agnes." Rachel was troubled by this information. "And thank you for what you are doing."

At that moment, the baby began to fuss, and Clara responded by gently starting to rock the little cradle.

"It is not a problem." Agnes smiled. "As you can see, I have a good helper."

"Yes, you do," Rachel said, slightly envious of Agnes and her children. "I'll check back with you when I know something more."

Chapter Nineteen

As Rachel drove out of Sugarcreek on Route 39, she stopped at the McDonald's outside of town. There she purchased the largest cup of coffee they offered. The only sleep she'd had was a two-hour nap before she went on duty last night. There had been times when she'd gone much longer without sleep, and she knew she could do it again. Besides, with the restaurant closed down for Christmas day, Joe was able to thoroughly enjoy being with Bobby. They didn't need her around in order to play with Bobby's Christmas toys.

Technically, she did not have to make this trip. She could have gone home and climbed into bed and dealt with it tomorrow. Or she could have handed it over to one of the other officers tomorrow, but this situation felt personal. She'd been the first cop on the scene and the vision of rain pouring down on that young mother's face wouldn't go away.

Until that sweet baby was settled and safe with, hopefully, loving family members, she would not be able to rest.

She did some quick calculations in her head. The drive to Cleveland only took about an hour and a half. If all went well, she'd be home in time to spend the rest of the evening with Bobby. He would probably want to play the Chinese checkers they had bought him, which were quickly becoming his latest obsession.

Chinese checkers, she could handle. There was actual strategy involved. It was his Candyland phase that had been rough on her. The day Bobby announced he was too big to play that "baby game" had been a happy day for her.

When she arrived at the address Ed had given her, she parked across the street and took a good look at the neighborhood. No doubt this had been a nice, blue-collar neighborhood once. Now it was a seedy, run-down place that gave the impression that the only people who still lived here were those who had lost hope of anything better.

She had not changed out of the civilian clothes she'd worn to her aunt's Christmas brunch. Slacks, a sweater, and a warm jacket. Having worked in Cleveland in past years, she had a hunch that whoever lived at this address was not gone but was just not willing to open the door to a uniformed police officer. If that was the case, she was hoping that a paper plate heaped with Lydia's cookies might help get her foot in the door. Before she stepped out of the car, she carefully secured her Glock beneath her sweater at the small of her back, just in case. It was, in her opinion, better to have a gun and not need it than to need a gun and not have it.

It looked as though whoever lived in this house cared at least a little about their home. There were a couple of dead plants in pots on the small porch, a couple of garden gnomes in a flowerbed in front, and an actual welcome mat outside the door. How welcome she would be, provided anyone was home, was anyone's guess.

She knocked on the door and, just like with the two street cops, no one answered. Then, out of the corner of her eye, she saw a curtain flicker. She took a couple steps back so the inhabitant could see that she was a just a non-threatening woman holding a plate of Christmas cookies.

She hoped there was nothing about her that shouted "cop." She'd also driven her classic silver blue Mustang. That was something she'd already begun to regret. It would not be a good idea to leave it parked on the street for too long while she was inside the house, assuming she was ever allowed inside.

She had placed a red bow on top of the cookies.

No cop here. Just a friendly neighborhood do-gooder.

Probably not something this neighborhood saw often… if at all.

She pasted a big grin on her face and hoped for the best.

A few minutes later, she heard a faint sound coming from within. She recognized it as the thump, drag, thump, drag sound of someone using a walker.

There was a great deal of fumbling on the other side of the door, as various locks were opened.

A thin, elderly woman with a deeply-lined face, unkempt gray hair, and wary eyes peeked through the small crack as she carefully opened the door.

"Are you Mabel Evans?" Rachel asked.

"I am."

"My name is Rachel Mattias," she said. "I'm from Sugarcreek, Ohio. If you have a minute or two, I'd like to talk to you."

"If you're trying to sell me something, I don't have any money."

"All I want is a little information."

The woman shrank back. "I don't know nothing."

"Okay, then." Rachel held the plate out toward the woman. "At least take these cookies. They are made with real butter and are some of the overflow of my Aunt Lydia's Christmas baking. You would be doing me a favor if you would take them. Lydia loves to bake. She never seems to know when to stop. I don't think my little boy can handle any more sugar, and I know that I don't need the calories."

"Well…" The woman wrestled with the decision of whether or not to unlatch the storm door. Finally, she did and held out her hand. "Okay."

Opening the storm door was a mistake. Smiling, Rachel held firmly onto the handle as she handed the woman the cookies.

"Merry Christmas!" she said. "Actually, I'm a cop from over in Sugarcreek. What I need to talk with you about is your car."

"What about my car?" Mabel said.

"Do you own a blue, '92 Buick?"

"Yes."

"Where do you usually keep it?"

"Out back, in the garage."

"Did you loan it to someone?"

Mabel hesitated. "No. Why?"

"Did you realize it was missing?"

"Missing?" The old woman said. "Not that I'm aware of."

"How long has it been since you went back there?"

"I don't know. A few weeks. I don't get around so good anymore."

"When was the last time it was driven?"

"My brother comes get it out of the garage and drives it around every now and then to make sure it still runs."

"When was the last time he was here?"

"Last month. He's been down in the back some lately."

"A vehicle matching the description of your car and bearing your car's license tags was found, wrecked, last night outside of Sugarcreek, Ohio. Any idea how it might have gotten there?"

"If you're a cop," Mabel said, "why aren't you dressed like one?"

"I'm not on duty today." Rachel pulled her badge out of her pocket and held it up for Mabel to inspect. The old woman steadied it with her hand and brought her nose up close to read it. Rachel realized that quite a lot might happen around her house without Mabel knowing it.

"Well, it looks official enough." She handed the badge back to Rachel and hobbled into the living room, sitting the cookies on a small table as she passed. "Come on in then, and lock the door. Some of my neighbors will steal me blind if I don't watch out."

"How long have you lived here?" Rachel asked.

"Nearly sixty years now. It was a good neighborhood once. Lots of nice young families. Now, I'm afraid to go outside unless my brother goes with me, and he's getting a little scared too."

Mabel had once been a tall woman, but not anymore. Her back was sharply curved and she seemed to be permanently bent over her walker. Still, even though she was obviously unable to do much in the way of house cleaning, Rachel was surprised to find the house well kept, and the smell was fresh and clean. It was definitely not the smell that she usually associated with an elderly woman's house—especially one who was infirm.

It was also sparser than most old people's houses she'd been in, but the couch that Rachel was directed to sit upon was comfortable. Mabel lowered herself onto an armchair.

"Go ahead," she said. "Ask whatever it is you want to ask."

By the time Rachel had explained the whole story, the old woman had grown pale.

"Do you have any idea who that young woman was who died?" Rachel asked. "We need to find the family."

There was a long hesitation while Rachel watched something play behind Mabel's eyes. There was a decision being made, and she was afraid she wasn't going to like it.

"No," Mabel said. "I have no idea. I don't know anyone who matches that description. Like I said, there are a lot of druggies around here. Probably one of them stole it."

"Does your brother, the one who sometimes drives your car, have a daughter or granddaughter who might fit the description?"

"My brother never married or had any children."

"Do you have children or grandchildren?" Rachel asked.

"No. Wish I did, but I don't."

"When I came up the sidewalk, I noticed your garage had a padlock on it. Do you always keep your garage locked?"

"Yes."

"Who has a key?"

"Just me."

"That's it?"

Another hesitation. "Yes."

"May I take a look inside your garage before I leave?"

Mabel thought about it for a moment, then dug into a drawer in the table beside where she was sitting and handed Rachel a key. "Suit yourself."

As Rachel went out to inspect the garage, she was puzzled by the fact that the garage was still padlocked, even though the car was gone. Thieves rarely bothered with keys. They used crowbars to pry a lock off, or special tools to cut it. And she couldn't imagine why car thieves would go to so much trouble for a vehicle that wasn't worth all that much. Nothing added up. Mabel was not telling her everything she knew.

She unlocked the padlock and opened the doors to the detached, single-car garage that was just big enough to park a car in with a couple feet on each side. The space in the middle was now empty. Up until this moment, she had thought there might have been a mistake about the license tags. Now she knew for certain that it was Mabel's car the girl had been driving. There had been no mistake.

In a TV drama, she would see a clue. Some left-behind piece of evidence that would help her solve the case, but there was nothing in here except a few yard tools. A couple rakes. A shovel. An old push mower.

Whoever took the car had unlocked the garage, backed it out, and then carefully returned the doors and padlock to their normal position. They might even have returned the key to its regular place beside

Mabel's chair unless there was another copy.

She supposed the brother could be suspected of some sort of wrong-doing. He seemed to be the only other person with access to the old Buick, but unless Mabel was lying about her brother, she couldn't see how he would be involved with Jane Doe and the baby.

Still, she was fairly certain that Mabel was hiding something. The question was, why? What would an old woman like her have to hide?

Mabel was waiting at the front door to receive the key after Rachel finished her investigation of the garage. As she handed over the key, Rachel also gave the old woman her business card. "Please call me if you can think of anything that will help us find out who the dead girl is who stole your car."

"Like I told you before," Mabel said. "I don't know nothing about it. Besides, I've learned to keep my nose out of my neighbors' business. It's a lot safer that way around here."

"This has something to do with a neighbor?" Rachel asked.

Mabel did not answer the question. Instead, she stuck her head out the door and craned her neck to look up and down the street as though to make sure the coast was clear. "You were smart not to wear your uniform."

"Why?"

"This neighborhood don't like cops. You seem like a nice woman. You said you have a little boy. Best for both of us if you never come back."

"My number is on my card. Call me if you think of something else that I need to know, or if you just need help."

"Yeah." Mabel ducked back inside. "Sure thing."

Rachel had parked on the street, directly across from Mabel's house. She got into her Mustang, started it up, and sat there for a few minutes checking her text messages.

As she sat there, she saw a young man walking down the street toward the house next to Mabel's. Late-twenties. From a distance, he did not look like he belonged in this neighborhood. Tall, well-built, short haircut, white. Someone who, from a distance, looked like he could have been an Eagle Scout at one time.

But that swagger did not come from attending scout meetings. That was street-level swagger. Cock-of-the-walk level. Alpha-male, I-own-everything-I-survey level. A gang member if she'd ever seen one.

It had been a long time since she had to use her knowledge about street gangs to assess a situation. Now, she tried to recall what she knew. This young man swaggering up the sidewalk probably wasn't a Heartless Felon, which from what she knew tended to be primarily made up of young black men. But she'd heard there was another gang in the city gaining prominence that was white, and every bit as tough and deadly.

The young man came to a stop in front of a house that was next-door to Mabel. Before going inside, he turned around and carefully surveyed the neighborhood. She knew the instant he marked her sitting there in her Mustang because the hair stood up on the back of her neck. Unless she missed her guess, Mabel's next-door-neighbor was one dangerous dude. No wonder Mabel had warned her not to come back.

One thing she could be absolutely certain of was that Mabel's dangerous-looking neighbor had not stolen her car. No self-respecting gang member would be caught dead in a grandma tank like the old Buick. Not to mention that they wouldn't have bothered to neatly lock up the garage after they'd taken it.

Her classic Mustang, however, was a very cool and memorable car. A gang member with taste might be interested. Since she would prefer not to be involved in a carjacking, she decided that, if and when she came back, she'd be driving Joe's beat-up truck, and she would definitely be packing more than one weapon.

Chapter Twenty

....

After discovering that Mabel, the owner of the car, had no knowledge of the baby's family, or at least professed to have no knowledge, she decided to try to make more permanent arrangements for the baby's care.

That involved a call to social services, which she made while picking up some fast food on the outskirts of Cleveland. It took a long time for someone to answer. Apparently, they were either completely closed down for the holiday, or understaffed and overwhelmed to the point they couldn't answer one more phone call.

If that was the case, she wouldn't be surprised. Christmas often brought out the worst in people. So often, the holidays created a culmination of drinking, broken dreams, disappointments, and guilt—which brought on dangerous domestic situations. Too often, couples took their sadness out on one another, and sometimes their children. The stress of the holiday was more than some people seemed able to handle.

Finally, Sally, a middle-aged social worker Rachel knew from church answered and Rachel told her what had happened.

"I know Keturah and her family," Sally said, after Rachel told her all that had happened. "Agnes fostered a couple of our high-risk babies before Clara was born. If the Hochstetler family doesn't mind keeping her, it would be a kindness to us to leave the baby there for a while longer. I still have to work my way through several cases where the children could be in actual danger. I know the baby will be safe and well cared for with Keturah and Agnes until you can find the poor little thing's family. I've really got to go now. Good luck!"

Rachel sighed as she hung up. Until they got the fingerprints of the young mother back from the lab, there was nothing else for her to go on. Even then, if the girl wasn't in the system, they would be no closer to determining her identity than when Keturah found her.

When Rachel got back to Sugarcreek, she stopped in at the police station to give a report to Ed if he was still there.

When she walked in, she was pleasantly surprised to see Carl Bateman and his dog, Shadow, there. Ed was down on one knee praising Shadow and, from what she could see, Shadow was lapping it up. If it was possible for a dog to smile, Shadow was smiling. She saw that Kim had come in for the afternoon shift and there was an air of celebration in the office.

"What's going on?" she asked.

Carl, who was holding the dog's leash, smiled at her. "Shadow's done it again."

"Done what?"

"Shadow found Ray Jones, the man with dementia who wandered away from his family's Christmas party this morning," Ed said. "The family was very relieved."

"Oh, good dog!" Rachel dropped to her knees and buried her face in Shadow's fur. "You are *such* a good dog!"

She meant it with all her heart. Shadow was an extraordinary animal, and so was the man who had trained him. Carl and Shadow had saved her life just over a year ago, at the risk of their own. In fact, Shadow had needed extensive surgery after the bullet he had taken.

"Was Ray okay?" she asked.

"Cold and extremely disoriented," Ed said. "But he'll be fine. His daughter was absolutely frantic with worry when I got there. Instead of going back over ground she and the rest of the family had covered, I called Carl. It took Shadow… what, fifteen minutes?"

"He does have a good nose," Carl said, modestly, but Rachel could see the pride in his eyes. He'd put his heart and soul into training Shadow, a dog he'd found scrounging in the trash, and it had paid off not only for her but for the whole community.

"Did you and Doc Peggy have a good honeymoon trip?" Rachel asked, as she stood up. "Bertha told me about the seashells you brought back for Anna. That was kind of you. Anna's excited about them."

"Peggy was the one who thought of it. Gathering those shells for Anna gave us a nice reason to walk the beach."

"Who took care of her animal clinic while you were gone?"

"Our daughter, Vicki," Carl said. "She just graduated with her DVM last spring. She and her husband and their two sons are staying with us through Christmas. In fact, they like it here so well, they are thinking seriously about staying on. Her husband is an accountant."

"I am so happy for you." Rachel had not missed the pride in his voice when he called Peggy's girl 'our daughter.'

"Yeah, I've got a new saying now that Peggy and I are married."

"What's that?"

"Life begins at sixty-two!"

It was a sad statement, but she knew what he meant. After twenty years in prison, if anyone deserved a second chance, it was Carl.

He seemed to read her thoughts. "It's okay, Rachel. Without those years in prison, learning how to work with those rescued dogs, I would never have met Peggy. And let me tell you something—*that* is a woman who was worth waiting for."

Shadow looked up at him, expectantly, as though saying, can we go home now?

"Say goodbye to the good people, Shadow."

At the command to say goodbye, Shadow lifted his paw and politely shook hands with each of them in turn.

"Sorry to be in a hurry," Carl said, "but Peggy has a ham in the oven, and after supper my son-in-law and I are going to watch the game together."

"If you don't mind, Ed," Kim said, "I'd like to leave, too. My family is getting together tonight at my mom's."

"Go ahead," Ed said. "The other two will be coming in soon. By the way, you did a good job calming down Ray's daughter today. I was afraid the woman was going to have a stroke, she was so worried."

"No problem." Kim followed Carl and Shadow out the door.

"I never thought I'd see the day when Kim made a good cop." Rachel fell into a chair near Ed's desk.

"And I never thought I'd see the day when I actually liked Carl," Ed said, after Carl and Shadow left. "He's a great example of what the prisoner and dog program can sometimes accomplish."

"And what Bertha's prayers and letters also accomplished," Rachel said. "Don't forget Bertha's part in Carl Bateman's redemption."

"Of course," Ed said. "Now, what did you find out in Cleveland?"

"Not much," Rachel said. "I did get Mabel to let me in but she didn't know the girl. Didn't know the car was missing. Always kept it locked away in a garage."

"Do you believe her?"

"Not entirely. I think she's lying about the car, but she seemed to be stunned by the young mother's death and trying not to show it."

Ed leaned back in his chair and clasped his hands behind his head. "What's your assessment?"

"Mabel knows a whole lot more than she is saying. She also seemed very frightened. That's not a normal reaction."

"Is there any chance the girl might have been a neighbor?"

"I don't think so. That's a bad neighborhood. Mabel had to unlock about a dozen locks to let me in. Very suspicious lady. I can't see her getting cozy with anyone."

"Okay, then." Ed nodded. "Let's check and see if any of Mabel's family members are the same age and gender as our Jane Doe."

"Good idea, even though she swears there isn't."

"How is the baby doing?"

"She's fine for now. Keturah and her daughter-in-law are taking excellent care of her and, of course, Doc Mike is next door. I get the feeling he's over at the Hochstetler's a lot."

"He grew up next door. They've always treated him like a son."

"I talked to Sally at social services. She said that she's fine with them continuing to care for the baby for now. Agnes used to take in foster children. The only thing I see wrong about leaving the baby with them is that little Clara is getting awfully attached—quite the little mother. If the baby stays with them much longer, I think it's going to be hard on both her and Agnes to let go."

"No doubt, but you can't help that and neither can I. Now go on home and get some sleep. You've done enough for one day."

Rachel did go home. When she got there, she was relieved that Joe, Darren, and Bobby had left a note that they had gone to the movies. No Chinese checkers tonight. Instead, she went into her bedroom and, fully clothed, she fell face down on her bed, and did not move or awaken until daybreak.

Chapter Twenty-One

A new birth usually left Keturah tired but happy the next day. Exuberant if the birth had gone well—and most went well. It was a joyous life she lived most of the time.

Who wouldn't love a life that involved helping ease new babies into the world? Getting to hold the precious newborn, cuddle, it, love it, admire the new little miracle along with the new mother and father. If the mother had not already had multiple births and was, therefore, not well-educated in the process of having babies, Keturah would give her advice about all the things involving the nurturing of new life.

Of course, being a midwife to the Amish meant that she was seldom the only other woman present with the new mother. There was almost always grandmothers and aunts and sisters present to help. Together, they would discuss the benefits of catnip tea versus stinging nettle tea or a myriad of other tinctures and herbs the Amish culture had depended on for generations.

Her people went to doctors, but only after every home remedy they knew or heard of was exhausted. Part of it was frugality. With no insurance, the cost of a doctor came directly out of their pocket. Part of it was a natural distrust of all things not Amish or Mennonite.

There had been a wonderful Mennonite doctor in their midst for a while, but he had retired. It had been such a comfort to talk with a doctor who spoke their language. It was tiresome to try to translate certain symptoms into English when one was ill.

Keturah had no more mothers close to birthing for the next couple weeks, and she was okay with that. The ordeal she had experienced had taken a toll on her body and mind, and she was grateful for the respite.

"Have you heard anything from the policewoman today?" Agnes asked.

"No." Keturah was trying to rock little Rosie to sleep. "I know she is trying to find the baby's family. I think she must have not found them yet."

"It feels very strange," Agnes said. "To have a beautiful new baby and no family. Not even a family name."

"I agree," Keturah said.

Among her Amish friends, information about a motherless child would be all through the various families and churches. They would know where the baby was, who was caring for it, and how it was faring.

But in the Englisch world... silence. There should be a family celebrating the birth of this child today instead of it being cared for by strangers. Hadn't anyone noticed that a pregnant daughter, or sister, or niece was missing?

She had a lot of things worrying her right now. Ivan had shared with her the fact that Noah had apparently begun walking out with Beth, the Yoder girl, who everyone had doubts about remaining Amish. That was a huge worry.

Having Michael living next door again was a wonderful thing, but where was that Englisch wife of his? Something was very wrong there. Michael had chosen not to confide in her, and that was as it should be. A man should be loyal to his wife and not say bad things about her even to his family, but really! What young woman in her right mind would not want to be with Michael? Why did she not quit her lawyer job and move here to be with her husband?

Keturah knew very little about the law, but she knew a great deal about the care and nurturing of a marriage. It was not wise for a man or a woman to choose their work over their mate. Keturah clucked her tongue. She did not understand Englisch people. What could be more important than one's vow to God to stay together until death? It was a puzzle—but then, so much of the Englisch world's choices puzzled her.

Michael had walked around like a lost soul yesterday, dark circles beneath his eyes, trying hard not to show that his heart was broken. The entire family noticed and remarked quietly about it to her. They all loved Michael and were worried about him. She was a gentle person, but she wished she could have a good hard talk with Michael's wife.

Chapter Twenty-Two

Michael needed to talk to someone. Someone who would care. Someone besides himself venting to the mirror as he shaved. Someone with good sense and sound advice.

Ivan and Noah ran one of the smaller dairy herds in the Holmes County area, but it provided a modest living for them. The Hochstetlers kept expenses down by growing and harvesting their own hay and corn for the cows, and the animals were exceptionally well-cared for and healthy.

It was five o'clock in the morning and still quite dark, but he knew right where to go. Grabbing his barn coat and shoving his feet into boots that had seen their share of cow manure, he walked through the snow and across the pasture that lay between his house and the Hochstetler property.

When he entered their barn, a feeling of peace descended upon him. His wife had once dabbled with aromatherapy. She came home with essence of lavender and said it was supposed to calm her nerves. Whether it did or didn't, he had no idea. What he did know was that the familiar smell of an old barn had an instantaneous calming effect on him. It always had.

Ivan was milking a cow while she calmly chewed her cud as Michael walked in.

"Good morning, Ivan. Could you use some help?"

"Pull up a stool." Ivan nodded at the cow next to the one he was milking. She was standing patiently, ready for her full-to bursting udder to be stripped. Noah was further down the line. He raised his hand in greeting, then leaned his head against the side of a lovely Guernsey cow and continued to milk.

Michael grabbed a galvanized bucket Ivan had placed, sterilized and ready to be filled on a nearby worktable. He positioned it beneath the cow, seated himself on an extra three-legged stool, and began the process. The wholesome smell of the healthy cow as he leaned his head into her warm flank and the rhythmic sound of strong streams of milk ringing against the sides of the bucket were a balm to his soul in this early-morning darkness.

Some Amish farmers had purchased milking machines, but Ivan had not yet chosen to do so. Michael had tried to talk him into it, but Ivan was slow to make changes. At this moment, Michael was grateful that he had resisted. Now, the action gave his hands something to do, and a reason not to look at his old friend as he shared with him the sore spot in his heart.

"Cassie wants a divorce."

He could not see Ivan, but he heard the sound of jets of milk hitting the side of the bucket cease while Ivan absorbed this information. Then the rhythmic sound started up again. It took a few moments for Ivan to respond.

"And do you want this divorce as well?"

"It's ripping my heart out."

"Have you told her this?"

"No."

"Then that's the first step," Ivan said. "You must tell her."

"Talking to Cassie doesn't help once she's made up her mind to do something."

"Then, perhaps you should find a way to un-make her mind."

Michael pondered this. The only thing he could imagine helping resolve this impasse was for him to apologize, abandon his dream of being a small-town vet, and live the rest of his life exactly the way Cassie told him to.

"I don't think she'll listen," Michael said.

"You have been apart for a long time," Ivan's voice was concerned. "That is not good for a husband and wife. Perhaps she should come here for a while so that you can work things out."

"Cassie won't be coming here," Michael said. "I can guarantee that. The only possibility of her taking me back is if I agree to move back to the city with her."

The sound of milk ceased again. He knew that Ivan did not like hearing about that possibility.

"But this is your home." The sound of milk ringing against the side of the bucket began again.

"She has a very important job. She's worked hard for it and she refuses to leave."

Ivan digested this information. "You have a wife who is unwilling to follow your leadership?"

The idea of Cassie *ever* considering to follow his leadership struck Michael as humorous. Without meaning to, he barked out a laugh. The cow he was milking twitched her tail, and glanced around at him.

"What is so funny?" Ivan asked.

"Cassie does not accept the idea of male leadership. She's a modern woman, Ivan. She's really strong, and very smart."

"My wife is also strong and smart, but she does not choose to divorce me because of it, nor do my strong, smart, daughters-in-law choose to leave my sons." Ivan sounded puzzled. "I think you must have chosen a wife poorly, son."

"Perhaps, but plenty of men would think they hit the jackpot if they got to live with someone as beautiful and successful as Cassie."

Ivan chose not to comment on this, and Michael knew why. Beauty and success wasn't supposed to be a priority for choosing a mate within the Amish community.

In fact, it was only against the backdrop of the old-fashioned Amish mindset that it seemed like he had made a mistake. Had he allowed his lifetime association with Hochstetlers to make him believe Cassie was in the wrong, when all along it was him?

But if he had made a mistake by leaving her to come here, it was a little late to come to that conclusion. He had already signed papers agreeing to purchase Doc Taylor's veterinarian practice. Doc Taylor had not left a big estate. All he had left his widow besides his good name was his veterinarian office on Main Street and the practice he had built up over the years. Widow Taylor was dependent financially on the monthly payments Michael would be giving her. He couldn't simply walk away from a responsibility like that.

"Do not worry," Ivan said. "Your wife is probably only being a little bit stubborn. Sometimes it takes a while for things to smooth out between young couples. Sometimes even young Amish couples remind me of two people competing in a three-legged potato-sack race. Both of them wanting to go in opposite directions, tripping and falling and arguing until they get the hang of running the race together. Keturah and I will be in prayer about this. You will see. Something good will happen."

Michael admired Ivan and Keturah's faith, but he had no doubt that Cassie would push through with this divorce no matter how many prayers the Hochstetlers said. They had not lived with her and seen her single-minded focus. He had.

Truth be told, he wasn't particularly fond of the steely-eyed woman he'd left behind in Columbus but, the longer he was away from her, the more he missed the friendship they had once shared. As he and Noah helped Ivan finish up in the barn, he wondered if there might still be a shred of that friendship left.

Chapter Twenty-Three

"And how did your holiday go?" Bradley Cooper asked Cassie, as she joined him in the conference room the day after Christmas.

"It was fine. I finished work on the Johnson case."

"Great! Did Michael come here or did you go see him in Sugarcreek?"

Cassie hesitated. She didn't like discussing personal things at work, but Bradley was her boss and a partner in the firm. It would be rude and unwise not to answer.

"I stayed home."

"Then he came here?" Bradley's question felt odd to her. They didn't have that kind of relationship. On the other hand, he'd overseen her work for the past five years. He probably felt like he had the right to show interest.

"No," Cassie admitted. "He stayed in Sugarcreek."

"Did some sort of animal emergency keep him there?"

"No."

"Oh." Bradley sat back in his seat as though absorbing the import of what she'd just revealed.

She was in her usual spot, just to his left, as they sat around the conference table during their office meetings. As usual, she and the always-punctual Bradley were the first to arrive.

"You know you can call me if you ever want to talk." Bradley astonished her by covering her hand with his own.

"Thanks." She heard what sounded like genuine kindness in his voice, but it felt creepy when he let his hand linger on hers. That was new. He jerked it away as two other attorneys arrived.

She hoped he wasn't anticipating the possibility of her being available for an office romance.

On the other hand, he and his wife had recently divorced. Office rumors said that his wife dumped him because she couldn't handle him never being home. Cassie had felt a jolt of sympathy for Bradley because Michael often complained of the same thing.

"I might as well live in Sugarcreek," Michael had thrown at her as he packed to leave. "I never see you anyway."

"If you would just be patient, I might make partner in a few years," Cassie had thrown back. "Then things will be different."

Michael had not responded.

It was so much easier to talk to the people at her office than it was to talk to Michael. Everyone at the office understood the pressure. Especially Bradley. He was one of the youngest to ever make partner in this firm. Of course, his father had been one of the founders, which didn't hurt.

Bradley didn't make her feel bad about her goals. To him, they made utter sense, and she liked that a lot. Nothing about being around Bradley ever made her feel guilty, except right now. As he started the meeting, the feel of his hand covering hers lingered long after it should have. It was not a good feel. His hand was too soft, a little moist, and his fingernails were nearly as manicured as her own.

Some women liked a man who was that fastidious. She would have expected to prefer it to Michael's somewhat rugged hands and neglected, chipped, fingernails. Instead, she was slightly repulsive and that surprised her.

She mentally shrugged it off and focused her attention on the meeting. This was not hard for her. Her well-honed ability to hyper-focus was one of her strengths but, when the meeting ended, Bradley asked her to stay for a moment, which she did, thinking he wanted to talk more about the Johnson case.

Instead, he invited her to dinner that night.

Red flags immediately went up. She had serious misgivings about accepting his invitation. She also worried about the possible repercussions if she turned him down. Office politics were as difficult to deal with as office romances and it was often hard to tell the difference. Things could get very sticky if she turned him down. Things could get even stickier if she accepted.

"It's just dinner, Cassie," he said, when she hesitated.

Bradley was a nice guy, she reassured herself. She'd known and worked with him for over five years. He was definitely no stranger. This was just a friendly dinner. It was fine, she told herself. Colleagues had dinner out all the time together.

"Of course," she said, ignoring the uneasy feeling in the pit of her stomach. "That would be nice."

Chapter Twenty-Four

It had been just over thirty hours since the wreck, and Rachel was no closer to finding out the identification of the mother of the baby. The only lead they had at this point was the fact that the car was licensed to Mabel, who was either clueless or hiding something. Rachel tended toward thinking the old woman was hiding something.

While Ed checked into more missing person's reports, she borrowed Joe's beat-up truck, which she thought would blend in well in Mabel's neighborhood. She donned winter gear involving a sock hat and some Carhart coveralls, filled a thermos with coffee, and went to do a little surveillance. She didn't know what she was expecting to discover, but she didn't have any better ideas.

Snowplows had been through the neighborhood, and she found a spot in front of an empty house with a "for sale" sign in front and parked there. She was partially hidden from Mabel's house by mounds of snow, and doubted anyone would notice Joe's pickup in this neighborhood anyway.

She had dressed warmly because she didn't trust Joe's heating system, but also because she would have to turn the truck engine off once she got there. A vehicle that wasn't running attracted less attention. Fortunately, within an hour, her surveillance paid off.

Walking down the opposite sidewalk, she saw what looked like another young gang member, but this one was carrying a snow shovel.

Without bothering to go up to Mabel's door, he methodically began to shovel the sidewalk in front of her house, clearing all the snow away. When he was finished, he grabbed a broom leaning against the side of the house, which he used to sweep off the porch and porch steps. He knocked down some icicles hanging from the eaves, then he repeated his actions for the house next door—the same one that the Eagle-Scout-looking guy had gone into yesterday—and then went inside.

After a few minutes, Mabel's personal snow shoveler came out of her next-door neighbor's house and went back the way he'd come. This time he was walking a little dreamily, as though he were high on something.

So, it was probably safe to assume the house next to Mabel's was a drug house, but it seemed strange that the kid was willing to shovel her snow before he went into her neighbor's for a fix.

It was time to pay Mabel another visit, and this time Rachel had brought one of Aunt Lydia's fresh apple pies with her. The kind with lattice work on top. She was fairly certain that Mabel would open up when she saw that. She started the truck, drove around the block to scout things out a bit more, and then she pulled into Mabel's newly pristine driveway.

Even though she was dressed very differently, it was only seconds after seeing that tell-tale flicker of the curtain, that she heard the thump, drag, thump, drag of the walker. Unless she was very much mistaken, Mabel was moving a little faster today. No doubt, she'd seen the pie.

Once again, there was the ritual of unlocking of several locks. Then Mabel's face peered out at her, only this time she wasn't looking at Rachel; her eyes were already on that pie.

"That for me?" Mabel asked.

"Sure is," Rachel said.

"I suppose you want to come in." Mabel's voice was grudging.

"I would appreciate it."

Mabel opened the door. Then she once again carefully looked up and down the street, as though trying to see if anyone was watching her let Rachel in.

"I saw a kid shoveling your driveway a few minutes ago." Rachel sat the pie on a small side-table.

"Yeah, the kid does some work for me sometimes," Mabel said. "I haven't had lunch yet. I think I'll go ahead and have some of this pie right now if you don't mind."

The old woman limped off to the kitchen. Rachel waited until Mabel had returned, sliced herself a large piece of pie, and was taking a bite.

"I also saw him shovel your sidewalk before going into your neighbor's house," she said. "Who lives next door?"

Bingo.

Mabel's eyes narrowed. She chewed slowly as she considered whether or not to answer the question. "Tony Maddox."

"Does he sell drugs out of his house?"

Mabel choked a little on her bite of pie and then swallowed. "It's time for you to leave."

"I need your help, Mabel," Rachel said. "A dead girl is lying in a morgue, and she has to belong to someone. The license plate of the car leads here. You and I both know this car was not a random theft. It was someone who knew you."

"How do you know that?"

"For one thing, no self-respecting car thief would steal a car that is so obviously an old-woman's car. For another thing, whoever stole your car put the padlock back on the garage and locked it. Thieves don't do that. You either gave someone the key, or someone knew where it was and cared enough about you to lock up after themselves. It's time for you to tell me what you know, Mabel. Who is the girl? And why is a gangbanger shoveling your driveway?"

"I don't know nothing." Mabel took another bite. "Good pie, by the way."

Rachel sighed. "The young woman was in her early twenties. She had short blonde hair and multiple piercings in her ears. There was no I.D. in the car or on her person. No cell phone. No purse. She was pregnant, Mabel. A local midwife was able to save the baby, but not the mother."

"Wait a minute!" Mabel's fork clattered onto the plate. She was visibly shocked. "Are you telling me that Lily's baby survived?"

"Who is Lily?"

Mabel looked stricken by her slip of the tongue.

"Uh huh," Rachel said. "I think it's time you came with me to the morgue. We need someone to identify the body."

Mabel shrank back. "I'm not going to no morgue."

"Why?"

"I—I just can't." Mabel shivered at the thought.

Rachel had had that reaction from people before. She'd been counting on it.

Some people were horrified at the thought of having to go identify a body.

"Who was Lily to you, Mabel? A relative? A neighbor? Tell me who the father of the baby is. I need a name and an address."

"You won't need an address," Mabel jerked her head toward the house next door. "It's Tony Maddox's baby. Lily lived there with him past couple of years."

"And who, exactly, is Tony?"

"He's... well, all I know is, if you treat him good, he'll take care of you. That's why I get my sidewalk shoveled. Tony makes somebody do that every time there's a snowstorm and then he gives them a little reward afterward. Makes sure my yard is mowed in the summer too. Tony is a good neighbor as long as you don't cross him."

"What does he do if you cross him?"

"Just… don't ever do it."

"Are you saying that Tony is violent?"

Mabel avoided Rachel's eyes by focusing on the pie again. She picked up the fork and toyed with the crust.

"If I have to haul you in front of a judge to get the information I need, I will." Rachel was losing patience.

"Well, okay then!" Mabel threw down her fork again, nearly in tears. "I never shoulda let you in here in the first place!"

"Just tell me what you know about Lily and I'll go away and leave you alone."

That wasn't strictly true. She might need Mabel again, but it was true that she would go away and leave her alone for *today.*

"Oh, okay. I guess it won't hurt nothing," Mabel sighed. "Lily was the sweetest thing. Kinda innocent, you know? She was a runaway. Tony found her wandering around near the bus station and took her home. She didn't have anywhere else to go. She didn't seem to know how to do much. Except she was good at cleaning house and cooking. Because of that, Tony let her stay even when he got tired of her as a girlfriend."

"Tony found a runaway who became his housekeeper and cook?"

"Yeah," Mabel said. "It was kinda like that. She kept house and cooked for him and any of his friends who wandered through. The girl didn't have much of an education or any job skills. She didn't have much gumption either, for that matter, or she would have gotten out of there sooner."

"Were you and her friends?"

"Seemed to me like we were. I think maybe I was her only friend. At least the only one Tony allowed her to have. Tony had plenty of other girlfriends who came and went, but he always kept a tight hold on her. Didn't want to lose his cook, is my opinion. He loved the homemade doughnuts she made. Loved them. He wanted them two or three times a week, she told me. About the only place Tony allowed her to go by herself was over here to visit me. I guess he didn't think an old woman like me would be a problem. She came over here nearly every day."

Mabel's voice choked up and Rachel saw that, underneath her cranky and suspicious exterior, the old woman truly cared about the girl.

"We would watch soaps together most days," Mabel said. "She loved *Days of Our Lives*. I miss her awful."

"Did you give her the keys to your garage that night?" Rachel asked.

"I did more than that." There was a touch of pride in Mabel's voice. "I taught the girl to drive."

"How was that?"

"She'd never had anyone to teach her, I guess. Tony sure wasn't gonna do it. One day he left for Florida. Some kind of a drug run he had to make. Wasn't gonna be back for a few days. She put my walker in the trunk of the car, I got in and told her what to do and she did it. Lily was quick study. Nothing wrong with her mind. My car was an automatic instead of a standard, so she didn't have to learn much except how to keep it on the road. By the time Tony was supposed to get back, she was driving real good. At least I thought she was. Looks now like she didn't learn as much as she should have, wrecking my car and all."

"It was raining Christmas Eve," Rachel said. "Anyone could have slid into that tree. Especially someone who didn't have much experience driving a car. Did you see her that night before she left?"

"No. I was at my brother's Christmas Eve. It was nearly midnight when he brought me back home. I didn't know nothing until you showed up. Didn't even know she was gone."

"Why do you think she waited until Christmas Eve to leave?"

"I don't know, except sometimes, if Tony was in a bad mood, he would knock her around some. Maybe she finally got the courage to get out of there. Women will be brave for their kids sometimes, even when they won't stand up for their own selves. Tony and his friends were probably out partying somewhere and she stayed home and grabbed her chance."

"Did she have a key to your house?" Rachel asked.

"No, but she knew where I hid it outside in case I got locked out. I always kept a spare hidden away. I knew an old woman who walked out on her porch to look at the thermometer in the middle of winter, got locked out of her house, and froze to death."

"So you think she might have come inside, grabbed the garage door key, backed the car out, locked the garage back up, and then put the key neatly away before she drove off? That's a lot of trouble for a car thief to go through."

"I don't know if that's the way it happened," Mabel shrugged. "But she was a tidy little thing."

"What was Lily's last name?"

"I don't know. I don't even know if Lily was her real name. Wasn't none of my business." Mabel brushed a crumb off her lap. "I do know she planned to name her baby Holly if it was a girl, because her due date was two weeks after Christmas."

"Did she ever say anything about her family? Where she came from? That sort of thing?"

"No. She was pretty closed mouth about all that. The only thing she ever told me was that she was the black sheep of the family and could never go home again."

"Tony will need to be told he has a child," Rachel said.

"I wouldn't do that if I were you," Mabel said. "He never wanted that kid to begin with. In fact, it's the only thing Lily ever fought him over. She was determined to have that baby no matter what."

"And yet he still let her stay?"

"He did, but she was on thin ice the whole time. Told me she stayed out of his sight as much as possible. Once she started to show, she either stayed in her room or came over here. She did her housework and cooking when Tony wasn't there."

"So, she had no family that would take her in, as far as you know," Rachel said. "Living at Tony's doesn't seem like much of a life. Did she ever ask to move in here with you instead?"

"We talked about it," Mabel said. "But we both knew Tony wouldn't stand for it. We'd both have been in deep trouble with him."

"If he didn't want the baby, and he didn't want her, why would both of you have been in trouble?"

This time, Rachel had to wait while Mabel finished her piece of pie. The old woman ate every bite, and then scraped at the plate until every crumb was gone. She placed her plate on the living-room table, carefully put the plastic wrap back over the remaining pie, and then looked Rachel in the eye.

"You ain't too bright." She brushed more crumbs off her light blue, polyester pants.

"Excuse me?"

"You ever heard of Ghosts Incorporated?"

"Ghosts Incorporated?" Rachel said. "No."

"It started out as a small street gang. Then it grew," Mabel said. "Kinda like the Heartless Felons, only the majority of the Ghosts are white. They got a few thousand members. Half of 'em probably in the prisons. Not been around as long as some of the others."

"And?"

"Tony's the head. Some people would call him the godfather."

Rachel's heart sank.

"Take my advice," Mabel said. "And leave sleeping dogs lie. Don't tell him he's got a kid. Find a nice family to raise that baby girl. And whatever you do, don't go straight from my house to his. Please. Tony will be mad if he finds out I was talking with a cop about him. Only reason he puts up with me now is I tried to be good to him when he was a kid. That mother of his is one crazy-rotten lady."

***

Instead of going next door to talk with Tony, Rachel took a trip downtown to talk to Bill Sherman, an old friend from her Cleveland days. They'd been partners once. She'd heard awhile back that Bill had been put in charge of the gang division.

"Tony Maddox," Bill said, when she found him in his office. "Yeah, I know the name. Never met the gentleman personally. What is your interest?"

Bill was in his mid-fifties, stocky, and balding. He was genial, loved his wife, and had five children he was hoping to somehow get through college. He was also smart and could, if necessary, be deadly. That was an attribute Rachel remembered a couple of bad guys not anticipating.

In other words, he was a man whom Rachel respected and trusted. She explained the situation with baby Holly while water gurgled through Bill's ever-present Mr. Coffee machine he kept on top of his file cabinet.

"That Amish midwife sounds like one tough cookie," Bill said. "I don't suppose she'd be willing to join the force? She could work undercover. No one would ever suspect an Amish grandmother being a cop. Tell her to think about it."

In Rachel's opinion, Bill's propensity to make lame jokes was one of the reasons he had not yet buckled under the pressure of his job.

"I'll make sure to give Keturah your message," Rachel said. "Now, what can you tell me about Tony?"

Bill swung his chair around, tapped a few keys on his computer, and then studied the screen. "Strong connections with Ghosts Incorporated. He has an attitude, but was never really written up for anything. He did spend time in juvenile detention, but that was before he turned eighteen. Those records are closed."

Bill's chair creaked as he shut down the computer and swung back around to face her.

"On paper, the guy looks okay. In reality, I've heard rumors that he's one of the kingpins of the organization. Lots of suspected drug activity, but nothing we can prove yet."

The coffee machine gave a loud, steamy sigh, signaling that it was finished.

He stood up, went to the file cabinet, and lifted the now-brimming carafe. "Fresh made. Want some?"

"No thanks." Rachel shook her head. "Already had my limit."

He poured coffee into a dirty red and white Ohio State University mug, took a gulp and sat back down at his desk.

"Is Tony dangerous?" she asked.

"Of course he's dangerous. You don't thrive on these streets without being dangerous, or at least having lots of dangerous friends."

"If you find out anything else about him, I'd appreciate knowing it." She stood up, ready to go.

Bill held his cup up in a salute as she left.

Going to see Tony was out of the question today for more reasons than Mabel's fear of him. Rachel wanted to talk this whole thing over with Ed before she made another move. The law was the law. A paternal father had rights with or without being married to the mother, but turning sweet baby Holly over to someone with Tony's background was not something she wanted to do.

Chapter Twenty-Five

Cassie had begun to feel uneasy within moments of agreeing to go out to dinner with Bradley. That feeling lasted all day. It was one thing to have an easy camaraderie with her boss at work. It was altogether another thing to agree to go out to dinner with him. At night. After dark.

As she got ready for the dinner date, she thought through their conversation, examining each word trying to discover why she—a strong, independent woman—had agreed to go out with him in spite of not wanting to do so.

He had caught her off guard, for one thing. He'd also made light of his invitation with his slightly demeaning, "It's only dinner, Cassie," remark.

On closer inspection, she also realized in that moment that her instincts told her that it would not be wise to turn him down. He was a nice enough person, but he *was* her boss. His father was a partner. If she thought about it long enough, he did hold her career in his hands.

It occurred to her that she had fallen into the same trap that so many other women had faced down through the years—saying yes to a boss when her common sense was yelling no.

While they were at dinner, she would make certain to show no romantic interest. She would ignore the topic of his recent divorce, and instead ask about his three small children. She would discuss work throughout the evening as much as possible and pretend that neither of them considered this a date.

Because it was *not* a date.

"It's only dinner, Cassie."

He'd said so himself. Then why did it feel like a date?

Just thinking about the corner he had backed her into made her want to say a few very unladylike words.

Instead, she chose her outfit carefully. More dressy than she wore for the office, but nothing clingy or low-cut. There was a tan, silk dress in the back of the closet that she no longer liked. It was an expensive brand and well-made but, the first time she caught a glance of herself in a store window, she realized the color washed her out and the cut of the dress made her look a bit matronly.

So… the tan dress, plain gold necklace and earrings, tan heels, hair pulled back in a low ponytail, her black-rimmed glasses instead of her contacts—her eyes needed a break from contacts anyway at this time of night. Elegant, but not quite date-worthy. She cocked her head to one side and studied herself in the mirror and almost laughed. She would describe the look she had achieved as that of a well-paid librarian. Expensive outfit, very intelligent… but mousey.

When the buzzer to her apartment complex went off, she took one regretful backward look at her dining-room table before she left. It was piled with work as usual. This evening was going to be such a waste of time.

Bradley was waiting on the sidewalk for her. He looked good, was wearing a dark, perfectly-tailored suit, and was quite the gentleman as he opened the passenger door of his sports car for her. Unfortunately, as she was hunting for the seatbelt, before he closed the door, he leaned in and gave her a quick peck on the lips.

"I'm so glad you decided to go out with me tonight, Cassie," he said. "I've admired you for so long."

Well, *that* was interesting and unwelcome. She fought the desire to scrub the kiss from her lips. As he slipped into the driver's seat, another vehicle drove in right behind them.

He hit the ignition of the low-slung car. She was not overly educated about cars, but it didn't take an expert to know that this one was special. The motor practically growled as it prowled away from the curb. The interior smelled of expensive leather.

This was not the kind of vehicle one purchased to cart around three little kids. This was the kind of car a man drove to impress a client... or a dinner date.

She couldn't help but think back to the hundreds of times she'd ridden in Michael's black, Ford truck over the years. He had always driven a truck, even in the city.

As soon as Bradley pulled away from the curb, he once again put his hand over hers. It felt creepy and she tensed up.

"Relax. We're going to have a good time tonight." He gave her a smoky look. "I promise."

She was grateful when he removed his hand in order to shift—his sports car was a manual, of course. Although he didn't wear any sort of cologne during working hours since some of the staff had allergies, he had made up for it tonight. The scent made a good attempt at being masculine, but it also made her slightly nauseous.

Michael had never worn cologne or any other sort of scent. He said the animals he worked with had such sensitive noses that strong, artificial smells were hard on them.

She found herself missing Michael. Quite a lot, actually. Perhaps she'd been a bit hasty...

As Bradley swung through the dark streets of Columbus, she felt her stomach start to churn and realized she had broken out into a cold sweat. As a kid she'd gotten car sick easily, and that's what this felt like now, only it was fast becoming the worst car sickness she'd ever experienced. Her stomach spasmed.

"I—I think you need to pull over," she said.

"Why?"

"I'm going to be sick."

"Oh, good grief." Instead of showing concern, he sounded exasperated.

They were on a side street in downtown Columbus and he pulled to the curb in front of a boarded-up store front.

She got out of the car in a flash, managed to walk toward the back of it for a little privacy, and then lost the contents of her stomach into the street gutter.

Bradley did not get out of the car to help in any way. Instead, he recoiled a little when she got back into the car.

"Do you want me to take you back to your apartment?"

"Please." She buckled her seatbelt back on, leaned her head back against the seat and cracked the window as he pulled away from the curb.

"Well, that's a couple reservations that'll go to waste," he said.

"I'm sorry."

"You should have told me you were feeling ill." He was plainly irritated.

"I wasn't ill before you came."

"You're blaming me for getting sick?"

"I think there might be something in your cologne I'm allergic to."

This did not set well with him. He drove in stony silence all the way back to her home.

When he pulled up to her apartment complex's front entrance, even though she had been ill, he did not get out and open the passenger car door for her. She barely had a chance to close it behind her before he drove off, leaving her alone on the sidewalk searching in her purse for her keys.

Tomorrow at work was going to be awkward, but she would handle it. She'd have to. If she was going to eventually make partner at this firm, she'd have to make sure to find a way to smooth his ruffled feathers.

One thing for sure, tonight had made her feel sorry for his sweet ex-wife.

As for her, she wouldn't be accepting any more one-on-one invitations to go to dinner with her boss. Of course, she would be very surprised if any other invitations were extended. This did not feel like a hardship to her. It was a relief.

Apparently, there was nothing like almost throwing up in a man's expensive car to cool his interest. She'd have to remember that ploy if she ever found herself needing to get out of future, similar situations.

Getting away from Bradley and the smell of his cloying cologne made her immediately feel better. As she rode up in her apartment's elevator, she couldn't help but compare Bradley's actions tonight against what she knew Michael's would have been. Had it been Michael tonight and she had asked him to pull over because she was sick, he would have been out of the car in a flash, holding back her hair, offering her his handkerchief to wipe her mouth, stopping at the nearest convenience store to purchase a bottle of water so she could rinse out her mouth. He'd probably even insist on purchasing a ginger ale to help settle her stomach as well. He would have made certain she got safely inside the apartment and well-settled before he left.

He would have cared about her.

She heaved a great sigh. Michael was a genuinely good guy in a world swimming with men like Bradley. Maybe there was some sort of compromise she and Michael could work out. If she worked extra hard at the firm during the week, maybe she could carve out some time on the weekends.

Those were her thoughts as she opened the door to her apartment and saw Michael standing in the middle of the living room.

He looked so good, so handsome, so strong… so *right*. There was no doubt about it. She had been a fool to let this fight between them go on so long.

"Michael!" She wanted to throw her arms around him, to tell him how much she'd missed him and apologize. "I'm so glad…"

His look of contempt stopped her cold.

"Well," he said. "I guess I know why you were so willing to stay here instead of coming to Sugarcreek with me. How long has this been going on?"

She was confused. "How long has what been going on?"

"I'm talking about your boss. I came to see if we could figure out a compromise of some kind; a way for us to be together. When I pulled up, I saw you getting into his car. He's the real reason you want a divorce, isn't it. He's been the problem all along."

"Michael, you're wrong, I…"

"Don't you dare say another word," he warned. "You reek of that man's cologne! I'm done. I'm finished. You two can have each other!"

She tried to wrap her mind around what was happening. "How long have you been here?"

"Why are you back so soon? Did you forget your toothbrush?"

"Michael! I never…"

"I saw him kiss you, Cassie!"

It took a lot to shock her into silence, but she was so astonished that she didn't even remember to close her mouth until he slammed the door behind him.

Chapter Twenty-Six

It began to snow again as Rachel drove home from Cleveland. Big, messy, flakes that plopped onto to her windshield and clung.

The rhythmic staccato of the wipers created a sort of mantra in her mind. "Don't. Let. Him. Have. My. Baby."

Obviously, Lily had been referring to Tony, but how was Rachel supposed to keep the baby away from the biological father? Tony might be the suspected godfather of Ghosts Inc. but gang leaders were not necessarily the ones with the longest criminal records. They needed to be smart enough to command absolute loyalty from their followers, and manipulative enough to get their underlings to do what needed to be done when it came to breaking the law.

As she entered Sugarcreek and drove down Main Street, the small downtown area looked like something from a painting. The street lights were all lit, the decorations still on display, the pretty buildings were covered in snow. All but one business was closed—her husband's. As she pulled into a parking space, she saw that the restaurant was bursting with noise and customers.

"Two Home Plate Specials," Joe called over his shoulder to Darren as Rachel came through the door. Then he saw her and his face lit up. "Rachel, could you get some water to those people at table four? I'm sorry, but I'm really short-handed right now."

"Sure thing." She shook the snow out of her hair, hurried to the backroom, tied on an apron and became an emergency waitress.

The place was hopping. After all the rich foods people were accustomed to eating during the Christmas holiday, it appeared that everyone in Sugarcreek was ravenous for a hamburger.

"Any news about our Jane Doe?" Darren asked, as he brought out a tray of soft drinks.

"Not much," Rachel said.

"The man at table two wants pumpkin pie and we're out." Lonny, one of the teenage waiters Joe employed after school, called out.

"What kind of pie do we have?" Darren asked.

"Apple," the boy said. "We still have apple pie. Everything else is gone."

"Then go tell him."

The worried-acting teen rushed off.

"Where is Bobby?" Rachel asked.

Joe nodded to a corner table where their son was happily coloring pictures with "Aunt" Marge, his teacher from Sunday school.

"Marge and Bill came in tonight?"

"They brought Bobby a coloring book and new crayons as a Christmas present."

"Ah," Rachel said. "That's sounds like something they would do."

"Word is out, by the way. Everyone who came in tonight was asking about your Jane Doe." Joe expertly flipped a dozen burgers on the grill. "What did you find out up in Cleveland?"

"She's no longer Jane Doe. Her name is Lily."

"Lily? Lily what?"

"I don't know."

"Let's get through this crush, and then I want to hear all about it."

Rachel was tired, but she didn't mind helping out. Most of the people there were regulars. Many were people she'd known most of her life. An hour later, the crowd had thinned, but Bill and Marge were still there. Bill reading a copy of *The Budget*, Bobby asleep on the bench with his head on Marge's lap. Marge sat with a sweet smile on her face as she smoothed the little boy's blond curls with her hand. With no children of her own, Marge poured her love into other people's.

Rachel was cleaning off the next-to-last table when Darren came staggering out of the kitchen. His face was pale, and his eyes wide, and he was holding the receiver to their restaurant landline.

"What's wrong?" Rachel asked.

"We just got a phone call," Darren said.

"We get a lot of phone calls." Joe was cleaning the grill. "It's closing time. Tell them it's too late for us to do a takeout order."

"That's not the kind of phone call we got." Darren's voice was shaking.

"Is Dad okay?" Joe stopped in mid scrape and focused on his brother.

"That wasn't about Dad," Darren said. "That was Kris Burkshire's assistant on the phone."

Rachel and Joe looked at him blankly.

"Kris Burkshire," Darren stated again. "You know. The chef?"

Rachel and Joe still didn't get it.

"Chef Burkshire walks into restaurants that are about to close and gives advice on how to turn them around, financially and food-wise. His show is on TV."

"So?" Rachel said.

"His home base is Columbus. Someone told him about us, and he drove in tonight to check us out. I was so busy in the kitchen, I didn't even see him. His assistant said that he thought the story behind Home Plate—how a baseball legend and his brother with no experience had started a successful hometown business—made for good TV. If Joe's Home Plate was doing well, he intended to do a story on what was working in this start-up business. If it was having troubles, he'd do a story about helping it become a success."

"So which did he decide?" Joe was holding his spatula in mid-air, waiting to hear.

"Neither," Darren said. "He wasn't particularly interested one way or another. He wants to interview our pie maker."

"Aunt Lydia?" Rachel said.

"Yeah."

"And by 'talk' he means..."

"He wants to bring a TV crew to film her technique and recipes for making pies."

"She would never allow herself to be filmed," Rachel said.

"I know," Darren said. "I told him that she was Old Order Amish, but Rachel... now he *really* wants to talk to her."

Chapter Twenty-Seven

There was a Starbucks that Cassie visited every workday morning as she walked from the parking garage to her office building. Her order was always the same; a Venti Caffe Latte. That large shot of strong espresso with a froth of milk each morning booted up her brain and kept it running at maximum speed well into the afternoon. She had become such a known regular that the barista had memorized her preference and began to create it every day the moment she walked through the door—and that made her happy.

"Here you go, Ma'am." The handsome barista handed it to her with a flourish. "Your usual. Just the way you like it."

"Thank you, Jeffrey." She stuffed a nice tip in the jar. It was worth every penny for the small ego stroke of having everyone in line—many of whom were employees of Blackwell, Hart & Cooper—see that she was a favorite with the staff.

In her early days of working here, Michael had gently pointed out that it would be less expensive to bring a thermos of coffee from home, which he had calculated would mean a saving of several hundred dollars a year. He even offered to fill the thermos for her each morning.

What Michael did not realize was that walking through the door with a leather briefcase in one hand and a large Starbucks coffee in the other was a sort of badge of honor. It subtly signaled the same thing as rolling up one's sleeves might have meant to a different generation.

Bringing homemade coffee in a thermos just didn't cut it.

Her mind flickered on Michael for a moment, and then she pushed the thought away. Last night was not something she wanted to think about—at least not now. It took all her focus to succeed in this high-powered place, and she couldn't allow Michael to distract her. His reaction to her coming in from her ridiculous date with Bradley still stung.

She stepped off the elevator and used her keycard to go through the bulletproof door. It had been installed after one of the lawyers had been physically threatened by a former client.

"Good morning," Sophie Jamison, the middle-aged assistant Cassie shared with two other attorneys, handed her a sheet of paper. "Your schedule for the day."

"Thank you," Cassie said, as she juggled her coffee long enough to glance at the sheet. As usual, the day was packed. First thing on the agenda was a meeting in the conference room in ten minutes.

She barely had time to take off her coat and drop her briefcase in her office before heading toward the conference room. It would be nice to have time to visit the bathroom, but there wasn't. She would simply have to hope the meeting wouldn't last too long. She also hoped that, when she saw Bradley, things wouldn't be too weird.

The deep maroon carpet in the hallway leading to the conference room was one of Cassie's favorite things about the upscale law offices where she worked. There was a richness to it that made working there feel like a luxury. Everything was topnotch in this office building. Even the elevator seemed to glide more smoothly and more quietly than other elevators. Cassie breathed in a feeling of stability and security every time she entered the building.

Bradley was already sitting in his usual place at the head of the conference room when she arrived. Unfortunately, they were the only ones in the room. Maybe she *should* have made time for that bathroom stop after all.

"Good morning." She seated herself at her usual place beside him.

"You are feeling better?"

"I am," she said. "Much better."

"Good. Shall we try it again New Year's Eve?" he asked. "I've been invited to a charity fundraising event and I need a dinner date. It's black tie. You might need to purchase a nice gown for it, unless you already have something appropriate."

The invitation came as a surprise, especially considering his reaction to her illness last night. Still, she wasn't as blindsided by his invitation this time.

"Thank you," she said, with a conciliatory smile. "I'm flattered you'd even ask me after what happened last night, but I've been thinking… perhaps it would be best if we didn't go out anymore under the circumstances."

"Oh?" Bradley raised an eyebrow. "What circumstances?"

"I'm sure there's a lot to sort out with your children after your recent divorce, and I'm not entirely sure what's going on between me and Michael. For now, it's probably best for you and I to just have a working relationship."

"It's only a charity dinner, Cassie," Bradley said, peevishly. "I need to take someone who'll make a nice appearance. It isn't like I'm asking you to marry me, for Pete's sake. Why make such a big deal about it?"

Cassie felt herself flushing from his dismissive tone.

Two other associates came through the door and found their seats, cutting off Cassie and Bradley's private conversation.

He began shuffling papers, preparing to head-up the meeting. She fought down the feeling of embarrassment their conversation had left her with. Her momentary embarrassment would go away, but continuing to go out with Bradley was unthinkable. Besides, in a few days or weeks, he would have already set his sights on someone younger and more malleable anyway. At least, she hoped so.

The day continued and she didn't see Bradley again. She was a little more tired than usual, but she chalked that up to what had happened the night before.

Lunch was a sandwich that Sophie ordered for her. She ate it at her desk while working her way through business emails, making every minute count, as usual.

Dinner was Chinese takeout, which she picked up on the way home. It was dark before she made it back to her apartment. As she walked through the door, she noticed a blinking light on her landline answering machine.

She expected it to be a telemarketer. Calls on her landline were rare. She pressed "play" and went to hang up her coat. Instead of a telemarketer, it was her gynecologist's nurse. She paused in the action of hanging up her coat and listened. The nurse was asking her to call the office.

That was a little disturbing.

Probably nothing.

And yet, she had trouble concentrating as she watched the news on television, and she had little appetite for the excellent General Tso's chicken she'd brought home for supper.

It was too late to call the doctor's office. They would have closed hours earlier. She put her barely-touched supper in the refrigerator, turned off the television, and tried to apply herself to the work she had brought home. Her powers of concentration were strong, but not quite strong enough to quiet the fear niggling at the back of her mind.

The doctor's office opened at nine o'clock in the morning. She intended to be the first call they received.

Chapter Twenty-Eight

Rachel was no expert on gangs but, when she was working in Cleveland years earlier, she'd had some brief dealings with the Heartless Felons. They had come out of the juvenile detention system almost twenty years earlier. The Heartless Felons were highly organized and they were deadly. They also had a strictly-enforced code of ethics. It involved only one principle. They must have absolute and unquestioned loyalty to the group.

"Do you remember what our youth minister, Scott, told us about his experience while he was working in the juvenile detention system?" she asked Joe, as she broke four eggs into the butter sizzling in a cast-iron skillet on the stove.

Joe glanced up from buttering a piece of toast. They were enjoying the luxury of an early breakfast together while Bobby slept in from his late night at the restaurant. It was a rare opportunity for them to talk without being interrupted by their son's almost constant questioning.

"Scott had a lot of experiences there." Joe rose and selected a jar of Mrs. Miller's blackberry jam from the refrigerator. "Which one are you talking about?"

"It was at last month's potluck. He was describing the hold that gang leaders have on their followers."

She brought the skillet of eggs over to the table and divided them between their two plates. It was useless to save any for Bobby. He would want toaster waffles with peanut butter, which was his latest food craze.

Joe reached for the salt and pepper. "Remind me what he said."

"Scott said they had a Heartless Felons leader in their detention center for a while. He said the kid was a great student. Brilliant, actually. He never got in trouble for anything the whole time he was there. If I remember correctly, Scott said he was quite a likeable kid. Quiet and unassuming, but he had such total control over the others that all he had to do was look at some kid and nod, and his minions would be all over him. Scott said that they preferred the odds of six on one. A classroom could erupt without warning, and six young men would begin beating up one unsuspecting youngster. The eighteen-year-old 'godfather' would just sit back, cross his arms, and watch it all happen."

"How did Scott even know for sure this godfather was the one causing the fights?"

"Scott said he got to talk with some of the boys while he was tutoring them one-on-one for their GED tests. Two of them trusted Scott enough to privately tell him about the control the boy had over the others. Those two were scared to death of the kid. There was nothing Scott could do about it. If he said anything, it would have gotten the other boys in trouble. Possibly even killed. The irony was that the Heartless Felon godfather got out early for good behavior."

"Scary stuff," Joe said.

"An old police buddy of mine tells me that there's a white version of the Heartless Felons called Ghosts Inc."

"And how does this affect your Jane Doe case?"

"Mabel says the baby's father, Tony Maddox, is her next-door neighbor, and also the godfather of Ghosts Inc. He does not yet know what happened Christmas morning. I think I'm going to have to go back up there, knock on his door, and tell him that his girlfriend died two days ago, but his baby survived."

"Does he have a legal right to take her?"

"He does. Paternity rights carry weight, even if the couple was never married. With no criminal past on record, and only rumors connecting him to the Ghosts Inc. I'm afraid it could be a slam-dunk for him… assuming he wants her."

***

In the end, she did not have to go back to Cleveland to talk to Tony after all. She was at the police station, still discussing her visit to Mabel with Ed, when her cell phone rang.

"Rachel here," she said. "How can I help you?"

There was a slight hesitation before a low voice said, "I'm Tony Maddox. My neighbor says you have Lily's body?"

"I do." Rachel's mind raced. What had Tony, or one of his henchmen, done to Mabel to get her to tell him? Was the old woman okay? "Can you come identify the body?"

Another pause. "Yes. I'll identify her."

She gave him the address. "Tell me when you're coming and I'll meet you there."

"Two hours." He hung up.

She stared at her phone.

"What?" Ed said.

Rachel glanced up. "It looks like I'll be meeting the Ghosts Inc. godfather in two hours at the morgue."

"Want me to go with you?" Ed asked.

"Tempting, but I don't think I want two alpha males in the same room under such emotional circumstances—especially if one is a criminal and one is a cop."

"I'm an alpha male?" Ed seemed pleased at the label.

"Tony's coming of his own free will, and I have no reason to arrest or accost him in any way," Rachel said. "But it might be wise to have some backup."

"I'll go," Kim looked up from some reports she'd been working on at her desk.

Kim was the opposite of an alpha male, and quite lovely. She had grown a lot as a cop over the past three years and, in Rachel's experience, was probably much better at defusing a tense situation than Ed.

"I'd appreciate that, Kim," Rachel said. "We'll leave after lunch."

"Got it." Kim went back to her work.

Visiting morgues was something Rachel dreaded. It was always so hard on the people she had to accompany, and their fear and nervousness bled over onto her. There was no way to lessen the emotional impact. Some people were stoic, some were highly emotional, and some passed out.

She was grateful Tony had called though. Maybe he would be willing to share some information about the young woman's family. The best-case scenario would be that Lily had some loving grandmother waiting in the wings to take over the baby's care, and that Tony was willing to let her.

But first, she needed to check on Mabel.

"Hello?" It was interesting the amount of suspicion and distrust the old woman put into that one word.

"This is Rachel. Are you okay?"

"Tony called you," Mabel said. "Didn't he?"

"I'm supposed to meet him in a couple hours to identify Lily's body. What happened, anyway? You warned me not to even tell him about Lily and the baby. How did you come to give him my number? Did he hurt you in some way?"

"No," Mabel said. "He didn't have to. I know better than to lie to

Tony. He saw you coming to my house. He saw your Mustang the first day, and then saw the old truck there the next. He doesn't miss much. He asked me to explain what was going on... so I did."

After a quick lunch at Joe and Darren's restaurant, she finished some paperwork, then she and Kim headed on over to Dover, where Union Hospital had the morgue that Tuscarawas County used. On the way there, she filled Kim in on everything that had happened so far.

They waited in the parking lot near the outdoor entrance in her squad car until she saw Tony and another young man emerge from a late-model black SUV and walk toward the door.

"That's him," Rachel said, nodding.

"And who is the human refrigerator standing next to him?" Kim asked.

"I have no idea," Rachel said. "As big as he is, it looks like he might be a bodyguard."

It was not hard to recognize Tony. He was tall, well-built, and was wearing a black leather jacket and jeans. Now that she could clearly see his face, he looked a few years older than she thought when she'd first seen him on the street. She now judged him to be mid-thirties. That was ancient by gang standards, where young boys assumed they'd be dead by twenty.

As she approached him, he looked her up and down, then treated her to a flat-fish stare. Tony's friend, or bodyguard, or whatever position the young man held in the gang, was as tall as Tony, but much more muscular and about a hundred pounds heavier. He had the bulk that only dedicated bodybuilders... or prison inmates trying to survive... ever achieved.

Even with Kim along, she was grateful for the reassuring weight of her Glock tucked into the back of her slacks beneath her coat.

"Mr. Maddox," she said. "I'm Officer Rachel Mattias. I was the first officer at the scene of your girlfriend's accident. This is Officer Kim Whitfield. Thank you for coming."

Tony showed little interesting in either of them. There was no warmth of greeting in those eyes—not that she'd expected any. She waited to give Tony a chance to introduce the man standing behind him. He chose not to. So be it.

"Shall we get this over with?" she said.

"Suits me," Tony said.

The refrigerator guy standing next to him blinked once, but was otherwise expressionless.

She didn't need to flash her badge at the middle-aged coroner. She'd been here before. He knew her by sight. She was surprised when, instead of taking them to the back of the morgue, he led them out back to a trailer with the words "Disaster Relief" on it.

"What's this?" she asked.

"We had to borrow a casualty trailer from the Department of Health. It's for overflow. I didn't have room in the morgue for all the bodies."

She was surprised. "But we haven't had any disasters."

"You're wrong," he said. "I had to call for this rig just last month. Our facilities weren't built to handle Carfentanil."

"Carfentanil?" she said. "I thought that fentanyl was the big threat these days."

"Yeah?" The coroner looked washed-out and wearier than the last time she'd seen him. "Well, we're starting to think of heroin and fentanyl use as something that happened in the good old days. Carfentanil is an animal tranquilizer about a hundred times more powerful than fentanyl. It's used on big animals like elephants. The druggies like to mix it with meth. Sometimes they do a lousy job of doing so. If you haven't heard of it yet, I envy you."

"I don't think it has hit Sugarcreek yet," she said.

"Just wait," the coroner said. "It will happen in Sugarcreek too. It probably already has."

Not on my watch, Rachel silently vowed.

"Lily." Tony was apparently uninterested and unimpressed with their topic of conversation. "I'm supposed to identify her."

The coroner opened the door to the refrigerated trailer. The space was limited. The smell of death was inside. As Kim, Tony, and she followed the coroner in, Tony didn't flinch. The bodyguard, or whatever he was, started to go inside, hesitated, changed his mind and stayed out.

"This is the Jane Doe we got from the car wreck in Sugarcreek," the coroner lifted a sheet, revealing only the face. "I finished the autopsy last night. My assistant dropped off the details at the police station a little while ago."

Tony stared silently at the young woman who was lying on what looked like one of multiple macabre metal bunk beds lining the walls. Rachel gave an involuntary shiver. Not from the cold. It was from the overwhelming sadness she felt over the county having to bring in a disaster trailer because of yet another new drug.

Tony seemed unaffected as he studied the woman's disfigured face.

"That's Lily," Tony's voice was steadier than Rachel expected. "Now what?"

Good question, Rachel thought. Now what, indeed?

"I need to ask you a few questions," Rachel said.

"You can use my office," the coroner said. "I have some paperwork you need to sign."

The office the coroner took them to was small. The coroner sat down behind his piled-up desk and waited. She and Tony sat in the only two other chairs available. Tony's bodyguard stood on one side of the door, and Kim stood vigil on the other.

"So tell me what you know about Lily?" Rachel said.

"I found her on the street," Tony said. "She'd just gotten off a bus. Wandering around like she didn't know what to do. I took her home. Told her she could stay awhile."

She noticed that Tony sat completely still. That was highly unusual. Most people fidgeted even under the best circumstances. If they were being interrogated, they fidgeted even more so. Picking at lint on their clothing. Snapping or unsnapping a coat. Crossing their legs and uncrossing them. Running their fingers back through their hair. She'd interrogated one teenager who had chewed on her long ponytail the entire time.

Not Tony. He sat loosely in the chair, feet on the floor, hands unclasped. It wasn't as though he was relaxed. Instead, he reminded her of a watchful animal, muscles tense, ready to spring or run away at any moment.

"You have any idea what her last name was?"

"She said it was Smith. Maybe it was. Maybe it wasn't."

"She ever talk about her folks?"

"No."

"Not at all?"

"Not at all. Never talked about her past. I didn't want to hear it, anyway."

"You don't seem like a man who has the time to go around rescuing strays. Why'd you take her in?" Rachel asked.

"I don't know," he said. "Kinda reminded me of my kid sister. Sarah used to be as clueless as Lily."

"How long did Lily stay with you?"

"About three years."

"And she was your girlfriend all that time?"

"She lived there, but she wasn't my girlfriend. At least, not all the time. I have a lot of girlfriends."

"Do they all stay with you?"

"No. I make them go home. With Lily it was different."

"Different how?"

"She could cook. Real food. Healthy stuff. Vegetables. None of that garbage everybody else lives on. She kept things clean. Didn't talk much. Didn't bother me if I didn't want to be bothered."

"How did you feel about her pregnancy?"

"I didn't want a kid," Tony frowned. "I wanted her to take care of things as soon as she told me, but she wouldn't. Said it was wrong."

"So, you didn't want the baby?" Rachel kept her voice steady, but her heart began to beat harder. If she could get Tony to sign away parental rights...

"Nah, I got too many responsibilities as it is."

Rachel refrained from asking him what kind of responsibilities he had. She was pretty sure she already knew. Running a gang must be quite a full-time job.

"Did you know she'd stolen Mabel's car?"

"No."

"Where did you think she'd gone when she disappeared?"

"How should I know?" He shrugged. "I had a party to go to that night. When I got back, the door to her room was closed. I didn't even know she was gone until yesterday."

"She had her own room?" Rachel asked.

"Yeah. It was real small, so I let her have it. Made it easier for me if she wasn't under foot all the time."

"Just to be clear," Rachel said. "Mabel told you that the baby survived?"

"Yeah, she told me I have a kid."

"You mentioned not wanting the baby because of all your responsibilities." Rachel was careful to keep her voice even. "There are a lot of people who'd be happy to adopt her. You'd have to formally give up parental rights, first. Are you willing to do that?"

He mulled it over. "I'll have to think about it."

Before she could say anything else, Tony stood up. "We done here?"

"Someone needs to take responsibility for the body." The coroner, who had been waiting for Rachel to finish her questioning, was anxious to get on with things.

Rachel saw a flicker of what looked like a shred of decency in Tony's eyes as he debated what to do. "How much will it cost to bury her?"

"Just a burial?" the coroner asked. "No funeral?"

"Yeah," Tony said. "No funeral."

"Probably under three thousand."

"Here." Tony pulled out a wad of cash. He peeled off thirty hundred-dollar bills and handed them to the coroner. "Take care of it."

"You don't want any kind of service?"

"Why would I?" Tony shrugged. "She's dead ain't she?"

As they started to leave the coroner's office, the big man who had come with Tony seemed to wake up. He pulled a hundred-dollar bill from his pocket and handed it to the coroner.

"Get her some flowers," he said. "Lily liked flowers."

Chapter Twenty-Nine

"I want a shower," Kim said, as Rachel drove back to Sugarcreek. "Then I'm going to burn all my clothes. Then I'll take another shower. Then I need a nap. Then one more shower... and I might start to feel normal again."

"First time at the morgue?" Rachel asked.

"Yes." Kim gave a shudder.

"It isn't easy for anyone," Rachel said. "But you did well. I'm grateful you were there. Thanks for having my back."

"You're welcome." Kim sounded pleased. They had come a long way since Kim's first days on the force when she had been little more than a major irritation to Rachel. "I'm glad I was able to help."

She dropped Kim off at her house then, just like Kim would be doing soon, she went straight home and took a long shower. She might not actually reek of the smell from the trailer, but it seemed like she did.

As soon as she had dried her hair and put on fresh clothes, she went straight to the Sugar Haus Inn. The visit was purely selfish and restorative on her part. She needed to spend time basking in Bertha's wisdom and strength and she was craving something sweet from Lydia's kitchen. Whenever she needed the world to feel like a safer, saner place, she went to visit her Amish aunts.

When she walked in, all three aunts were engrossed in a one-thousand-piece jigsaw puzzle spread out on the kitchen table. It was a scene involving a barn, blue morning glories, a birdhouse, and a farm wagon. No people, of course. Even with their jigsaw puzzles, they avoided pictures of faces.

"I'm a good jigsaw puzzle doer," Anna informed her as she came through the door. Anna had several random puzzle pieces in front of her and was fitting them together. Whether they actually fit or not was not of great importance to Anna.

"So, what's been going on in your Englisch world?" Bertha was collecting all the blue pieces since she was intent on completing the flowers. "Have you found the baby's relatives yet?"

Rachel told them about her visit to Mabel and to the coroner's office.

"That Tony person didn't even ask to see his baby?" Bertha asked.

"Not yet." Rachel found a corner piece and completed the frame.

"So, you didn't have to tell him who has the baby?" Lydia was in the process of cornering the market on all the red barn pieces. Rachel noticed that Lydia was also soaking her feet in a pan of water beneath the table.

"No. He didn't seem to be interested, so I didn't offer," she said. "I didn't tell him the specifics. I didn't want to accidentally make trouble for Keturah's family."

"Do you really think he'll sign away his paternity rights?" Bertha asked.

"I think there is a chance."

"Ah hah!" Bertha crowed, as she found the right spot for one of her blue puzzle pieces. "Another one! I'm gaining on you, Lydia!"

"Imagine," Lydia said, wistfully. "Someone not wanting that sweet little baby."

"So, what happens if he does give up his rights?" Bertha asked. "What happens to the baby then?"

"I suppose she will become available for adoption."

"Oh, Rachel!" Lydia gasped. "Do you suppose…?"

"I know what you're thinking, but there are so many other families on waiting lists for babies. Joe and I wouldn't stand a chance. Especially since we already have Bobby."

"Where is Bobby?" Bertha asked. "Public school isn't back in session yet, is it?"

"He's with Joe and Darren," Rachel said. "Probably taste-testing the breakfast menu they are trying to put together."

"The restaurant is doing well then?" Lydia asked.

"Joe says we're actually turning a profit," Rachel said, proudly. "That's unusual for a new restaurant."

"*Ach!*" Bertha's voice held a gentle reprimand. "Pride is a dangerous thing."

"You're right," Rachel said. "Let me put it a different way. We have been blessed by God against all expectations."

"Good." Bertha nodded. "That is okay then."

"Do you have anything sweet to eat, Lydia?" Rachel asked. "Cookies? Leftover pies?"

"I'm afraid not," Lydia said. "It is all I can do to keep up with the orders I'm getting from the restaurant. Darren was just here and picked up another dozen pies. My feet are sore from standing."

It was the first time in Rachel's life that Lydia did not have some sort of bakery item to offer when she came by. It was quite a shock. It also reminded her of the news Darren had given them the night before about the TV chef.

"Did Darren tell you about Chef Burkshire?"

"That television person who wants to come and film Lydia making pies?" Bertha sounded disgusted.

"That's the one."

"Lydia does not wish to do such a thing," Bertha said. "It would create much strife within the church if she did."

"It's only pie-making," Rachel pointed out.

"The people who make the show will make fun of this old Amish woman who bakes her pies in a wood stove, and who rides in a horse and buggy, and who wears funny clothing," Bertha argued. "I have heard stories. We cannot trust Englisch TV. Some of our people have learned this the hard way. The people they trusted made our ways look foolish."

"I can't argue with that, Bertha," Rachel said. "But I imagine Darren was disappointed when you turned him down."

"A little disappointment will not kill him," Bertha said. "Darren has many big ideas. Too many, I think."

She noticed that Lydia had not said a word.

"How do you feel about this, Lydia?" Rachel asked.

"I would not mind if this TV person wanted to take a picture of my hands as I make a pie," Lydia said, in a quiet voice. "Maybe Englisch people need to learn how to make a pie. I don't think that would be wrong or prideful, do you?"

Rachel noticed the sharp look that Bertha gave her younger sister. She had a feeling that those two were going to have a long, hard talk after she left, which would probably end in Bertha convincing Lydia that having the television people in her home was a mistake.

"Can I pour some more hot water into your footbath before I go, Lydia? I need to go check in at the station. Ed's going to want to know how things went."

"I would not mind if you warmed it up a little," Lydia said. "The tea kettle on the back of the stove should be hot again by now."

Rachel carefully added the steaming water to Lydia's foot bath before leaving. It was the first time she'd ever known Lydia to complain of foot trouble.

Chapter Thirty

"How did things go?" Ed asked, as he entered the tiny police station. He was studying a couple sheets of paper that he held in his hands.

"Next time *you* get to go do the morgue run," she said.

"I know it's not your favorite part of the job," Ed said. "I'll do it next time. What is your opinion of Tony Maddox?"

"He gives me the creeps," she said.

"What is it about him that gives you the creeps," Ed asked, still studying the paper.

"His stillness. It's unnatural. He reminds me of a cat watching a mouse. Ready to spring, but not moving a muscle until he decides to pounce."

"And you felt like the mouse?"

"Little bit."

"Autopsy report." Ed handed her the papers. "You aren't going to like it."

She skimmed the words. It said that Lily had been repeatedly battered.

Rachel closed her eyes against a wave of sadness and anger that washed over her. "So that is what she was running away from when she stole Mabel's car."

"Maybe. Maybe not."

"What do you mean?"

"Look closer. The breaks are old. They are probably the reason she was a runaway when Tony found her."

"But her last words to Keturah was not to let him have her baby. She was afraid that he would hurt her."

"She was afraid that *someone* would hurt her. Maybe it was Tony, maybe it wasn't. Maybe it was someone from her past; a relative, maybe. Perhaps that's why she was so secretive about where she came from. Maybe Tony is the lesser of evils. So far, we're still working in the dark."

Visions of that sweet, vulnerable infant rose in her mind. She wanted to protect the baby girl, but how? And from whom?

"I need to go see the Hochstetlers and let them know what's been happening," Rachel said. "My friend, Sally, from social services, said its okay for the baby to continue to stay with Keturah and Agnes for now until we find out more about the baby's family situation."

When Rachel arrived at the Hochstetlers, she found Keturah holding little Holly while also keeping an eye on Agnes's two-month-old Rosie, asleep on a blanket on the floor. Agnes was slicing bread and cheese for a platter of sandwiches that she was building.

"Do you want a sandwich?" Agnes asked, holding the knife ready to slice more.

"Actually, yes," Rachel said. "If you have enough."

"Are you suggesting that an Amish woman might not have enough food to feed a guest?" Agnes laughed. "You know us better than that."

"In that case, I would really appreciate one." Rachel smiled. "They look delicious."

"Have you brought news?" Keturah asked.

"I found the baby's father."

"And?" Agnes stood still and taunt. "Is he coming for her?"

"Not yet," Rachel said. "He identified Lily's body, but he didn't seem terribly upset by her death, or all that interested in the fact that he had a child. Do you mind caring for her a few more days while I try to get this sorted out?"

"Of course not." The Amish women spoke in unison.

Ivan and Noah burst through the door at that moment, followed by Aaron and Benjamin, bringing a swirl of cold wind with them. As soon as the door was closed, they began the process of stamping snow-covered boots, unwrapping coats, scarfs, and taking off gloves. A few pieces of hay from their clothing scattered onto the floor. As they came into the house, Ivan and Noah were finishing up their conversation about a certain cow that they thought might be developing mastitis.

Neither Keturah nor Agnes chastised them. Men bringing snow and hay into a house was not an issue to a dairy farmer's wife. It was part of a normal day's work.

"Supper is almost ready." Agnes lifted the lid off a pot on the stove, stirred and tasted. Benjamin came over to his mother and peeked into the kettle.

"*Bist du hungrig?*" Agnes said.

"*Ja,*" Benjamin said, rubbing his stomach.

"Clara!" Agnes called up the stairs. "*Bitte komm und hif mir beim Tischdecken!*"

The four-year-old came clattering down the stairs and began setting the table.

"Aaron," Agnes said. "*Lasse das Wasser.*"

The little boy began filling water glasses at the sink and placing them on the table.

Ivan and Noah greeted Rachel, then poured themselves cups of coffee from the enamelware coffeepot simmering on the back of the woodstove, sat down at one corner of the table, and continued their conversation. This time about the merits of planting a different kind of field corn for their cows the coming spring.

Rachel walked over and caressed the downy head of the two-day-old baby. If only the infant could have a family such as this, where people spoke to one another with respect, where decency and kindness were the rule, and where good food was always abundant. If every child grew up in this environment, she seriously doubted street gangs or drug addiction would be a problem.

The baby grasped her finger when she touched its tiny fist. That small grip weakened Rachel's knees, but it stiffened her resolve. She would do everything within her power to make certain this helpless baby girl ended up being raised by someone who would love and take care of her. Somehow, she did not see that being a possibility with Tony.

Chapter Thirty-One

· ·

"We got the results of your biopsy back," the nurse said the next morning when Cassie returned the doctor's office call. "Dr. Baker would like for you to come into the office so he can talk with you. We have an opening at two o'clock today."

Two o'clock. Smack in the middle of the day.

Why would the doctor have to talk to her face-to-face? Why couldn't they simply tell her the results over the phone?

"I have a very heavy workload today," Cassie said. "Can't you give me the results over the phone?"

"The doctor thinks it would be best for you to come into the office."

Cassie's stomach lurched. That meant it had to be bad news.

"I'll be there," she said.

It was going to be difficult to concentrate for the next five hours.

The thought that she might have breast cancer was overwhelming. How could she continue to meet the high expectations of her job if that were true?

Not only was she frightened, she simply didn't have *time* to have cancer.

***

Getting fingerprint results usually took around two to four days.

Considering that they were dealing with the aftermath of the holiday season, Rachel was pleased that they had gotten Lily's fingerprints back after only seventy-two hours. The results, however, were disappointing. Apparently, Lily had never had reason to be fingerprinted. No surprise there.

Dental records were not going to be helpful without a narrower location to search. According to Mabel, Tony had found Lily wandering around the bus station. She could have come from anywhere. Since there was no national database for dental records, targeting a particular dentist to request them from would be akin to throwing a dart at a map of the United States. Even then, there was no guarantee that Lily had ever visited a dentist. The autopsy had shown that there had been no dental work done, or needed.

So Rachel had spent every spare minute for the past four days searching the National Unidentified Missing Persons Data System or NamUs. Using what information she had from Mabel, in addition to her own observations, she had been going back three years, searching for a teenager matching Lily's description.

It was truly astonishing and saddening how many missing persons there were.

But at least those people who had been registered as missing had someone in their life who had actually missed them enough to alert the police.

Saddest of all were the reports from coroners around the country reporting unclaimed bodies of human beings who had once been alive, with thoughts and feelings and hopes and dreams, but who didn't have even one person who cared enough to claim responsibility for them.

So much loneliness in the world. It boggled her mind.

Rachel thanked God for her family, her friends, and for a community where she had people who would notice and worry if she didn't show up.

She had people who would grieve and investigate if she went missing.

She typed in Lily's name and known statistics into a different search engine. Perhaps this was futile, or a mistake. Now that the autopsy showed severe abuse in Lily's past, Rachel wasn't even sure she wanted to make a connection with Lily's family of origin. But there was protocol to follow, which meant doing her level best to find Lily's relatives.

"Put a picture of her in the paper," Ed suggested. "Offer a reward. It doesn't have to be much. A lot of people would turn in their own grandmother for twenty bucks."

"The only picture I have is from the wreck. I took it with my cell phone after she was dead. It is not exactly a picture people will want to run across while eating their breakfast."

"Is there a chance Tony Maddox or Mabel might have one?"

"I'll call and see."

Mabel was not home. Or else the old woman had chosen not to answer the phone today. There was no telling what was going on when it came to Mabel. Rachel had better luck when she dialed Tony's cell phone—the number he had used when he called her.

"This is Rachel Mattias," she said, when a man's voice answered. "Is this Tony Maddox?"

"Depends," Tony drawled. "You the hot girl cop I saw yesterday?"

She had no idea what he was trying to do. Impress a buddy listening on the other end? Actually hitting on her? Or was he letting her know that he was not impressed with the fact that she was a law officer. Probably all three. She ignored his rude comment.

"I accompanied you when you identified Lily's body. I need a good photograph of her. Do you have one?"

"What's it worth to you?"

She held onto her temper by counting to three slowly before she responded.

"Do you have one or not?" she asked. "We can negotiate price later."

At that, Tony started laughing until he choked. After a coughing fit, his voice and attitude changed. He seemed to be the kind of person whose personality and attitude could turn on a dime. No doubt it kept his minions on their toes.

"I'm just messing with you, Officer," he said. "There's no pictures of her. It was the only thing she insisted on besides hanging onto the baby. It's a real shame because she was a pretty girl."

"Do you have any idea why she didn't want her picture taken?"

"She never said."

"You ever ask her?"

"People I hang with say they don't want pictures, I don't argue. I figure they got reasons."

Rachel tried to stamp down her frustration. This man had lived with Lily for three years. He'd fathered a child with her. He must know something about her that would make it possible to track down her family.

"Do you know why she had a news clipping with her about my husband's restaurant when she crashed?"

"No clue. You gotta understand, Officer, me and Lily, we weren't close."

"But you fathered a child with her."

"Well, yeah. But it's not like we sat around chit-chatting or anything."

"I understand. Thank you." She clicked off.

"Find out anything?" Ed asked.

"Yes," she said. "Tony is a jerk, and Lily was definitely hiding from someone. There are no photos of her, because she didn't want any. Did you ever meet a teenage girl who didn't want her picture taken? Ever?"

"She was definitely running," Ed said. "And it had to be for a bad reason if living with Tony looked like a good alternative."

Chapter Thirty-Two

Cassie felt so strange when she got out of bed the morning after being told by her doctor that she had an aggressive form of breast cancer. The earth had shifted on its axis and, if the doctor was right, nothing would ever again be the same.

Her night had consisted of staring at her ceiling, telling herself that everything was going to be okay. Pacing the floor, trying to calm herself with the hope that the lab had gotten things wrong. Watching the hours evaporate while berating herself for not being able to relax enough to get to sleep.

The reality was that her mother had died of the same form of breast cancer that Cassie now had. This knowledge was a sword that had been hanging over Cassie's head ever since she was sixteen and became her mother's caretaker for the few short months she had lingered.

That which Cassie had feared, had come to pass.

The routine of her daily schedule kept her moving through the morning in spite of being upset. She showered and brushed her teeth at the usual time, dressed in the outfit she had chosen the night before.

The classic charcoal skirt and jacket she had chosen fit her perfectly. As she dressed, she couldn't help but wonder what Michael would think of her after a surgery that she was fairly certain would be inevitable. Maybe it was a good thing that they were getting divorced. At least now she would never have to see disappointment in his eyes when he looked at her. Although, with Michael, it was hard to tell. He wasn't like the men her mother had dated.

She had noted and admired the choice that the actress Angelina Jolie had made, choosing to have a double mastectomy rather than risk a future where the fear of breast cancer would always be lurking. In the back of her mind, she had known that she too might have to make that same decision someday.

Her mother had made the opposite choice. She had been too frightened that, if she chose surgery, the Prince Charming she had been waiting for her whole life would not want her.

Her mother had chosen a fantasy over fighting to live for her sixteen-year-old daughter's sake. Cassie had never forgiven her for that.

Her morning routine was one that she had developed in order to be as organized and efficient as possible. Now, she realized that, when one experienced tragic news or a traumatic event, having routines in place was even more important because it took away some of the need to think. It was possible to at least give the appearance of normality and continue to walk through her day even if her mind was partially disengaged.

Her purse and briefcase were already packed and ready. Her car keys hung on a hook beside the door.

She drove to work. She parked her car. She walked to Starbucks. She carried her coffee cup to the third floor of Blackwell, Hart & Cooper and stepped out of the elevator. She thanked her assistant, Sophie, for handing her the schedule for the day. She walked into her office and closed the door. She hung up her coat. Sat down at her desk. Stared at her Starbucks coffee cup and tried to push this brain fog away that had descended on her.

Taking a deep breath, she carefully placed her coffee to the left side of her immaculate desk, turned on her computer, and reached for her briefcase.

It wasn't there. It was back at the apartment. Still sitting on her kitchen table. She had forgotten the second most important tool in her arsenal. The first, of course, was her cell phone. At least it was in the inner pocket of her suit jacket. She pulled it out and stared at it. News like she had received needed to have someone at the other end of the phone willing to listen and grieve. She did know people she could call who would verbally express sympathy and compassion. The problem was, she couldn't think of one person who would truly care.

Creating the kind of career she had took one's complete focus. Making the kind of grades that she had made in school while competing against so many other smart young law students had taken everything she had. Achieving her goals did not leave time for long lunches with girlfriends or hanging out with friends over the weekend. It was a marvel that she had even managed to shoehorn Michael into her life.

The pull was strong to call Michael, but how could she? Especially now? He would think the only reason she was reaching out to him was because she was sick. Even though he would be angry, he would feel honor-bound to take care of her. That was the kind of man he was.

She had no intention of becoming an object of her estranged husband's pity. No. Calling Michael was not an option. She would figure out a way to take care of herself by herself.

There would be surgery, radiation, chemo, nausea, loss of hair... her mind did not allow her to pull any punches or lessen the blow. She needed to face reality so that she could make plans.

But how could someone make plans for something like this? People's bodies responded in different ways, there was no set schedule. She would have to ask for a medical leave of absence. Bradley would not be happy about it, but he had to realize that this was not something over which she had any control. It wasn't as though she were asking for a vacation.

Come to think of it, she did have nearly a month of vacation leave saved up. That would help. Assuming she survived. If she didn't survive, it wouldn't exactly be an issue.

She pushed a button on her phone. "Please hold any calls this morning, Sophie. I have some important things that I need to focus on this morning."

"No problem," her assistant said.

Cassie locked her office door. Then she went to her third-floor window and looked down at the street. There were quite a few people walking on the sidewalks and others driving along in their cars. All of them with lives and projects and private worries. She wondered how many had ever dealt with something like what she was going through.

She had worked for so long to create this life—the kind of life that she had envisioned since childhood. How long had she planned for a good-paying career? If she remembered correctly, it had been in third grade that some of the girls in her school had called her "trailer trash." She had walked home that day and seen the broken-down trailer park where she and her mother lived for what it was—a place for poor people to live. That was when she vowed to herself that, when she grew up, no one could ever make fun of her again. She had carried that resolve with her ever since. It had not been easy, but she had been true to her vow. She had made it.

Now, unless her body responded extremely well to treatment, it appeared that her life might be over before it had truly begun. She was only twenty-nine years old and most of those years had been spent getting ready to begin her life. There were so many things she had wanted to do; now it was anyone's guess as to whether or not she would ever get to do any of them.

Making the effort to go back to her apartment to retrieve her briefcase suddenly seemed overwhelming. It was a small thing to cry over, but she felt her throat closing up and tears began to well behind her eyes.

The charcoal-gray suit she was wearing had been specifically tailored for her body. It was one of her favorite outfits. A power suit, so to speak, and she was very careful with it. Her shoes had been carefully chosen to match. Even on sale they had cost several hundred dollars. Her manicure was perfect, as was her carefully-highlighted auburn hair.

And yet none of it meant anything to her as she ignored her expensive clothes, crumpled to the heavily-carpeted floor, and began to cry. There were all sorts of people buzzing around inside this office building. There were people milling about on the sidewalks and the streets. She was surrounded with people, and yet she felt completely alone.

Chapter Thirty-Three

Cassie cried until she was sick. Fortunately, her office included a small bathroom. She had been pleased just over a year ago when she got high enough in the pecking order to have an office that included a view *and* a private bathroom.

When everything was over and the tears stopped, she washed her face, blew her nose, and reapplied her makeup from a kit she kept in a drawer. The makeup was good, but it wasn't quite good enough.

When she finished, her eyes were still red and swollen, her skin was still blotchy, and she was furious with herself. Other women might fall apart emotionally, but she did not. She couldn't even remember the last time she'd actually cried. She considered crying a waste of time. Quickly, she rummaged around in her purse for a pair of sunglasses to hide the damage. She had been a fool to try to come in to work today.

With sunglasses in place, a scarf wound around her head and her coat buttoned up to her chin, she applied a layer of lipstick and left her office.

"Going out to lunch?" Sophie asked as Cassie passed by her desk. "You don't want me to order anything for you?"

"I'm not feeling very well," Cassie said. "I might have a touch of flu. I'm going home to keep from spreading it around."

"Your nose is red," Sophie said. "I hope you feel better soon."

"If you would reschedule my afternoon appointments, I would

appreciate it."

It was the first time since she had begun to work here five years ago that she had taken a sick day.

"You going out for lunch?" Bradley said, as he came around the corner and found her waiting at the elevator. "Mind if I join you?"

Cassie debated. It was one thing to turn down his dinner invitation. It was entirely another to turn down a friendly lunch. Right now, talking to Bradley was the last thing she wanted to do but he would have to know what was going on with her, especially if she was going to have to ask him for leave of absence. The surgery was scheduled in four days. Her doctor had felt there was no time to waste. She couldn't put off telling her boss.

"Of course," she said. "There are some things I need to discuss with you anyway."

Bradley had his coat draped over his arm. It was cashmere, she noticed. Of *course* it was cashmere. How could Bradley possibly wear anything less?

She could hear the sarcasm in her head. Why was she so annoyed with him? Was it because Michael had routinely worn an old, tan Carhartt barn coat? She had always hated that coat. Now, she wished she could bury her face in it and feel Michael's arms around her.

"You look like an old-time movie star with that scarf and sunglasses," Bradley said, as they left the building.

"That's the look I was going for," she said, lightly.

There was a small restaurant two blocks away that had excellent soups and sandwiches. Her mind was so full of how to explain what was going to happen in the next few weeks to Bradley that she neglected to discuss their destination. She simply plunged her hands into her coat pockets and headed in that direction.

"You do know your own mind don't you." Bradley laughed. "Do you want to let me in on where we are going?"

"I'm sorry. I'm a little preoccupied today," she said. "Soup sounded good to me."

"It sounds perfect to me too," Bradley said. "I think it's going to start snowing again. Nothing like hot soup on a snowy day."

It was not a fancy establishment that she had chosen. One chose a tray and then guided it along while pointing at the various foods one wanted. It reminded her of a school cafeteria. Perhaps that's why she liked it. When she was a child, the food she got for lunch at the cafeteria was often the only thing she had to eat all day, especially toward the end of the month.

Without giving it much thought, she chose comfort food. A bowl of chicken noodle soup and a baguette of sourdough bread.

"That's quite a load of carbs," Bradley pointed out as they sat down. "I'm surprised you can keep your figure eating like that."

"Not in the mood for a salad today," she said.

"I'll overlook it this one time," he teased. "Now what was it that you wanted to discuss with me? I hope it wasn't another lecture on why we should not be dating. That's a little hard on a man's ego."

She took off her sunglasses and stared across the table at him. His ego was the least of her worries.

"I have breast cancer, Bradley. It's aggressive. In four days I'm scheduled to have surgery. After that there will be chemo, and possibly radiation. I'm going to need to take a leave of absence."

Bradley recoiled. He even placed his hands on the table and pushed himself back away from her as though her cancer might be catching.

"This is quite a shock," he said.

"Yes," she said, simply. "It is."

Maybe she had been a bit abrupt, but she didn't know how to candy-coat it, and she didn't want to. It was an ugly thing she would be going through. A leave of absence in their busy office was asking a lot. Her boss needed to know the reality.

"How long have you known?" he asked.

"I saw the doctor yesterday."

Bradley crossed his arms. His food forgotten. "And you'll be out how long?"

"A few weeks, a couple months, I don't know," Cassie said. "It depends on how my body responds. Whether or not the cancer has spread. No one can predict the time trajectory."

"You have quite a few projects that you're working on."

"I should be able to finish them. There will be some good days in between the surgery and treatments. I will be able to work at home, but just not at my usual pace. I might even be able to come into the office some of the time."

"Yes, yes." Bradley picked up a fork and toyed with it. "I'm sure."

He glanced around the room, suddenly agitated. "Do you mind if I head back to the office? I just remembered a meeting I have with a client. You know how it is."

She nodded. Yes, she knew how it was. Nothing like the mention of breast cancer to cool a man's interest. In a way, it was a relief to see him react this way. She would never have to worry about turning down his advances ever again. He hadn't even expressed any compassion or concern for her. The only thing he had seemed to have on his mind was how her illness might affect the completion of the firm's projects that she had been assigned to.

After he left, she watched the snow begin to fall outside the large window onto all the other office workers going to and fro on the sidewalk. Everyone was so busy. In such a hurry. Just like her until she hit the brick wall of preparing for the possibility of a terminal illness.

She tore a piece off her half loaf of sourdough bread, picked up her knife and buttered it. It would be wise to get as many calories in as possible while she still could. From caring for her mother, she knew that too much weight loss would soon become an issue.

As she chewed, she noticed a calendar nailed to the wall to her right. The coming year was going to be a challenge. If things went well, she would still be alive to choose a new calendar for her office next year. She really hoped she would get to do that. Funny how quickly one's goals could change.

Chapter Thirty-Four

Rachel was playing Chinese checkers with Bobby. Since she had no new clues to follow up on about the baby, it seemed as good an idea as any to make some popcorn and enjoy being with her son. Sometimes her brain came up with answers better if she wasn't concentrating so hard on a problem.

Besides, Bobby had been spending way too much time at the restaurant with Joe and Darren during this Christmas school break. Most of the time the little guy liked being there with his dad, but after a while she knew it could become wearying for a small boy.

"Can we play a long time?" Bobby asked. "You don't have to go catch bad guys or anything?"

"Nope. We can play until bedtime. Kim is patrolling tonight," she said.

"But she's not as good a police girl as you are, is she?" Bobby said.

"Where did you get that idea?"

"I heard you talking to Daddy. You said she wasn't very good at her job."

When would she learn that Bobby heard everything, and paid more attention than she realized?

"Kim hasn't been a cop as long as me, but she's getting better at it every day. Like you practicing your alphabet, or learning how to name some of the stars from your daddy."

"But she'll never be as good as you, will she, Mommy?"

There was that 'Mommy' again. She loved it when he said that. It usually came only when she was paying a lot of attention to him, like now.

It was tempting to boast that, no, Kim would never be as good. Rachel wanted to be a hero to her son just like any other parent. But her Amish background had taught her that pride was unwise.

"Kim's becoming a very good cop," Rachel said. "But we have different strengths."

He changed the subject, as only a seven-year-old could. "Why can't I go to Aunt Anna's school?"

"It's only supposed to be for Amish boys and girls." She jumped two of his yellow marbles with her black.

Bobby contemplated the board. "Did you go to an Amish school when you were little?"

"Yes."

"Did you like it?"

"Very much."

"Then how come I can't go?" He jumped three of her blacks and ended up with a marble in her space. She needed to pay more attention. This little guy was getting better. "Aunt Anna goes there, and she's not even a kid."

It was true. Anna, with her child-like mind, was fascinated with the school that had been built next door to the Sugar Haus Inn, and she enjoyed being with the children. Fortunately, Naomi, who was the teacher, understood Anna's curiosity and mental capacity, and kept an adult-sized desk and chair available and filled with crayons and coloring pages so that Anna could happily go to school whenever she liked.

Rachel was trying to form a plausible reason that Bobby could not go to an Amish school, when her cell phone rang.

"Rachel!" Darren shouted over the din in the background. "Can you go over to Lydia's and see if she has any more pies ready? We're completely out."

"I thought Joe picked up a dozen this morning. That's nearly a hundred pieces. It's always more than enough."

"It's not been enough today," Darren said. "We're completely sold out and it's still four hours to closing time."

"What's going on?" she asked.

"Remember that TV chef who wanted to film Lydia making pies, but she and Bertha turned him down?"

"Yes."

"Turns out he's also a columnist for the Columbus Dispatch. He wrote a whole article about our restaurant, but mainly he focused on the pies. He said that they were the best he'd ever eaten, and they were made by an elusive, elderly Amish woman, who wouldn't allow herself to be interviewed, and who refused to give away her secret recipes."

"Aunt Lydia has secret recipes?"

"It's a mess over here," Darren said. "Our regulars are complaining and the out-of-towners are upset that they drove all this way for a real Amish pie and we're out. I'd be happy if it were our hamburgers or potato salad the chef wrote about. I'd be thrilled. Joe and I could make more, but all the customers coming in here today just seem to want pie and they're leaving mad."

Rachel glanced down at Bobby. "You want to go over to Aunt Anna's?"

"Yay!" Bobby jumped up so quickly from the game that he spilled marbles everywhere. The white cat he'd gotten from Anna started batting them around with her paws.

"I'm sorry." Bobby looked stricken. "I'll pick them up."

"Don't worry about it right now, son," Rachel said. "I think we'd better hurry."

The kitchen was Lydia's undisputed kingdom. She planned the meals, she cooked the meals, and Bertha and Anna helped by washing the dishes afterward. This evening, however, when Rachel and Bobby arrived, Anna was washing a sink full of apples. Bertha was up to her elbows peeling them, and Lydia was rolling out pie crusts and draping them over multiple pie pans lined up on the table. No one looked happy.

"Darren told me what was happening at the restaurant," Rachel said. "Can I help?"

"Your help will be much appreciated," Bertha said. "Anna should go lie down now. She has done enough for someone with a weak heart."

"No!" Anna said. "I want to help."

"And you can, dear," Rachel said. "But let me take over and help Lydia for you so you can take a break. Besides, Bobby brought his book of seashells again. He'll be disappointed if you don't look at it with him."

The look of relief on Anna's face was great. She dried her hands, then she and Bobby went into the living room. Bobby cuddled up beside her, and opened his book. Anna's favorite pet, Gray Cat, leaped up on the couch and settled on her lap. She began to stroke it, and Rachel could hear the cat's purr clear across the room.

Now for those pies.

"What do I need to do?" she asked.

"Bring in an armload of that good oak kindling Joe split for me last week. The stove needs to be much hotter. Then help Bertha peel and slice the apples while I mix the flour, sugar, and spices. I will have six ready in about an hour. You can take them over when you leave."

Rachel did everything Lydia asked, quietly and competently, but her attempts at conversation with Bertha and Lydia fell flat. The joy had gone out of Lydia's baking, and they all felt the loss.

After Lydia pulled the last pie out of the stove, she packed all six into boxes, ready for Rachel to carry them out to the car. Rachel loaded the boxes into the trunk, and then came back inside for Bobby.

Lydia was sitting at the table, wearily fanning herself.

"Give Joe and Darren a message from me," Bertha said.

"What's that?" Rachel said.

"Tell them to double the price," Bertha said, wearily. "Maybe that'll make customers think twice before ordering more pie!"

Chapter Thirty-Five

As Cassie moved through her early morning routine, she steeled her resolve and made her plans. There would be no more tearful breakdowns like she'd had yesterday. Self-pity was a luxury she could not afford. Continuing to work would be her salvation.

Cassie had always dealt with emotional trauma by working harder. When she was a kid and things were bad at home, she had worked especially hard. Since things were nearly always bad at home, she graduated from high school with a perfect 4.0 grade point average. This she accomplished in spite of chaos at home, poor lighting at night, and frequent hunger. Her powers of concentration were finely tuned, carefully honed in a downtrodden community where there was never any lack of freeloading men for her mother to fall in love with.

"I think this is the one!" her mother gushed each time a new man came into her life. "I think he really loves me. This one is going to be my Prince Charming!"

There had been no Prince Charming. Cassie had been the one to take her mother to the doctor, for surgery, for chemo, to the hospital. No one at the graduation ceremony had a clue what she'd been through while making the grades to become Valedictorian her senior year.

She had never known her father. He had been serving a life sentence when she was born. While she was learning to crawl, he had died from a well-placed knife to the ribs. Her mother never talked about him. She didn't seem to have known him well, but Cassie sometimes wondered about his IQ. The school counselor, trying to encourage her to go to college, told her that hers was exceptionally high. Her mother's, unfortunately, was not. Sometimes Cassie had wondered if her mom was slightly substandard retarded because her attitude and mind was so childlike. She was a pretty woman, so men didn't seem to care.

Those powers of concentration she'd developed as a kid would have to serve her well during these next difficult weeks and months. There were cases she needed to research; work she was going to be expected to accomplish. She was determined not to let cancer keep her from providing her law firm with the best she was capable of. It occurred to her that, if she refused pain medications, it would help keep her mind clear enough to work. She thought she might be tough enough to endure the pain if it meant keeping her mind sharp.

One thing she knew, a law firm like the one she worked for was not a compassionate entity. She would either have to deliver, or they would eventually find someone who could. Cassie planned to deliver no matter what. She'd worked too hard for this position to lose it due to illness.

That was one reason she was coming in on a Saturday morning. Blackwell, Hart & Cooper did not require their employees to work on Saturdays, but they always had some staff on hand to keep things going in case someone like her wanted to come in and get some work done. The firm stressed the fact that they did not expect their attorneys to work six days a week, but everyone who worked there knew that it did not hurt one's standing in the company to do so.

They made it possible for their employees to access the building on Sundays also. Michael had put his foot down on that. She did not go in on Sundays as long as she and Michael were together—but it made her a little nervous not to do so.

Again, she contemplated telling Michael what she was facing, and once again rejected it. Even though she had not moved forward with the divorce, he was probably still angry at her. That was okay. She much preferred anger over pity right now.

Anger she was trained to deal with. Pity brought on flashbacks of being the recipient of a local church's Christmas coat drive and their annual Thanksgiving food basket program. Her mother had been grateful. Cassie had been humiliated.

As she walked from her car to Starbucks, to her office building, the winter wind whipped around her as she remembered that church coat. It had been warm and smelled new. She had learned then that it was possible to be humiliated and grateful at the same time.

Without thinking, she slid her ID card through the slot that would open the door to the wing of offices where she worked.

Today, of all days, it decided not to work. How frustrating! She took a good look at her ID card, made sure the electronic tape was facing the correct way, and slid it through again. It still didn't work.

There was a buzzer on the thick, glass door. Irritated, she pressed it, signaling her assistant to come open the door. When Sophie saw her, instead of coming to open the door, she looked scared, immediately glanced away, and got ultra-busy at her desk.

Puzzled and angry, Cassie was about to push the buzzer again when she saw two clean-cut security guards coming toward her. She knew these guys. She'd even exchanged pleasantries with them from time to time. One was carrying a large box. Perhaps the box held the necessary tools to fix or replace the obviously broken card-swipe gadget.

The tallest one opened the door for her. Finally! Now she could get to work.

"Thanks, Jeff," she said. "When did this thing break?"

Instead of allowing her to walk past him, he held his arm out like a traffic cop. "I'm sorry, ma'am. I can't let you enter."

"What on earth are you talking about?" she said. "I need to get to my office."

"You've been let go," he said. "We were instructed to pack up your desk and escort you back to your car."

"I've been let go?" she was stunned. "As in fired? Are you telling me that I've been *fired*? That's not possible. There's been some mistake!"

"I'm sorry," Jeff said, still barring the door. "My instructions were to pack up the personal items from your office and accompany you back to your car."

"But why?" she said. "I've done nothing wrong."

"Again," Jeff said. "I was not given any reasons. Larry and I are just following instructions."

"Can I at least download some work from my computer?"

"That is not allowed, ma'am. I was clearly instructed not to allow you access to your work computer."

"But I have unfinished cases…"

"Mr. Cooper did say to tell you that he apologizes for the inconvenience."

"Inconvenience? Bradley calls this an *inconvenience*?"

"Please, ma'am. I'm only doing my job. Mr. Cooper also said that you are to leave behind any files you might have in your briefcase."

"Which files?"

"He said anything pertaining to company business."

Cassie had been up late last night working hard. Always the good girl. Still trying to make straight As. Still trying to prove to the world that she was worthy of people's respect.

They said she'd been "let go." Bradley apologized for the "inconvenience." Bradley then, was the one behind this. Bradley was the only one to whom she had confided her prognosis. Bradley, who had recoiled from her when she told him, as though cancer was catching.

She had given five years of her life to this firm. She had allowed her loyalty to it to destroy her marriage. And just like that... they locked her out. No warning. No conversation. No chance to reason with Bradley or anyone else.

Things were beginning to make sense. She, who had gone from annoyed, to puzzled, to bewilderment, to understanding, crossed over the line into fury.

She had become a liability the moment she told Bradley she needed to take some sick leave. Smart, well-educated, *healthy* young lawyers were a dime a dozen. Fool that she was, she had not thought to create a chain of emails about her need for sick leave. Had she done so, she would have had a solid lawsuit against Blackwell, Hart & Cooper. As it was, Bradley had deniability. He could say that he had not known about her diagnosis. It was her word against his, and he was a founding partner's son.

For the first time since she'd started college, her carefully-hidden, hardscrabble personality took over.

"Here, hold this." She shoved her Starbucks coffee cup into Jeff's hand.

He was surprised, but he held onto it.

Then she opened her briefcase, held it above her head, turned it upside down and shook all her carefully-organized files onto the floor. Papers and legal documents flew everywhere.

"May I have my coffee back now?" she asked, sweetly.

Stunned by what she'd just done, Jeff handed it to her.

She took the cap off her still-full cup of Starbucks and poured it all over the contents of her briefcase. In doing so, she destroyed approximately ninety hours of work.

Feeling slightly better, she cheerfully motioned the other security guard to follow her.

"Come on, Larry, I'm not mad at you," she said. "My car is not far."

Knowing that Bradley—that coward—was no doubt watching the security cameras to see how she would react, she made a rude gesture with both hands as she turned to leave, and she maintained that gesture until she knew Bradley could no longer see her.

Chapter Thirty-Six

The supper dishes were washed and put away. The linoleum floor swept. The fire in the woodstove was banked and giving off a constant, comforting heat. It was so silent in Keturah's old kitchen that she could almost hear the snowflakes landing on the glass of the kitchen windows.

It was a church Sunday for her and her family. They had just gotten back from having services in a young couple's workshop so newly built that it still smelled of freshly-sawed wood.

She was seated in the rocking chair in which she had rocked her three sons. It was the same rocking chair in which her mother-in-law had rocked baby Ivan nearly seventy years ago.

Seventy years. Time passed so swiftly. One of the pieces of wisdom that age brought—and could never be taught to the young—was how quickly it all went and how important it was not to squander a minute.

The minutes that ticked away as she rocked the little Christmas baby were not squandered. Snuggling this newborn was something she savored. Did the need to nurture a baby, for women who knew what it was to love a baby, ever go away? She thought not. But this one was special. This was the one whom she had saved. This was the one whose flickering flame of life she had personally kept from being snuffed out.

What great things did this baby girl have in front of her to do? Had her little life been saved for a special reason? Keturah would never know. What she did know was that she did not believe it had been a coincidence that she had been on that road at that specific moment in time. Or that she had felt compelled to purchase such a fine razor for Ivan and hide it in her midwife bag. Or that she had known enough of mothers and babies that she was able to bring the baby into this world without damage.

Ah, look at that. The little thing was sucking her thumb again. Was there anything more precious?

"Where is John?" Ivan walked into the kitchen. "He was going to help me with the evening milking before he went home."

"John took Agnes and the children out to the woodshed to see the new puppies that Bonnie had last night. Noah just found them."

"Bonnie had puppies?" Ivan said. "I did not expect them so soon. Did you help her?"

"No," Keturah said. "Apparently she had everything under control."

"We are blessed by being surrounded by so much new life at our age," Ivan gazed down at the baby Keturah held in her arms. "Look at this little one. Only six days old. It takes me back."

"It takes me back too," Keturah said. "But from what Bertha's Rachel has said, I don't think the baby's father is a good man, or even a kind one. I can't stand to think of placing her in the arms of someone who won't love and care for her, Ivan."

"Nor can I, but there is nothing we can do. We have no control. The law is the law. You know that."

"Is it?" Keturah asked.

Ivan was surprised at her question. He sat down on one of the kitchen chairs. "What are you thinking?"

"There is a greater law than the one you are talking about," she said. "Do you agree?"

"You know I do."

"Would we be obeying that greater law if we gave this baby over to people who will not care for her or who might possibly even hurt her?"

"Probably not," Ivan said.

"Have you noticed that she looks like just another little Amish baby lying here in my arms?" Keturah smoothed the tiny strings on the baby's white kapp. "I don't think an Englisch person could ever tell the difference. Not even her own father. He's never even seen her and babies change so much from one day to the next when they are this young."

"One could spend time in jail for doing what you're thinking, Keturah," he warned.

She shrugged. "When have our people ever been fearful of jail when it comes to doing God's will?"

"That's the problem, Keturah. How will you know for certain you are doing God's will? We do not know this man, her father. We do not know his heart."

"Bertha's Rachel tells me that he is not sure if he wants her, and so now we have to wait to see what he decides." Keturah held the baby a little closer. "What kind of father does not want his own child the moment he learns that her heart still beats? A good man would rush to see her at once. This father did not. Agnes and I have discussed this problem at length. We are very worried. How can we bear to give this precious little soul up to such a man?"

"Perhaps he is not really a bad man," Ivan said. "Perhaps he is just young and unsure of his ability to give her a good home."

"And perhaps this baby girl came into my hands for safe keeping. Perhaps God knew that she would need my protection. All of our protection."

"I would like to discuss this with Bishop Yost," Ivan said. "It does not matter how pure our motives. If we are forced to hide the child among us to protect her, it will affect our whole church. This is not a decision we can make alone."

"Do not take this to Bishop Yost quite yet," Keturah said. "For now we pray that God has a better plan than the one I'm thinking."

"That is a good idea," Ivan said. "But for now, while you pray for God's wisdom, I will go help my grandchildren enjoy the treasure of new puppies."

Chapter Thirty-Seven

Michael, the only child of a widowed mother, had always wanted a large family when he grew up. At least four children. Maybe more if his wife was willing. Cassie was an only child too. Before they got married, she said she also wanted children.

Apparently, she'd either changed her mind or maybe she intended to have that family with Bradley Cooper. It hurt to even think about it.

It looked like he was going to have to find someone else to build a family with, but the thought of going through the ritual of finding, courting, and marrying another woman did not excite him. About the only emotion he felt as he thought about it was... tired. He had loved Cassie with his whole heart and yet their marriage had ended. Adjusting to someone else seemed hardly worth the effort when he had no idea if that marriage would last either.

Tonight was New Year's Eve. Keturah and Ivan had not invited him over, although they would not have turned him away, but he did not want to wear out his welcome. He probably tended to go over there too much as it was.

Still, sitting at home alone on New Year's Eve seemed particularly pitiful. With nothing better to do, he decided to go to Joe's Home Plate for a late supper. He had heard that they were keeping the restaurant open until past midnight tonight.

When he got there, the place was packed, but he found one

unoccupied seat in the corner where he could have a good view of the giant TV screen while he ate his meal. The TV was tuned in to the huge New York Time's Square celebration. A hand-lettered sign below the TV announced that they were out of pie. Funny thing, he had not been thinking about pie when he entered the restaurant, but now that he knew there was none available he wanted some.

Even without pie, everyone at the restaurant seemed to be enjoying themselves and in a festive mood. It was not as good as having Cassie beside him like when they were still a couple, but it was a whole lot better than nothing. At least he was not completely alone.

About ten minutes before midnight, Joe announced that everyone who wanted to was welcome to walk across the road with him and watch Sugarcreek's famous giant cuckoo clock strike twelve. Even though everyone had seen the cuckoo clock multiple times, the restaurant immediately cleared out and Michael went with them, part of a laughing, joking crowd as they crossed the dark, deserted street and lined up on the sidewalk in front of the huge clock.

The mayor was already positioned beside the clock and, as the crowd gathered, he began the countdown. "Ten. Nine. Eight..."

Everyone joined in chanting the numbers. "Four. Three. Two. One..."

There was a long silence as everyone waited. It wasn't as dramatic as the giant silver ball dropping in Time's Square but, sure enough, a small door in the clock opened, and a group of painted, wooden, mechanical musicians came out and began playing loud polka music while little wooden dancers spun around and around. The mayor, who was far from a young man, began dancing the polka with his wife, which inspired several of the others to dance a jig or two in the street. As soon as the short piece was over and the carved, wooden figures disappeared back into the clock, everyone shouted "Happy New Year!" and several couples kissed.

Michael had no one to kiss, and felt the lack deeply. On a whim, he reached for his cell phone, which he usually kept in his inside coat pocket. He figured it wouldn't hurt to just call and wish Cassie a Happy New Year.

The phone was not there. Without waiting for the others, he ran back to the restaurant and checked the table where he'd been sitting. Sure enough, there was his cell phone. He breathed a sigh of relief, pocketed the phone, paid his bill, left a tip on the table for the high-school girl who had served him, and drove home. By the time he let himself in the front door, the desire to call Cassie had gone. After all, he still had some pride and it was very late.

***

Once Cassie calmed down, she acknowledged to herself that, in some ways, getting fired was a relief. As angry as she was over the way it had been executed, at least she wouldn't have to struggle to continue to work while enduring the surgery and all that was involved in recovery. Perhaps having that particular stress temporarily eliminated from her life might help her body recuperate a little faster.

The abrupt way she had been fired gave her a little time to prepare for what she knew would be an ordeal. Remembering her mother's lack of appetite and nausea, she stocked the apartment pantry and refrigerator with every nutritious and tasty thing she could think of. She even purchased several bottles of vitamin-enriched drink. It had been the only thing her mother could stomach toward the end.

The next thing she chose to do for herself was go to a bookstore and purchase several books by popular authors. She chose books that weren't heavy intellectually or physically. Books that would be fun to read. Books that she looked forward to reading. She also bought a dozen magazines.

Easy-to-read things. Nothing political. Everything from People to Better Homes & Gardens. Just something to flip through.

It had been years since she had allowed herself to read anything for sheer enjoyment. Knowing that she would be spending days in the apartment without going out, she made a rare stop at Walmart and purchased flannel PJs and fluffy slippers. One of the few perks about living alone was that at least she wouldn't have to look good for anyone for a while.

Plenty of lip promenade for the dry mouth that she knew would be part of this process, and the final preparation—the one she had been dreading—she went to her hairdresser and asked him to cut off all her hair.

"All of it?" Her regular hairdresser, a young, black man named Diamond, was perplexed. "But you have such beautiful hair."

"I don't want to deal with long hair when the chemo kicks in."

"Oh, sweetie," he said. "I'm so sorry."

"It's not your fault," she said, grimly. "Cut it off."

She sat stoically while the hairdresser pulled her lovely, auburn hair into a ponytail with two elastic bands. Then he cut at the root of the ponytail until it all came off. He held it up, showing her its length in the mirror.

"The people from Locks of Love would appreciate this. It would make someone a fine wig."

Cassie was staring at herself in the mirror. It felt strange to have the weight of all that hair off of her head. She had worn it long as far back as she could remember. Her mother had loved braiding it before she went to school each day. That was one of her good memories about her mother.

"Give it to whomever you wish," she said. "I don't care."

The hairdresser went to get a gallon zip-lock bag to put it in. While he was gone, Cassie looked in the mirror and wrestled with herself. She knew she should ask him to simply shave it. But she wasn't sure she could face that just yet. There would be such a long time of wearing caps and scarves to cover her baldness. She found herself longing to look somewhat normal for as long as possible.

"Now what?" Diamond asked.

"A pixie cut would be nice, for now." she said. "I don't think I can handle being completely bald quite yet."

"I think that's a good plan." Diamond held up a pair of scissors and a comb, ready to begin.

He did the best he could and it was a good cut, but she could not hide how dismayed she was with not having her former mane of hair.

"Oh, honey!" Diamond saw her hesitation about her reflection, and jumped in with enthusiastic encouragement. "You look so cute!"

Cute was not a word she normally longed for, but at the moment she would take what she could get. It might be a long time before anyone thought she was cute again.

By the time Cassie had carried her groceries, her new pajamas, and her books and magazines up to her apartment, she was tired but satisfied. It had been a long day but she had done the best she knew how to prepare.

After putting everything away, she settled down on her balcony with a cup of tea to watch the sunset. She was hungry but, with surgery in the morning, she was not allowed to eat anything tonight. It was cold outside but, instead of going in, she put on her down coat and wrapped a blanket around her legs. She did not know how many more sunsets she had left. It could be a long lifetime, or it could be a few months.

If she survived, she would need to go about finding another job. She supposed she should feel bad for allowing herself that temper tantrum back at the law firm, but it had felt awfully good. Deep down, she wondered if she had been wanting to do that for a long time. Would another firm hire her? Maybe. Maybe not. Bradley and his father had a lot of pull in the corporate law community. She might be waiting tables for all she knew. It was not an alien concept. That's how she'd put herself through college.

Shoving that thought aside, she concentrated on making plans for survival for the next few weeks. She would drive herself to her appointments for as long as possible. She would hire a taxi or Uber when she was too shaky to drive herself. The local grocery store had begun a program recently where one could order items online, and the order would be ready for curbside pickup a short time later. After the provisions she'd just purchased ran out, she would use that method to replenish her food supplies until she was well again.

Fireworks startled her, lighting up the night sky. Car horns began to blow from down below in the street. She heard people cheering.

She had been so sunk in her own misery, she had nearly forgotten that it was New Year's Eve.

What a terrible night to be alone!

The frigid air had found its way through her coat and blanket, and she realized she was chilled. She went inside and closed and locked the sliding glass door. Then she pulled her cell phone out of her pocket. It wouldn't hurt just to call and wish Michael a happy new year. It was a civil thing to do. She wouldn't have to let him know that she desperately just wanted to hear his voice tonight. She would say nothing about being ill.

The phone rang a long time. Michael always made sure it wouldn't cut off after only two or three rings. She was so startled when a young woman's voice answered the phone instead of Michael that she hung up immediately. Just to be sure, she checked the log on her phone to make absolutely certain she hadn't called someone else by accident. No. It was no accident. That was Michael's number, and some woman had answered.

Her heart hurt at the sound of that voice. What had she expected? Of *course* there was a possibility that a woman would answer. After all, it was New Year's Eve. A night when no one really wanted to be alone.

She tried to calm her nerves by taking a hot bath. This was something she almost never did because it took more time than jumping in the shower. After she'd toweled off, she donned her soft, new, pajamas.

Before crawling into bed, she set her alarm for 4:30 a.m. As soon as she awoke, she would shower, pack a small suitcase and have an Uber driver take her to the James Cancer Center. Even though it would be New Year's Day, her doctor thought it critical to operate a soon as possible. He had scheduled surgery for 7:30 a.m.

Sleep was impossible. All she could think about was Michael and how foolish she had been to lose someone she loved, just because of her job. A job that had unexpectedly been ripped out of her hands.

Scared, sick, unemployed, lonely, and facing the biggest fight of her life, she curled into a fetal position and tried not to cry.

Chapter Thirty-Eight

Rachel was cuddled with Bobby on the couch. They were celebrating New Year's Eve with cocoa, cookies, and an attempt to make cranes from an origami kit Santa Claus had left under the tree at Christmas. It was more advanced for Bobby's age than she'd realized when she purchased it, but she thought maybe, with her help, he could achieve learning to create a couple of the simpler ones. It was a lot harder than it looked.

"Is this good?" Bobby asked, holding up his third crane.

"You're getting it." Rachel gave his lopsided attempt her undivided attention.

Tonight was a big night for Joe and Darren, and she was using the chance to enjoy her stepson for the evening. They were keeping the restaurant open until midnight, when the mayor promised to dance the polka in front of the huge, outdoor, cuckoo clock. It was Sugarcreek's equivalent of watching the Times Square silver ball dropping on the stroke of midnight.

She loved being part of this small village where they could create their own traditions—even if they were a little non-traditional. Bobby wanted to go over in a bit to be part of the celebration. That would be fine, assuming he was still awake. He'd been having a growth spurt lately, and needing more sleep than usual.

The TV was still on from where Bobby had been watching cartoons earlier. With Joe gone, it helped the house not feel empty. They had been getting a little lax lately about Bobby's TV watching. It was supposed to be no more than an hour per day, but sometimes they neglected to turn it off.

One thing they were more careful about was not allowing the news to be on when he was in the room. They wanted their son to have as innocent a childhood as possible. Bobby was very smart, picked up on everything, and absorbed other people's grief too deeply to have a diet of real-life tragedy and adult worry.

She was attempting a particularly complicated origami fold when she was surprised to hear the intro music announcing the 11 o'clock news. Before she could get up, grab the remote and turn the news off, a familiar face filled the screen. It was Tony Maddox.

Instead of turning off the TV, she turned up the volume.

"Tony Maddox, a known leader of the street gang, Ghosts Inc. was shot and killed last night at his home," the news anchor said. "Police have no leads on who is responsible..."

Quickly, she switched the news off before Bobby could be subjected to more details on the violence. She was grateful that he was so absorbed in his origami creation that he hadn't seemed to notice.

"You good there for a while, buddy?" she asked. "I need to make a phone call."

He had discarded the crane, she noticed. Now he was concentrating on making a paper airplane. She didn't blame him. She liked making paper airplanes too.

She dialed Mabel's number and was relieved when the old woman answered.

"This is Rachel." She walked into the kitchen for privacy. "I just saw Tony's face on the news tonight. Can you tell me what happened?"

"Someone shot him. I heard a gunshot about eight. It sounded like it came from Tony's place. I went to the window, but I couldn't see anything. Then someone came running out and they kept running."

"Could you tell who it was?"

"No. It was dark and they went the other way."

"Were you the one who called the police?"

Big hesitation. "No."

"Why not?"

"Like I told you before, it's not smart to get involved with things that happen in that house."

"You heard a gunshot and you ignored it?"

"I'm an old woman. I stay out of other people's business."

Rachel sighed.

"Did the police come talk to you?"

"Yeah, but I didn't open the door and they went away."

"They should have brought baked goods."

"It would have helped," Mabel agreed. "What do you think will happen to Lily's baby now that Tony's gone?"

"I wish I knew. Does he have any close family members who would be trustworthy enough to care for a newborn?"

"Tony had family," Mabel said. "But not anyone I can think of who Lily would want her baby left with."

Chapter Thirty-Nine

The next morning, Rachel called Bill Sherman, her old friend from her Cleveland cop days, and made arrangements for him to meet her at Tony's house. He promised to allow her access so she could try to discover if there was anything in that house that might give her a clue to Lily's identity.

As far as Tony's death went—that was what the homicide detectives were for.

Rachel was on her way to Cleveland when she received a call from Sally, the social worker.

"Did you hear about Tony Maddox's death?" Sally asked.

"Yes. I'm headed up there right now."

"Good news," Sally said. "Tony's mother, the baby's grandmother, is willing to take her. She contacted us early this morning and wants her grandchild brought to her as soon as possible."

A long pause while Rachel thought this through.

"What do you know about her?" Rachel said.

"Not much, except she doesn't have a criminal record. In my line of work, that alone is something to celebrate."

"It doesn't necessarily mean she is someone you'd want in charge of a baby."

"No, but she must have had Tony when she was a teenager. She's still in her forties and young enough to be able to care for a child. She has a daughter too."

"Does she have a job?"

"Doesn't seem to," Sally said. "Apparently she got a large settlement from a grocery store for a slip-and-fall suit. Ended up with a permanent back injury."

"If she has a back injury, can she even lift a child?"

"I don't know," Sally said. "I'll need to check things out a little more before we hand the baby over, of course. I just called to let you know where we were on this case."

"Thanks," Rachel said. "Please keep me informed."

The professional cop in her wanted to rejoice in the fact that there was a relative willing to care for the baby. The unofficial side of her wanted to grab that infant and run. She wasn't sure how well the woman who had raised a street-gang leader would care for a child, and there was also the comment Mabel had made that Tony's mother was crazy-rotten.

When she arrived, Bill was waiting behind the crime-scene tape.

"Homicide has been here," he said. "We've dusted for fingerprints, etc. You can look into anything you want."

"Any luck finding anything?"

"My guess is there will be too many fingerprints to do much good. With all the traffic the neighbors say was going on in that house, I'm thinking it'll just be a Who's Who of Ghosts Inc. gang members."

"So you cleared it for me to go in?"

"Sure," he said. "But I don't think you'll find much. It looks like your girl had her own room, so you might want to start there."

The house was not the pig's sty Rachel had seen in so many other houses where drugs were sold. The furnishings were old, but clean and well-polished. What appeared to be Lily's room off the kitchen was not much more than a closet. Rachel suspected it had, at one time, been a pantry. Inside Lily's room, there were no photos of family members, or herself. Instead, Lily had cut out dozens of pictures of flowers from magazines and taped them to the walls.

There was not much in the way of furnishings in the little room. A cot-sized bed, a small bureau, a miniscule closet, and one small bookcase. It was stuffed to overflowing with paperbacks. Rachel squatted down to read the titles. She saw that the bookcase was mostly crammed with fictional novels about the Amish. Many had price tags on them of a quarter or a dime. Probably picked up at garage sales or thrift stores.

From the looks of the contents of her bookcase, Lily liked to escape into Amish fiction. Rachel could understand. Those books must have shown her a way of life much different from what she had in this house. Perhaps that was why Lily had been trying to get to Amish country, and why she'd also cut out that article about Joe's restaurant.

The thing Rachel couldn't figure out about that newspaper article was why Joe's restaurant in particular? Where was the connection? There were plenty of restaurants in Amish country, many of them Amish run. Again, why Joe?

The article had mentioned that Joe's wife was a cop. Had Lily thought Rachel would help protect her and the baby? If that was the case, Rachel wished she had been able to have gotten to her without wrecking. Lily wouldn't be the first pregnant girl she had helped.

"From what I've seen," Bill said, "your girl was part Tony's girlfriend, part unpaid housekeeper."

"And his cook," Rachel said. "Tony told me that was why she got to live here when his other girlfriends were not allowed. He said it was because she cooked 'real' food."

"Girl must've loved flowers."

"Looks like it."

"Seems like there should be something more personal in this room than just her paperbacks, furniture, and pictures on the wall."

"Especially at her age," Rachel said. "And did you notice that there aren't any baby things? Most mothers are buying little outfits long before they are full-term."

"She didn't have many clothes of her own," Bill said, drawing back a curtain, revealing the tiny closet where a handful of tops and bottoms hung.

"If she liked to read, maybe she liked to write. Did anyone find a journal or diary?"

"Nope," Bill said. "But I'll help you look."

Five minutes later, they'd been through all the bits and pieces of jewelry, clothing and underwear in the bureau drawers. All items were folded neatly. They turned the mattress over and looked beneath for anything that might have been hidden. They looked behind the headboard and in a small footlocker that held two pairs of shoes and a worn pair of boots.

The room was so small, it was hard for two people to move around without bumping into one another. It did not take long to search every inch. It was almost as though the girl had not wanted to leave anything behind that could identify her. No family photos, no keepsakes. It was disappointing. Rachel's hopes had been high that she would find some clue here. Now, she saw that she would not.

"It's as though she was trying to erase her whole identity," she told Bill.

"Or didn't have one to begin with."

"What do you mean?"

"Sometimes people can become so bowed down by circumstances or mental abuse that they almost cease to exist even to themselves. You told me that Tony said he'd found her on the street. That means she was running away from something or someone. More than likely, someone. Tony took her in and she traded her ability to cook and more intimate favors for a roof over her head and food to eat. Tony's was a powerful personality. He kept his followers frightened, loyal, and in awe of him, and some of them are bad dudes. I can see why someone like Lily didn't have a chance."

"Do you suppose Lily was her real name?" Rachel asked.

"What do you mean?"

"All these pictures of flowers she pasted to the wall. Maybe she just chose to call herself by one of them."

"There's a good chance we'll never know," Bill said. "You might have to give this one up, Rachel."

"That would be easy to do, but I keep thinking of her little girl. When she grows up, she'll want to know who her mother was. She'll want to know whether or not she had grandparents, cousins."

"I suppose, but I dunno if that's always a good thing." He scratched his head. "I get the feeling that God has a wicked sense of humor every time my family gets together at holidays at my grandma's. Craziest bunch I ever saw."

"And yet you love them," Rachel said

"Yeah," Bill conceded. "I do. Want to check out the kitchen? Lily must have spent a lot of time in there."

"Sure," Rachel said. "Might as well."

The kitchen did not reveal anything except that Lily had all the basics she needed to make decent meals. She might have been a good cook in Tony's eyes, but there was nothing gourmet or out-of-the ordinary in the supplies or equipment. Apparently, to Tony, any woman who could make mashed potatoes from real potatoes was a rarity and a gem.

"Since she could cook, maybe she thought she could get a job at your husband's restaurant."

"You could be right, but why leave here on Christmas Eve? If she was looking for a job, she couldn't come at a worse time. Joe's Home Plate would have been closed."

"Maybe she didn't think she had a choice," Bill said.

"Maybe she didn't. Any idea of who Tony's killer was?"

"Not yet."

Rachel heard a commotion in the front yard. Someone was out there yelling and swearing.

"I got a right to go in," a coarse voice screamed. "It was my son's house and now it's mine!"

"Not yet, ma'am," one of the two cops who had been guarding the place tried to calm the woman down. "The police have not yet finished their investigations."

"They don't have to investigate. I know who killed my son. I can tell them who it is too."

Rachel glanced out the door. The woman looked like she could be in her forties, but she must have lived a hard life. She was the kind of skinny Rachel associated with heroin or meth use. She had frizzy, unkempt hair that was dyed an unflattering shade of red. Tight black leggings and a t-shirt sporting a picture of a marijuana plant completed her ensemble.

Not exactly the kind of nurturing grandmother Rachel had been hoping to find.

"Is that Tony's mother?"

"Afraid so. Gertie Maddox. She's been making our lives miserable ever since she got word that Tony got killed last night. Funny thing though, from what I hear, it seems like she's not nearly as upset at his death as she is furious that we've not allowed her to go inside the house. Absolutely determined to get in here. I get the feeling there's something in here she wants, bad."

"Or something she thinks might be in there," Rachel said. "Have they found any money? Drugs?"

"Plenty, but it's with the Vice Unit right now. We haven't told her that yet though."

"Is there any chance that she does know who shot him?"

"Probably not. So far she's named about a dozen people she wants us to investigate. We are taking her accusations seriously, but some of them are pretty random. She even accused an old neighbor lady; a woman in her eighties who has to use a walker to get around."

"Mabel?"

"I think that's the name."

"I know her. I'm planning to go over there and talk with her when I finish here. It was her car that Lily stole."

"That's interesting. Let me know if you find out anything valuable."

"Of course. I think I'll go out the back door and see if I can avoid Gertie for now."

"Wish I could avoid her," Bill said.

Chapter Forty

"No pie?" Mabel said, when she opened the door to Rachel. "No cookies? I'm disappointed in you."

"My aunt is a little under the weather." Rachel held out a box of Krispie Kreme doughnuts. "Will these do? I picked them up on the way here."

Mabel unlatched the storm door.

"No walker today?" Rachel asked, handing Mabel the box.

"My hip is feeling some better. Thought I'd give my cane a try." Mabel glanced out at the commotion in the yard next door. "Gertie at it again?'

"She wants to get inside the house. The police aren't letting her."

"She wants to get at Tony's money."

"There isn't any left. The cops found it all; the drugs too."

"Doubt it. Tony had special-made places to hide his drugs and money. Gertie knows that. Lily told me Gertie was one of the main people he was hiding things from. He didn't trust her, and Lily said he had good reason. Last year Gertie got hold of his credit card and bought herself a giant flat-screen television set with it."

"Tony had a credit card?" Rachel asked.

"Not after that."

"Gertie told the cops you might have been the one who shot him."

Mabel was startled. "Me?"

"You, and about a dozen other people she suggested. Do you have a gun?"

"Of course, but I had no call to kill Tony. He looked after me... in his own way. That's why me and Lily got to know each other in the beginning. He sent her over here to check on me."

"Did you give her the keys to your car that night?"

"No, but she knew where the keys were. I'd told her, if things ever got really bad with Tony, she was welcome to use it. I promised I wouldn't call the police on her."

"Did she ever give you any indication where she was from?" Rachel asked.

"No. Funny thing. She'd chat with me all day about those paperbacks she read. She'd tell me the whole plot of one while she washed dishes or made me some soup or something. I don't read so good anymore, so I liked that a lot, but she never told me anything personal from before we met. I asked her one time where she'd learned to cook so good and she said her grandmother had taught her. That's the most she ever said about her past."

"If Tony didn't let her go out much, where did she get the books?"

"There's a thrift store up the street he allowed her to walk to. She could buy a paperback for pocket change. There were always a lot of people coming and going at Tony's house. She said she almost always found a quarter or two in the couch after some of them left. She could buy a paperback for fifty cents. She was always wanting to be reading them Amish stories."

"Did she ever tell you why she liked Amish novels so much?" Rachel said.

"I asked her once. She said she didn't know, except she felt safe when she was reading them."

"Safe?"

"That's what she said. Didn't make any sense to me, but I was glad it helped her."

Mabel began to eye the bakery box again.

"Just a couple more questions, Mabel, and then I'm out of here," Rachel said. "We found a clipping of a newspaper story in the car, about me, and my husband's restaurant. She'd circled the address. Do you know anything about that?"

"Oh, was that you?" Mabel asked.

"What do you mean?"

"Lily cut that article out of one of my newspapers a while back. Said 'Sugarcreek' sounded like a nice place to live. If I remember right, the article said that you'd risked your life to save your little boy only the night before your husband was scheduled to open the restaurant?"

"That's true," Rachel said.

"Lily started talking about wanting to go visit Sugarcreek sometime. She wanted to see the restaurant, meet your husband, the famous base-ball player, and maybe meet you too. She brought it up several times. I think she knew that raising a baby in Tony's house wouldn't work. She talked about maybe getting a job there as a cook. I asked her what she'd do with the baby if she had to work. She said maybe there would be an Amish family who would watch the baby for her."

It hurt Rachel to think of that poor girl reading a newspaper arti-cle and daydreaming about coming to work at Joe's Home Plate. If she could turn back time, knowing what she did now, she would have driven straight to Tony's weeks ago, loaded up Lily, and taken her home with her.

Instead, she would be going to the gravesite tomorrow to watch Lily's cheap casket being lowered into the ground.

"The social worker in Tuscarawas County called me on the way here," Rachel said. "Tony's mom has already laid claim to her granddaughter."

"Gertie?" Mabel looked astonished. "Gertie wants to raise Lily's baby?"

"She seems to think she does."

"Gertie is a terrible woman, Rachel. My guess is that the only reason she's going after the baby is because she's figured some way to make money from it."

"Welfare?"

"No," Mabel said. "She's got too much money to qualify for welfare. She won a slip-and-fall lawsuit last year. Got herself a big house with it. Got some money out of a whiplash incident too. There's something else up her sleeve."

"You don't think she's capable of simply wanting the baby because she's the grandmother and loves her?"

"Gertie's one of them—what do you call it—sociopaths. Doesn't care about anything except herself. Talk to her daughter sometime if you get a chance. Gertie shouldn't be allowed to own a junkyard dog, let alone a baby."

If what Mabel was saying was true, and there was no reason for her to lie, Rachel felt her stomach churn. Once again she wished she could take that sweet baby girl and run.

Rachel was more concerned than ever now. It sounded as though, as bad as Tony had been, his mother was even worse and, if Gertie didn't have a record, there was an excellent chance a judge would turn the baby over to her.

"Thanks for the information, Mabel," Rachel said. "You've been really helpful. I think that's about it for now, except you might want to know that the funeral home is going to bury Lily tomorrow. There won't be any kind of service, but I planned to go be there. If your brother wanted to bring you, it would be okay."

"There's no need," Mabel said. "I'd rather just keep the memory of

Lily sitting here watching TV with me."

"I understand."

"Before you go," Mabel rose from the table, limped over to the couch and brought back a fluffy, pink afghan. "I made it for Lily's baby. Even though Lily is gone, I'd appreciate it if you'd take it to whoever is taking care of her. I'd like to think that something I knitted for her will keep Lily's baby warm."

Chapter Forty-One

It was late afternoon by the time Rachel got to Joe's Home Plate. Normally, this wasn't a busy time for the restaurant but, with it being New Year's Day, people were off work and it was packed.

While his father and uncle helped cook and serve, Bobby helped clear tables. He was a conscientious little guy who felt a great deal of ownership of the restaurant.

She stood inside the door watching her stepson for a moment. Some people might feel that allowing him to help as much as he did was wrong, but she had grown up with the work ethic of the Amish and had seen the results. They were a people who were very deliberate in teaching their children how to work from the time they were toddlers. It created a culture of extremely competent people who could support themselves no matter where they were.

Toward this end, Joe and she had purchased their son a small notebook that he kept in a desk drawer in the back. This was the notebook in which he kept track of his hours. Since he could not yet tell time, keeping track of his hours meant bringing the notebook to his dad or uncle and asking them how many minutes he had worked, but then he'd get to mark down the number. Joe carefully counted out Bobby's salary at the end of each week.

And yet, even though he was growing up, Bobby was still a little boy with a little boy's heart. When he saw Rachel, he came barreling toward her. "Mommy!"

Everyone within earshot smiled. Many of the customers knew how much being called 'Mommy' meant to her. She had been 'Rachel' for a long time, and for a while had to listen to him frequently talk about his 'real' mommy after her and Joe's marriage. When that little boy slammed into her, everything became right again, as she lifted him up and his arms went around her neck.

"I'm going to head over to check on baby Holly and give her a present. Do you want to go with me?"

"Can I stay a little longer?" Bobby said. "Uncle Darren and daddy really need me today." He looked around importantly. "I just don't know who will take care of things if I'm not here."

"Go ahead," she said. "I need to go get a hug from your dad, and then I'll be back later to take you home."

Bobby scampered off and she greeted various townspeople as she walked through the crowd toward the kitchen. As she walked through the swinging doors, she found Joe mixing up another batch of his famous burgers. He had about five pounds of hamburger into which he was mixing in his special mix of spices. This was one job that Joe allowed no one else to do, except sometimes his brother. The various hamburger recipes that they used, some of which had been created by their mother, were his and Darren's secret. They did not share them with any of the help they hired.

Not sharing the recipes had worked out well. News had traveled fast that Joe kept the recipes in his head and shared them with no one. It added a certain cachet to the restaurant, she thought. Patrons liked to tease Joe about sharing his recipes with them whenever he would come out to mingle with the guests.

With his hands covered with hamburger meat, he didn't try to hug her but he leaned over and gave her a kiss as he continued to work.

"Tough day?" he asked.

She put her arms around his waist from behind and leaned her cheek against his strong back. "Very."

"What did you find out?" he asked.

"I found out that Tony's mother is someone I wish would go away. She wants the baby."

"And you don't think she should have her?"

"I think Holly is going to have a very hard life if she ends up being raised by Gertie."

"Is there nothing you can do about it?"

"I'm working on it."

"Are you hungry, sweetheart?"

"I am," she said. "I thought I would make a peanut butter and jelly sandwich when I got home. I don't feel much like cooking."

"Darren," Joe said. "Your hands are clean. Make a plate for Rachel. My wife needs sustenance, and she has come to the right place. Now," Joe nodded his head at a stool near him. "Sit down and start telling me everything that happened today. Maybe I can help you figure things out."

Joe's brother brought Rachel a plate of food and gave her a hug, both of which she gratefully accepted. Joe's brother was quickly becoming one of her favorite people—especially since Joe's Home Plate was initially Darren's idea and it had turned out so well.

One bite of the burger and a forkful of potato salad and she groaned with pleasure. "Oh, wow, that's good. You guys oughta start a restaurant or something."

"Enjoy!" Darren said. "But whatever you do, don't expect any pie. Ever since that newspaper article, we can't keep a pie in the place. If people see one here now, they don't just buy a slice, they buy the whole thing and take it home with them. All twelve pies I picked up from Lydia today were gone in the first hour even though I've doubled the price."

Rachel was worried. She couldn't allow Lydia to have this kind of pressure day in and day out. Lydia loved to bake, and she loved making some money to send to the children in Haiti, but twelve pies a day was a lot. Rachel knew her aunt was at capacity and possibly beyond.

However, that was not something she could do anything about right now.

"I need to get over to the Hochstetlers," she told Joe, after she'd bolted the plate of food. "I have to let them know about the latest development with Holly's father."

"They don't know about the shooting yet?" Joe asked.

"Not yet, and at this point, it's anybody's guess what's going to happen." She jumped off the stool and grabbed her hat and coat. "I'll stop by soon to pick up Bobby if you can get along without him."

Chapter Forty-Two

Keturah was in front of the stove, stirring up a special lotion to give to her mothers to help them prepare their perineum for an easier childbirth, when there was a knock on her kitchen door.

Her potion was at a fragile stage in the simmering/stirring process and she did not want to leave it for even a second. Agnes was tending to a naked baby with a dirty bottom lying on a blanket on the couch. Neither were in a position to open the door.

"Come in!" Keturah shouted. "Our door is not locked."

"Is your door ever locked?" Rachel asked, letting herself in.

"At night sometimes… if Ivan remembers," Keturah said. "There seems to be no point. A robber could easily break in a window if he wanted to come in. Ivan says there would be less for him to repair if the robber would use the door. Anyone is welcome to what we have anyway. But I don't think we have anything a thief would want these days. Don't today's robbers prefer to steal TVs and computers? We have nothing like that. Nor do we have any jewelry. I think they would not want our clothing, or the kindling Ivan keeps stored behind the stove, or our kerosene lamps."

"Probably not." Rachel laughed.

"See?" Keturah teased. "It is better to be Amish. Then no one wants anything you have."

"Your quilts?"

Keturah thought it over. "Yes, a robber, if he were smart, might want our quilts—but he would have to take them off our beds first and I don't think Ivan would give up his covers easily on a cold night."

"You still need to lock your door at night," Rachel said. "Tell Ivan I said so."

"I will give my husband your message." Keturah scooted the potion to the back where the stovetop was barely warm. "It is good to see you, Rachel. You look cold. Come warm yourself in front of the stove. Are you hungry? There are fresh oatmeal cookies on the plate on the table. Help yourself."

"Thanks," Rachel said. "But I'd like to see little Holly first."

She walked over to where Agnes was folding the cloth diaper on her lap just so. The baby was kicking her feet, enjoying the feeling of air on her bare bottom. Rosie was sleeping on a pallet made of blankets on the floor.

"She's a good eater, and is such a contented baby," Agnes said, fondly, pinning the diaper on. "She's an easy baby to care for."

Agnes finished her diapering job, she brought Holly and the rest of her clothing into the kitchen. She sat down at the kitchen table where she could finish dressing her and still keep an eye on Rosie.

Rachel also drew out a chair from the kitchen table and sat down. She laid the pink afghan on the table.

"Mabel, the woman whose car Lily wrecked, sent that along for the baby. I just came from there."

"That was nice of her." Keturah came over to finger and admire the afghan. "This is done well. Your friend, Mabel, is a very good knitter."

Rachel nodded. The afghan was adorable, but not her top priority.

"Is there some news?" Keturah asked, sensing her mood. "Is something wrong?"

"I'm afraid so."

"Bad news?"

"Yes."

"Then tell us," Agnes said. "We will face it together."

"Holly's father was killed last night."

"What happened?" Keturah asked, as she watched Agnes pull a tiny white shirt over the baby's head.

"We don't know everything yet," Rachel said. "The thing is, now Tony's mother wants the baby."

Keturah digested this information while she went to the sink and filled a tall glass with water.

"Nursing two babies required a lot of water, daughter." Keturah sat the glass in front of Agnes. "You work so hard, you too often forget to replenish the liquid in your body."

"*Danke.* I get so busy with the babies, I forget." Agnes said, and took a long swallow.

Keturah's attention turned again to Rachel's news. "But surely Holly's grandmother being willing to care for her is a good thing?"

"If the grandmother was like you, then having her take the baby would be a wonderful thing. But Gertie Maddox is not a good woman, or even a kind one from what Mabel, the next-door neighbor, told me. Mabel has known that family for a long time. She's afraid Gertie will mistreat the baby, like she did her own son and daughter."

"But surely we will not have to give this baby to someone who will treat her badly?" Agnes drained her glass.

"Of course not. I called Sally, the social worker. I told her what I'd heard from Mabel. Tried to slow things down until she and I can investigate further, but Gertie told the social worker, if she doesn't have the baby within forty-eight hours, she'll sue for custody."

"Who is she going to sue?" Agnes asked.

"I have no idea," Rachel said. "I'm not sure even she knows. Gertie is unpredictable and volatile and apparently she really enjoys suing people."

"What would you advise us to do?" Keturah asked.

"I told Sally to keep your name out of this for now," Rachel said. "I don't want Gertie to know where the baby is being kept. You have already done so much, you should not have to also deal with a hysterical or angry woman at your door. I'm hoping her demands and threats are just from the first waves of grief. People change. Perhaps she'll turn out to be the kind of grandmother who can raise a baby well."

"But you don't think so," Keturah said.

"I don't think so at all," Rachel admitted.

Agnes put Holly in a tiny, white handmade nightgown, tied a pair of fuzzy, white baby booties on her little feet, snuggled a white, knit cap onto her head, and then wrapped her in the pink afghan. "She's ready for bed. Do you want to hold her for a minute before I take her upstairs?"

"I'd love to," Rachel said.

Little Holly was so adorable wrapped in the pink afghan and wearing her white-knit cap. Rachel was dead tired but holding that newborn close made her feel much better. Holly yawned hugely, then the little butterfly eyelashes fluttered a few times before they stopped and rested on the baby's cheeks—tiny, blonde crescents. Rachel kissed both eyes and the tiny nose before handing her back to Agnes.

"As adorable as this baby is, I have a seven-year-old son at the restaurant who needs to be taken home and read a bedtime story before he goes to sleep. It is our special time together. Sometimes my job gets in the way, but I try not to let it."

Agnes walked with her to the door. "Let us know the minute you hear anything."

"Thank you for what you're doing," Rachel said. "I know it is a burden caring for two infants at once."

"It is not a burden when it is the work that God has given me," Agnes smiled. "That makes the burden lighter. Besides that, I really love babies."

***

As soon as Rachel was out of the driveway, Agnes turned to Keturah, sorrow written on her face.

"I can hand this baby to an Englisch relative, if that relative will take good care of her," Agnes said. "Part of my heart will go with her, but I know the need for family to be with family. But to give her to a bad woman? Someone truly evil?" She looked down into the baby's sleeping face. "How could I ever do that?"

"You couldn't." The moment Rachel mentioned that Gertie might bring harm to the baby, Keturah had begun to make a plan. "And I could not let you. I did not save this baby's life for such a fate."

"But if the law says I have to..."

"Which law?" Keturah said.

Agnes was puzzled. "What do you mean?"

"Which law? God's or man's?" Keturah said. "I have been talking about this with Ivan. Which laws do our people follow?"

"God's, of course, but we are still a very law-abiding people."

"We are, as long as the law is just." Keturah stroked the baby's soft cheek. "In this case, I am not at all sure that the Englisch law will be just."

Chapter Forty-Three

It had been several days since Michael's disastrous trip to Columbus to attempt to reconcile with Cassie. Trying to surprise her had obviously been a big mistake, but he'd at least expected her to call him before now to nag him to get on with the divorce. Cassie was nothing if not efficient. Why hadn't she contacted him?

Whether she called or didn't, he knew he needed to talk with her. He could not live in this unsettled state for much longer. So, why was he putting it off and drawing this out? If she didn't want him, why bother with her? There were surely a few other women who would think he was a catch. Maybe even someone nice who wouldn't think that living in Sugarcreek was such a big sacrifice.

Okay then. He'd do it.

He scribbled his signature on the divorce papers, put them in an envelope, stuck a stamp on it and carried it out to the mailbox. The mailman could take it tomorrow when he came. There. It was finished. He wasn't certain about what came next, but he thought he'd probably have to meet with Cassie and some lawyer to finish things. Since it appeared that there was nothing for them to fight over, the whole thing should be relatively quick and easy.

He walked back to the house, sat down on his porch steps and stared at the mailbox and its red flag standing straight up. It shouldn't be that easy to dissolve a marriage. At least, it shouldn't be that easy to dissolve his and Cassie's. They had truly loved each other at one time. Truth be told, he still did love her, even though he was angry at her for causing this mess. If only she had agreed to move here with him, had agreed to even *try* living here. He had lived the life she wanted. He'd been miserable, but he had loved her enough to at least try. Wasn't it only fair that she give him the same courtesy?

Office hours were over and he was hungry. He fixed a bowl of instant oatmeal for supper and didn't eat it. Fixed a cup of coffee and poured it down the sink. Turned on the TV and stared at the screen, his eyes and mind registering absolutely nothing he was watching.

Finally, he walked out to the mailbox, pulled out the envelope, brought it back into the house and fed it to the shredder beside his desk.

Even though he was still angry with her about whatever it was that had happened, or not happened, with Bradley—if Cassie wanted a divorce from him, he wasn't going to make it easy for her. He would not allow her to do it in such a bloodless, emotionless way. Their relationship meant more to him than that. She was going to have to fight him for it.

Part of him wanted to drive to Columbus again to have it out with her once and for all. Face to face. He wanted to hear her tell him that she no longer loved him. Wanted to look into her eyes and see for himself if it was true. He could be there, have it out with her, and be back within five or six hours.

Except for one thing. He had promised to head over to David Yost's this evening and help him keep vigil over a favorite broodmare that was ready to foal. The mare was acting more nervous than with her other two colts. David had sunk a lot of money into the stud fee; more than he could afford to lose. This new colt could make or break his chances of the first-rate horse farm he was trying to build. Of course, there was no guarantee that the mare would foal tonight. Or even this week, for all he knew. David just said he had a gut feeling she was getting close.

A thought struck. Why did he have to go to Cassie? Why did he have to abandon his patients to go seek her out? She was the one who wanted the divorce. It wouldn't hurt her to come here to him.

He decided to call and tell her that, if she wanted the divorce, she'd have to come and deal with him face-to-face. As far as he was concerned, she could come hang out at the barn with him and David tonight if she was so anxious to get this over with.

When he called her cell phone, he was annoyed that it went straight to her voicemail. He didn't want to leave a message. He wanted to talk to *her*. It was rare, but sometimes she did leave her cell phone behind in her car or at the apartment. When she was too engrossed in a project, she could become a little absentminded about matters like cell phones and car keys.

He glanced at his watch. It was only four-thirty. Cassie's firm didn't close their doors until six. They didn't even close their doors for some of the national holidays—like New Year's Day. Other law firms might be more lenient, but it did not pay to have a hangover the morning after New Year's Eve if one worked for Blackwell, Hart & Cooper.

Cassie would be at work. Cassie was always at work.

Calls to her office were always answered by her shared assistant, Sophie, who would then transfer them to her. He did not have to look up the number as he still had it memorized.

"Hello, you have reached the law offices of Blackwell, Hart & Cooper. This is Sophie. How may I direct your call?"

"Michael Reynolds here," he said. "Please put me through to my wife."

There was a long silence on the other end of the phone.

"Sophie?" he said. "Are you still there?"

"I—I…" Sophie stuttered a little. "Excuse me, but how long has it been since you talked to Cassie?"

He didn't see how their marital issues could be any of her business. "Please just put me through to her."

More silence. What on earth had Cassie said to her assistant about him to make Sophie act so odd? Had she instructed Sophie not to allow him to speak to her? That really would be the last straw. He wasn't some weird stalker. He was her husband.

"Sophie?"

"I don't know if I'm supposed to tell you this, but Cassie doesn't work here anymore."

His mind swirled. What Sophie was saying did not compute.

"I don't understand," he said. "Did she take a job with someone else?"

"I don't know," Sophie said. "The only thing I know for sure is that I saw two security guards clear her office and walk her out to her car. She is no longer allowed access to the building."

He was stunned. "What happened?"

"I can't tell you," Sophie said.

"Is that because you don't know or you can't say?"

"I don't know what she did wrong..." Sophie, who Michael had never found to be the sharpest knife in the drawer, seemed to warm to the subject. The chance to gossip a bit was just too strong. "But I know one thing for sure, she won't ever work for this company again."

"How do you know?"

"That's what Mr. Cooper said after your wife poured coffee all over the papers in her briefcase before the security guards escorted her out."

"Cassie did WHAT?"

"I *know!*" Sophie said. "That's how I felt too! I couldn't believe it either. I've never seen any of the lawyers act like that before around here, or seen Mr. Cooper so angry."

Michael was shaken. He couldn't begin to come up with a scenario in which Cassie would have been fired, let alone behaving like that at work. "You've been very helpful, Sophie. I'll try to get hold of her at home."

Chapter Forty-Four

As Rachel stood shivering in the corner of the cemetery, waiting for Lily's body to be laid to rest, she found herself envious of the snowbirds—those retirees who spent spring, summer, and fall in Sugarcreek, but lived all winter in Florida.

There was no sunshine today. She'd always thought that a burial was slightly easier to endure if there was sunshine, but the sky was depressingly gray and overcast, as though it too was weary of winter. She thought she detected the scent of more snow to come in the air and was grateful she'd worn warm leggings and a long-sleeved knit top beneath her Sugarcreek police uniform.

The small, gravesite funeral being held for Lily was almost as sparse as the information Rachel had managed to gather on her. The coroner had contacted Smith Funeral Home in Sugarcreek, and they had taken over once Tony identified the body. There was a modest spray of pink roses and greenery resting on top. It looked pretty on the plain, white, casket.

Lily liked flowers.

Yes, she did. To the point that the poor girl had cut out pictures of flowers from magazines and glued them to the walls of her room.

Because she had thought it would just be her, the funeral director, and the two workmen who were in charge of closing the grave, she had not planned on any sort of service. Then at the last minute, Joe had chosen to accompany her.

However, in thinking there would be no need for any type of service, she had not counted on the compassion of the Amish. Somehow, they heard that the Christmas baby's mother was going to be buried today. Black buggies began showing up. A couple, then more. By the time they stopped coming, fifteen buggies and nearly forty people had respectfully shown up in their black, Sunday-best, clothing.

Keturah, Ivan, and Agnes were among those who came. Agnes carried little Holly, and Ivan held two-month-old Rosie in his arms. John held the hands of the two boys. Clara clung to her grandmother's hand. Reuben and Betty were there as well. For the first time, Rachel saw that Betty was pregnant. Everyone was heavily bundled against the cold.

"We brought the baby," Keturah whispered. We thought someday it would give little Holly comfort to know that she had attended her mother's funeral."

"You're right," Rachel said. "I didn't even think about that."

The weather was cold, but not quite as frigid as it had been. Some of the snow had melted. What with the buggies and vehicles, the cemetery was becoming a quagmire of earth and mud. Because neither she nor the funeral director had expected for there to be anyone else there, they had contacted no minister, and yet now there was a small crowd standing solemnly around the gravesite, waiting for something to happen.

"Is anyone going to do something?" Joe whispered.

"I didn't think anyone would be here except us," she whispered back. "I've got nothing."

"Okay, then. I'll take care of it." Joe turned to face the group. "Thank you for coming. I apologize for our lack of preparation. We did not expect anyone except us to be here, so there's no service planned, but I've had something on my heart these past few days I would like to share if that's okay."

He glanced at Rachel. She nodded encouragement.

"The young mother's name we are burying today was Lily. That's all we know. Rachel thinks she may have run away from the home where she was living in order to protect her baby. For reasons we don't understand, Lily chose to come to Sugarcreek early Christmas morning. Most of you know that Keturah Hochstetler saved the life of baby Holly here and took her home with her. Agnes has been caring for her ever since."

Joe reached out his arms for baby Holly. "May I?"

"Of course." Agnes handed the baby to him.

Joe pulled the blanket away from the baby's tiny sleeping face, and held her up in the crook of his arm in such a way that all the people could see her.

"Another baby was born over two-thousand years ago while his mother was on a long journey. We all know the story of how there was no room for them at the inn. Mary had her baby inside a primitive stable. She did not have a midwife. It was just her and Joseph doing the best they could. It couldn't have been all that comfortable, and definitely not at all sterile. Mary deserved better, and her baby deserved better. Just like Lily and her baby deserved better."

Joe kissed the baby on her forehead and handed her back to Agnes.

"When I was a little boy, every time I heard this story, I wanted to go back in time and fix things. I wanted to give up my bed for Mary and the baby. I wanted my mother to fix them nourishing food. I knew that my father, who loved children, would have rocked the baby while Mary and Joseph got some rest.

"But none of us can go back and help Mary and the baby Jesus. Nor can we do anything to take away the tragedy of this young mother's death today. But there is a difference. Everything that can be done has been done. In the book of Matthew, Jesus says, 'I was hungry and you gave me something to eat, I was thirsty and you gave me something to drink, I was a stranger and you invited me in.'

"This tiny baby—from the moment she drew her first breath, she was taken in, loved, fed, and protected..."

At that moment, a car sped into the cemetery entrance, and a disheveled, rail-thin middle-aged woman jumped out. Rachel's heart sank when she saw who it was.

Gertie wore tight jeans with rips in the knees, a t-shirt that barely covered her navel, and a long, red coat that hung open. The coat had definitely seen better days, and so had Gertie.

"I know you." She pointed at Rachel. "I saw you sneaking around Tony's house. I came to get his kid. Mabel said you'd be here."

Rachel couldn't be sure, but she thought Gertie was either intoxicated or high on something. Before anyone could respond, Gertie caught sight of Holly. "Is that it? She reached her hands out. "Bring it here. I want my grandbaby!"

Agnes backed away, clutching little Holly protectively.

"No." Ivan quickly stepped in front of Agnes. "Stop." He was a tall man, and still powerfully built. Noah silently came to his father's side; Reuben on the other. Together, they created a wall between Gertie and Agnes while John hurriedly got his three older children into the family buggy.

"We have cared for this little one since the moment she was born," Ivan gently told Gertie. "But we do not know you. We do not know what kind of a person you are. Maybe you are a good person. Maybe you are not. Until we know more, you may not take the baby. Not yet."

Rachel wanted to shout "Bravo!"

With the exception of John and the children, the group of Amish had quietly closed in around Gertie and the Hochstetlers during this interchange. Rachel knew it was not meant as a threat. They were simply curious about this odd-looking woman who had suddenly appeared in their midst, and they were also worried about Ivan as he tried to guard the baby. A girl had come with Gertie whom Rachel suspected might be Tony's sister. She stood on the fringes of the crowd, her shoulders hunched. Gertie glanced around. She suddenly seemed intimidated by the presence of so many black-clad Amish people standing so close to her and began to push through the crowd.

"I'm not finished with you," she threatened, as she went toward her car. "My lawyer will sue the pants off of all of you for this. Come on, Tonya!"

Everyone was silent as Gertie climbed into the passenger seat, and then they watched them leave, the daughter driving.

"That woman should never have the care of a child," Keturah said.

"And yet," Rachel said. "Right now, she is the one with the most legitimate claim."

Keturah glanced at Agnes as she stroked the baby's soft cheek. "Have you not been wanting to go to Florida to visit your sister for some time now?"

Rachel realized what Keturah was saying.

"Not yet, Keturah," she said. "Gertie doesn't have custody yet. Until then, let's keep the baby here."

Chapter Forty-Five

. . . .

"My new mare isn't feeling so good, Doc." It was David Yost again, and his voice coming over the phone was shaking. "I was just out to the barn, and I need for you to come take a look at her."

Michael had planned to go to the cemetery with Keturah and Ivan but, from the sound of the man's voice, this might have to take priority.

"What are you seeing?" Michael asked.

"Her temp is a hundred and four. She's started coughing, and there's a discharge from her eyes and nose. I think it might be the horse flu."

Equine Influenza. Highly contagious. Sometimes the younger horses and the older ones didn't recover... and David had that new foal he thought might come any minute.

"Is this the mare you went down to Lexington to pick up a few days before Christmas?"

"Yes. She's a pretty thing. Seemed healthy enough when I picked her up."

"Horse flu has an incubation period of ten days," Michael said.

"I know." Misery laced his words. "She must have had it before she got here. Now all my horses will be exposed."

"How is your brood mare?"

"Getting that look in her eye that she might drop that foal any minute. I cleaned out her stall and put down fresh bedding this morning. I've got everything ready."

"I'll be over as soon as I can," Michael said. "Tell Jenny to make a pot of coffee. We're both going to need it before this day is over."

"Thanks, doc," David said. "We'll make some sandwiches too."

As puzzled as Michael was about what he'd just learned about Cassie, his first responsibility was to David Yost and those horses. This was exactly the kind of situation that had compelled him to come back to Sugarcreek and take over this practice. That new foal and the sick mare represented nearly every dime David had. Keeping those two animals and the rest of the stock alive and well could make the difference between David's dream of running a horse farm succeeding, or failing.

If this was equine influenza, and he wasn't able to stop it at David's farm, there could be an outbreak in the whole area. This was Amish country, and there were hundreds, if not thousands of horses. Unlike non-Amish people's automobiles, Amish horses were not insured. The loss of a well-trained standard-bred buggy horse was a great loss, the Belgian and Percheron draft horses an even greater one.

It really was a life or death situation. Trying to figure out what Cassie was up to would just have to wait.

Word got out quickly that a case of equine influenza had been confirmed in David Yost's newest purchase from Lexington. Michael was swamped for the next few days going from farm to farm, listening to massive chests for pneumonia, and reassuring nervous farmers.

He did call Cassie several times in-between farm visits. He got little sleep but left several messages on her two answering machines. She did not call him back.

This worried him. If she was no longer going into work, was there anyone who would pay attention to whether or not she was okay? Apparently, Bradley wouldn't be checking on her, not if what Sophie had told him was true. It wasn't as though Cassie had any girlfriends who would stop in. That wasn't the kind of life Cassie lived. Nor did she have a mother or sister to check on her.

With all his heart, Michael knew that his work was important, and he truly loved every minute of it, but the satisfaction in helping the animals and farmers of the Sugarcreek area was marred by wondering if Cassie was okay, and wondering what had happened to make her walk away from the law firm that had been part of the reason for the destruction of their marriage.

Chapter Forty-Six

"Rachel?" Noah Hochstetler's voice was nervous. "Daett told me to call and ask you to come quick. A social worker and that woman who says she's Holly's grandmother are at our house."

"I'll be right there."

The scene, as she let herself into the Hochstetler home, was about what she expected.

There was Gertie, red-faced and furious. Sally, the social worker, looking worn out and frazzled. Agnes, sitting in the rocking chair, holding Rosie. And Ivan, Keturah, and Noah seated on the couch all in a row. The older children were not visible, nor was baby Holly.

"You won't get away with this," Gertie was saying.

"What's going on?" Rachel asked, as she let herself into the Hochstetler's unlocked house.

"I'm glad you're here, Rachel," Sally said. "Gertie has a court order saying that she is the legal guardian of her new granddaughter. She's come to get her, but the Hochstetlers won't tell us where the baby is."

"Let me see the court order," Rachel said.

Gertie dug into a large, green, tote bag, brought it out and stuck it in her face. "Here! See?"

Rachel's eyes scanned it. Sure enough, the woman had somehow managed to get a court order saying that she was the legal guardian of her son's child.

Apparently, the Hochstetlers had decided to dig in their heels and defy it. She couldn't much blame them, but she wondered if they realized the legal ramifications if they did.

Keturah, Agnes, Ivan, and Noah were looking at her like she held the keys of life and death for the baby, and perhaps she did. She wanted Gertie to take Holly home with her even less than they did—if that was possible. She knew first-hand the kind of things that happened to help-less infants in homes where addicts lived.

"Where is the baby?" she asked Keturah.

"She is with a relative."

"Is this relative Amish?"

"Yes."

"Is the baby getting good care?"

"Wonderful good care."

"Is the baby dressed Amish?"

"Yes," Keturah said. "And it has been a busy season for babies."

"Gertie has a court order, Ivan." Sally said. "I know she isn't the most ideal guardian for an infant but, if you don't give her Tony's baby, you and your whole family will be in contempt of court."

"That is not a term I am familiar with," Ivan said. "We are a simple people. We know little about your court system."

"Is she here?" Gertie demanded. "Have you hidden her in this house? I bet she's upstairs."

Noah, who had been silently watching things play out, quickly moved in front of the staircase, his arms crossed, his muscular body effectively blocking her from going to the upstairs bedrooms.

"I don't know what you and your family have done with the baby," Sally said. "But Gertie has the law on her side. Tell them, Rachel. You know the law. Tell the Hochstetlers that they have no choice. They have to give the baby up or they could be charged with kidnapping."

"I do know the law," Rachel said. "And one thing I know for certain is that Gertie does not have the right to search this house. I will arrest her for trespassing if she tries."

"Can I talk to you outside, Rachel?" Sally asked.

"Sure." Rachel went out the door and Sally followed. "Make it quick. I don't want to leave that woman in there with the Hochstetlers alone."

"Gertie won't quit until she gets her hands on that baby," Sally said, once they were outside and the door was closed. "I know she's a mess, but somehow she's managed to retain a hair-trigger lawyer who'll slap a lawsuit on Ivan and Keturah so fast it'll make your head spin. She's talking of suing our agency as well, and we work on a shoestring budget. Her lawyer has won cases for her before. Several, in fact. Slip and fall. Whiplash. You name it. It's what she lives on. He's good."

"I'm curious," Rachel said. "She doesn't seem to have any particular feelings for the baby. Why is she doing this?"

"I haven't figured that one out yet, either," Sally said. "I've been to her house though. There are worse homes than Gertie's. I don't like her either, but I think the baby will probably be okay there."

"You *think* the baby will be *okay*?" Rachel said. "That's not good enough, Sally. We are both better than that. I think you and Gertie need to leave."

"What are you going to do?" Sally said.

"Keep going through missing persons reports to see if I can find out who Lily was, and then investigate to see if there isn't someone with more nurturing capability on her side of the family than Tony's. That's all I got."

Chapter Forty-Seven

....

As far as Michael could tell, he was past the worst of the equine influenza scare. He still had not gotten through to Cassie. Even though a trip to Columbus might be a waste of time, he decided to head there anyway. If she wasn't at the apartment, he still had a key, and he could let himself in. He might even find a clue as to what had happened and where she was. If she was fine, and merely ignoring his calls, he'd gather up some fishing equipment he'd left behind and come home. When spring came he did intend to do some fishing, and it was as good of an excuse as any to go see her.

All the way there he tried to figure out what to say to Cassie if she was home. They were in such an odd stalemate with their marriage that nothing he could think of seemed appropriate.

Each apartment had an open parking garage; a sort of shelter to keep the snow and ice off the resident's vehicles. There was room for two cars for each apartment. He slid in beside of Cassie's Lexus, pleased to see that she was home. It might be painful but at least the trip would not be wasted.

Even though he still had a key, he did not let himself in once he stepped off the elevator. Instead, he stood at the door and politely knocked. No one came. He waited a decent amount of time and then he knocked again, louder.

For safety's sake, at the beginning of their marriage, he and Cassie had developed a special knock so that she would know it was him standing outside the door before she opened it. He did not use this knock this time. He was afraid that she would not answer if she knew it was him.

Again he knocked, and pushed the buzzer.

There was no sound of anyone stirring within. Perhaps she was taking a shower or a nap. Except it was an odd time for Cassie to be taking a shower, and she never took naps. Not even if she was ill, or worn out. He waited a couple more minutes and then he inserted his key into the lock.

He opened the door slowly. "Cassie?"

She did have a handgun and he didn't want to startle her or make her think that he was an intruder.

"Cassie?" He took a step into the room and closed the door behind him "It's me, Michael. I've come to pick up my fishing gear."

Silence.

He moved further into the room and what he saw disturbed him. The room was far from being a shambles but in Cassie's carefully-ordered universe it was close to being so.

She owned a quilt of her grandmother's that normally laid across the foot of their bed, and was rarely used. Now, it was lying crumpled on the couch. A pillow from their bed was also on the couch. A pair of slippers lay on the floor beside it. Several prescription bottles littered the side table, along with a box of tissues. There was also a stack of magazines on the coffee table and the TV remote.

He walked over to the side table, then picked up and glanced at each prescription bottle. Because of his medical training as a veterinarian, he knew that these were used for cancer treatment and pain management. Each one had Cassie's name on it.

A trashcan lined with plastic liner had been positioned close to the couch. One of the prescription bottles was for nausea.

Heartsick at what he'd found, he walked back toward their bedroom.

"Cassie, honey? It's Michael."

The bedroom, so familiar to him from the years that he slept there beside of her, was darkened. This also was unusual. Cassie normally preferred light and sunshine. Living on the eighth floor, she nearly always kept the blinds open to the sky. Now the curtains were pulled and the room was pitched in twilight. A small figure lay alone in the king-sized bed.

"Michael." Cassie said, in a soft voice and held her hand out to him. "What are you doing here?"

Cassie's body seemed so small and alone in that giant expanse. She looked like she had lost weight, and she had not had any spare weight to lose. Her hair was cut shockingly close to her scalp. He had never known her without long hair. For the first time, he realized that Cassie, because of her bigger-than-life personality, had always seemed larger to him than she actually was. He sat down on the edge of the bed, and gazed into the saddest eyes he had ever seen.

"I was worried. What's going on with you?"

"Breast cancer."

Deep regret washed over him, followed by the most intense love he had ever felt, even as his heart shattered over the realization of what she had been trying to go through without him.

"Oh honey," he said. "Why didn't you tell me? Why didn't you call me? Why didn't you even answer your *phone*?"

"I didn't want you to know."

"You've been alone all this time?" He took her hand in his. It was so cold. He chaffed it, trying to warm it. "You tried to get through this all by yourself? Why?"

"I thought I was strong enough." Her cheeks began to glisten with tears. "I was wrong. It is good to see you, Michael."

"Oh sweetheart." He started to pull her close, but she grimaced and cried out.

"What did I do wrong?" he said.

"They had to do a double mastectomy," she said. "I'm a little... sore."

The thought of her going through all that just about did him in. "I would have come, Cassie. You *know* I would have come."

"I know, Michael. That's why I didn't call."

He could not bear another second in this darkened bedroom. He was a strong man, used to doing heavy work. It was no effort at all to gently gather his wife in his arms and carry her into the living room, into the light. He sat down on the couch with her in his lap and gingerly pulled the quilt up around her, careful not to touch any incisions. Then he asked a question to which he dreaded the answer.

"What do the doctors say?"

"They think they got it all." Her face was pressed against his shoulder. Her tears dampened his shirt. "But I still have to go through the treatments. It's going to be rough for a while."

"But you don't have to face it alone now," he said. "I'll take care of you."

"How can you?" She shook her head. "You just started your new practice in Sugarcreek. I cannot ask you to give that up. I never should have. I'm so sorry for the way I acted, Michael."

"Shhhh. Let's not talk about that now. All I want is for you to get well."

Tears continued to quietly leak down her face. With a corner of the quilt he dried her tears and kissed her cheek. Then, suddenly, his stomach gave a loud growl. Even he was startled by it.

"You're hungry," she said. "There's plenty of food in the kitchen, but I'm afraid you will have to fix it."

"I'll make something for both of us. What would you like?"

"Right before you came," she said. "I was lying there, wishing I had the energy to make a box of chicken-noodle soup mix. My mom always fixed that for me when I was a kid and not feeling good. I've been craving it."

"That's easy enough." He slid out from under her and tucked the quilt in around her. "You want to watch TV while I make lunch?"

"No. I've had more than enough TV. It'll be nice just to lie here and listen to you banging around in the kitchen."

"I'll try not to bang too hard. I don't want to break anything."

"Doesn't matter." Tears began to seep from the corners of her eyes again. "Break anything you want. Break all of it. Nothing in that kitchen matters to me anymore."

Of all the things she'd said so far, this one shook him the most. She rarely cooked, but she had always been ultra-fussy about her kitchen, buying only the best, keeping it immaculate. He'd always felt clumsy and fearful of damaging something whenever he tried to cook in it.

He caressed her face with his hand. "I'll be careful, anyway."

As he filled a small cooking pot with water, she called in from the living room. "I just can't get over the fact that you're *here*, and that you didn't run away the minute you saw me. That's what my mom's boyfriend did when she was battling cancer."

"Your mom's boyfriend? Wait a minute." Michael turned off the water, and stepped back into the living room to see her. "I thought your mom and dad were killed in a car wreck. Both at the same time."

"That was a lie, Michael. Pretty much everything I told you about my past was a lie." Cassie closed her eyes in weariness. "There is so much we need to talk about, but not now. I just don't have the strength to go into it right now."

Michael was no cook, but he could boil water and dump a Lipton soup mix into it. While the water came to a boil he sliced cheese and found some fancy crackers. There were some nice-looking grapes in the refrigerator. He rinsed them off in the sink and let them drain on a clean towel he placed on the counter.

"Are you strong enough to sit at the table?" he asked, as he set out their simple lunch. "I could bring you a tray if you'd rather."

"I think it would feel good to sit at the table. It will feel like maybe things are starting to get back to normal. Healthy people don't appreciate normal enough, you know."

"No doubt. Let me help you to the table."

"No—I can do this." She pushed the quilt away, stood slowly, and wandered over. "I'm weak, and I won't be running races anytime soon, but I can walk. This looks really good, Michael. *You* look really good."

"And here I was hoping you wouldn't shoot me when I came through the door."

"Never." She put a napkin on her lap. "Thank you, Michael. Thank you for coming here."

Chapter Forty-Eight

Rachel dropped in to the Sugar Haus Inn to check on her aunts after her upsetting visit to the Hochstetlers. As usual, ever since the newspaper article came out about her Joe's Home Plate, Lydia was in the process of turning out pies.

"What kind are you making today?" Rachel asked.

"Chocolate Meringue," Lydia answered. "They sell really well."

"If I remember right, you make the chocolate filling from scratch?" Rachel said.

"Of course." Lydia nodded toward Bertha who was stirring something in a huge pot. "But it has to be stirred constantly or it will scorch. Be careful, Bertha. I don't have enough ingredients to make another batch."

"I *am* being careful," Bertha grumbled.

"How are you feeling?" Rachel asked. "Is your arthritis acting up?"

"My arthritis is always acting up," Lydia said, peevishly.

Although the kitchen looked and smelled the same as always, the atmosphere had changed. Instead of being joyful as she bustled about the kitchen, Lydia was acting as though making pies was drudgery. Instead of being wise and interested in what was going on in everyone's life, Bertha was turning into a grumpy old woman. Instead of being joyful and happy to see her, Anna was sitting in one corner counting her seashells over and over; something she did whenever she was upset.

"I can stop this, Lydia," Rachel said. "Any time you want. Joe's restaurant won't fail if he orders his pies from a different bakery instead of from you."

"She won't listen to reason," Bertha said, from her place at the stove. "So you may as well save your breath. I think it's ready, Lydia. Come look at it."

Lydia went to the stove, took the large wooden spoon from Bertha, dipped it into the chocolate pie mixture, stirred it a couple times and declared the consistency to be adequate.

Rachel helped ladle the pie mixture into the already-baked pie crusts that Lydia had lined up on the long kitchen table. The smell of chocolate and fresh pie crust was intoxicating.

"Want me to scrape that pot out for you?" Rachel asked, hopefully. "I'd be happy to eat that leftover pie filling."

"Go ahead." Lydia handed her the bowl and a spatula. "I'll let the pies cool while I beat up the meringue. Darren will be here soon to pick them up."

Lydia's voice was flat.

Lydia's voice was never flat.

This was disturbing.

"I need to rest my bad leg," Bertha said. "Come into the front room with me, Rachel, and keep me company while Lydia finishes."

Rachel obediently followed her aunt into the front room, carrying the spatula and the pot with her.

Considering all that had been going on—dead bodies, drug houses, at-risk babies—getting to simply lick the chocolate pudding off the spatula like she had done when she was a kid sounded like a wonderful idea.

Bertha sat in the Amish-made, wooden glider, and rested her foot on the matching brown footstool.

"Lydia is wearing out," Bertha said. "I think making all these pies is going to kill her. Helping her with them is starting to kill me."

Rachel looked up from scooping up a spatula of chocolate heaven. Bertha was serious. She sat the pot on the floor and gave her aunt her full attention.

"Then why does she continue to do it?" Rachel asked. "I've offered repeatedly to get Joe to purchase pies from one of the other bakers in town."

"It's the money," Bertha said. "Joe and Darren pay her on a per pie basis. She carefully divides it up. Cash for more baking supplies goes into an unused cookie jar in the kitchen; all profit left over is stashed in a box underneath her bed. Once a month, she goes to the bank, deposits it, and sends a check to the Mennonite Haitian orphanage we help support.

"To Lydia, each pie she makes represents several meals that will fill hungry children's bellies. For a while, that gave her great joy. Now that Joe's Home Plate is able to sell every pie she makes, she's afraid that, if she stops or cuts back, she's allowing a child to go hungry. You *know* how strongly Lydia feels about no one ever going hungry."

"What should I do?" Rachel said.

"I have no idea," Bertha said. "But we need to think of something before she ends up in the hospital."

"I'll talk to Joe."

"Good. You do that." Bertha pulled her black choring sweater out of the mending basket beside her chair and handed Rachel a needle and a length of string. "Now thread this. It will save me having to use my magnifying glass. Then I want you to tell me about your visit with Keturah and Ivan today."

"I just came from there. How on earth did you find out so soon?"

"Don't you remember the Amish grapevine?"

"Cousin Eli stopped by on his way back from auction, didn't he?" Rachel said. "I thought I saw him drive by when I was going in."

"Exactly. The Amish grapevine." Bertha smiled. "Eli does his part."

"I love Eli but, you have to admit, he is awfully nosey," Rachel said. "And he gossips."

"True, but if Eli had not been nosey about your Joe and Bobby, and brought them to our inn when Joe's truck broke down, you would not have such a fine husband, or such a beautiful son."

"True," Rachel conceded.

"So, tell me about your visit with the Hochstetlers."

Rachel picked up her spatula and pot again and, between bites, recounted everything that had happened in exactly the way Bertha preferred, which meant leaving nothing out. Bertha always wanted to know the details.

"So, Keturah and Ivan have hidden the baby with one of their relatives?"

"They certainly gave that impression," Rachel said.

"Have you talked with Keturah since?"

"I went back after Gertie and Sally left so, yes, I've talked with her. I asked her to tell me where the baby is. Keturah was respectful, but firm. She said it was best that I not know. I think I might have made a mistake in telling her about Mabel saying Gertie wasn't fit to raise a child."

"Have you changed your opinion about Gertie?"

"No."

"Then Keturah's family is doing what they believe to be right, and she's being protective of you by not telling you more."

"That's true," Rachel said. "But I never dreamed the Hochstetlers would do something so close to kidnapping a baby. If we don't get this resolved, things could get truly ugly for them."

"I'm not the least surprised by their actions," Bertha said. "That's been our way down through history. As long as we believe the civil law to be just, we do our best to obey it. If it goes against our perception of what God has commanded, we will go to jail rather than go against our conscience. Or we will find a way around it—like how so many of our men served as non-combatants during some of the wars into which they were drafted."

"What if I'm asked to arrest them?" Rachel said. "Gertie had a court order to take Holly, and the Hochstetlers refused to obey it."

"If you have to arrest them, then that is what you do," Bertha said. "They know what they are risking."

"But, knowing why they are doing it, how can I do that?"

"God will give you the answer when you need it," Bertha said. "But you must understand, midwives will always protect the babies. It is, how do you say it about your computers—hardwired into them? Keturah is like Shiphrah and Puah. She is hardwired to protect that baby."

"Never heard of them. Do they live around here?"

"They were the Hebrew midwives in the Bible who were commanded to kill all the boy babies they helped birth. It was Pharaohs' idea of birth control. He didn't want the Hebrew population to get any bigger. He thought there were too many of them and that they would grow to a point where they were a threat to his people. The midwives risked their lives when they disobeyed the Pharaoh. They still served the Hebrew women, they continued to let the boys live—and then they lied to the king about it. They told him that their women gave birth too quickly for them to get there in time."

"So, what are you saying?"

"I'm saying that it would be wise for you and the courts not to underestimate Keturah. To the marrow of her bones, she is a dedicated and caring midwife. She will risk her own life, her freedom, and maybe even lie right to your face if doing so will protect that baby she brought into the world."

Chapter Forty-Nine

Michael was grateful when Cassie managed to eat most of the bowl of soup he had made for her.

"It tastes so good," she said. "Thank you, Michael."

She even ate a couple bites of cracker and two grapes before she said that she was full and needed to rest.

While she lay on the couch, he cleaned up the kitchen. He had brought no extra clothes, no toothbrush, no razor, and he had no idea what to do about tomorrow—except he knew he could not leave her here alone. He didn't *want* to leave her here alone.

The problem was, he did have people relying on him to care for their livestock and pets back home. Would Doc Peggy be able to cover for him? She had a busy business herself over in Millersburg. But maybe she and her new husband could help out for a day or two if things didn't get too bad.

***

The reassuring sound of Michael's voice awoke Cassie. He was in the kitchen, speaking with someone on the phone. Awakening to the knowledge that he was nearby was one of the most comforting things she had ever experienced.

She focused on his words and realized that he was speaking with another veterinarian. Sounded like he was trying to make arrangements for someone to temporarily take over his practice while he took care of her.

On the day he walked out, he had made it abundantly clear how much he disliked living here. He had tried to tell her before, but she had not wanted to listen. Even so, he'd stuck it out for five years. How long those five years must have seemed to him. Now, it sounded like he was setting things up so that he could stay here with her indefinitely, until she got through this. That could take a long time. He knew enough about medicine to know that.

She did not want him to do this. Yes, she needed more help than she had realized, but not at the expense of his job. Not at the expense of *him*.

He hung up the phone and came in to check on her.

"You're awake," he dropped into the easy chair he had always preferred. "How are you feeling?"

"Who was that on the phone?" she asked.

"Another veterinarian who works in Millersburg," he said. "The residents call her Doc Peggy. Her husband is her assistant. I was asking if she could help with my practice for a while so I could stay with you. It turns out that her daughter, who recently graduated from veterinarian school, has come for a visit. The three of them are willing to cover for me."

"Michael," Cassie said. "If I asked you for a favor, would you do something for me?"

"If it is within my power, of course I will."

"I've been thinking. Would you mind taking me home?"

"Home?" He was puzzled.

"Sugarcreek. Your old farmhouse in Sugarcreek."

"Are you sure?"

"I'm sure."

And she *was* very sure. Cows. Manure. Horse flies. Amish buggies.

No corporate law firm to work at. She didn't care. As she'd lain in that giant bed, sick and alone, she'd realized that she didn't care about anything except getting well and being with Michael. Hearing him trying to make arrangements to stay here with her had erased any doubt. Sugarcreek was not her home, Columbus was not her home, her mother's impoverished little trailer in eastern Ohio was not her home. *Michael* was her home. Being with him was the only real home she had ever experienced.

"But you need to be here with your doctors."

"Not all the time. There will be several days between treatments. We could go back and forth. I mean, if that works for you. I'm kind of the one on the receiving end here. It's whatever you want to do."

"Do you think you'll be strong enough to make the trip tomorrow morning?"

"I'd like to try."

"A good night's sleep will help."

"I'll take some sleeping meds."

"Before you go to sleep, would you mind telling me about that temper tantrum you threw when you left Blackwell, Hart & Cooper?"

"How do you know about that?"

"Sophie told me," he said.

"I had no idea Sophie could be so chatty."

"I think you definitely made an impression on her."

"It was not my finest moment."

"Maybe not, but apparently one of your more memorable ones."

"I'm just hoping it doesn't end up on YouTube. I'm really tired, Michael. How about I explain it all to you tomorrow on the ride home. Actually, there's quite a lot I need to tell you."

"Does some of it have to do with this past you say you lied to me about?"

"Yes. There's a lot to explain."

"I'll listen as long as it takes."

He helped her into bed, made certain she had everything she needed on her bed stand, kissed her on her forehead, and then gathered a pillow from his old side of the bed to go sleep on the couch.

"This is a large bed," she said. "It won't bother me if you sleep here."

"It will bother me," he said. "I won't sleep a wink for fear that I'll roll over and accidently hurt you. I'll leave the door open so you can call for me if you need me."

"Thank you, Michael."

Cassie took one pain pill, but discovered that she did not need any sleeping meds after all. With Michael close by, she was so grateful and relieved that she fell asleep instantly and awoke the next morning feeling much better.

Chapter Fifty

"Well, would you come look at that," Ivan said, gazing out the side window. "That's a sight I didn't think I would ever see."

Keturah had just come inside with a basket of stiff and frozen cloth diapers from the outdoor clothesline. She sat the basket down and went to stand beside Ivan.

"Is that Cassie?" she asked. "It's been a long time since I saw her, but she looks a lot different."

"Hair's been cut," Ivan said. "Really short. Looks like she might have lost weight too. Doesn't seem to be feeling all that good. Look at how Michael's helping her up those few front steps. That is not a well woman."

"What do you suppose is going on?" Keturah said. "Should we go over there and see if we can help?"

"My guess is, not yet," Ivan said. "Let them get settled a bit first."

"I bet Michael doesn't have anything to eat in that house," Keturah mused. "He never did learn to cook very well, even though I tried to teach him. He's been so busy fighting that horse flu, I doubt he's brought any groceries into the house."

"They probably won't starve in the next half-hour," Ivan said. "Let's leave them alone for now."

"I have that soup left over from last night, and I just finished my baking for the week. I have fresh loaves of bread still warm. You know how much Michael loves my homemade bread."

"Yes, I do," Ivan said. "I also know you are not paying a bit of attention to what I am saying."

"I think they might appreciate a pot of soup and a loaf of bread. I won't go in. I'll just run it over, knock on the door, and leave. That way they'll have something nice to share without him having to go out and buy it. I have a small crock of fresh butter too. I'll add that and a quart of applesauce. I think it will fit nicely into that basket your sister gave me."

She bustled off, still talking.

"Your mother." Ivan grinned at Noah, who was repairing a harness at the kitchen table. "What is a man to do? She does not follow my advice on this."

"And probably a good thing she doesn't sometimes," Noah pointed out. "But I think she's giving our supper away."

"Not if she leaves a loaf of bread behind," Ivan said. "Keturah's bread and some cold milk makes a fine meal."

Ivan continued to watch out the window as Michael carried several pieces of luggage from the car into the house. Apparently, Cassie was coming to stay. At that moment, Ivan saw that Keturah was already walking toward Michael's with a large basket on her arm.

"That basket your mother is carrying looks heavy," he observed. "I think I should go help her with it."

"You are as curious about Michael's wife as I am," Noah said. "Admit it."

"I am," Ivan said, as he put on his coat. "But that does not make the basket any lighter."

***

Cassie had seen the old house before, of course, but always with a feeling of detachment. Although she knew that Michael had enormous nostalgia for his childhood home, she could never muster up any enthusiasm for the place. It was just a big, white, square farmhouse, much like every other big, white, square farmhouse in Amish country.

Today was different. Today, when she entered, it felt like the old house gave her a hug and welcomed her home. It felt like it had a heart and soul and was trying to give her comfort—and it did give her comfort. She was worn out from the two-hour trip. She was grateful to be here.

Huge windows, all with a view of rolling hills and pastures. Wallpaper covered all the walls. It was lightly sprigged with spring-green willow leaves. No one used wallpaper anymore, which made it feel quaint and old-fashioned. White-painted woodwork. A comfortable old greenvelvet couch piled with brightly-quilted pillows. Multiple photographs of Michael's family on the walls. A wide-planked, oak floor, aged with at least a century's worth of wear.

"The house will be warm soon," Michael said. "It got a little chilly while I was gone."

Michael made sure she was comfortably seated in a cushy old armchair, her feet on a footstool, with an afghan tucked around her before he went back outside for her luggage. He sat it inside the door of the downstairs bedroom, then headed toward the basement.

"I'll unpack for you as soon as I get a fire started in the wood stove downstairs," he said. "In the winter, the gas furnace doesn't always heat as well as I'd like. This is an old house. There are drafts. I'll be right back."

In a few moments, she heard him banging around in the basement, directly beneath where she was sitting. It was a walk-out basement, and she heard the door slam shut multiple times as he brought in firewood from where he kept it stacked outside the basement walls.

She had heard of women who only truly fell in love with their husbands after being married several years. Now she understood. Never had she thought the sound of a man starting a fire just to keep her warm would bring tears to her eyes, but it did now. For a woman who rarely cried, she didn't seem to be able to stop ever since Michael showed up on her doorstep.

He had barely gotten back up the stairs when there was a knock at the door. She wasn't used to having people come to her home, but he showed no surprise at all.

"I wondered how long it would take," he said, good-naturedly, as he went to the door. "It's been nearly a whole half-hour since we pulled in the driveway. Ivan must have made Keturah wait to give us a chance to get settled."

When he opened the door, an older Amish couple stood outside looking very sober and solemn. She had met Keturah and Ivan before, briefly, but did not know them well. Ivan was holding a large basket, and Cassie could smell the fragrance of fresh-baked bread wafting from beneath a large, white dishtowel.

"I tried to hold her back," Ivan said, as Michael invited them in. "But you know how Keturah is. She was afraid you and your wife would starve to death if she waited a minute longer."

"That is not true," Keturah said. "I knew you would not have anything nice for your wife to eat unless I brought it. It is good to see you again, Cassie. Are you hungry?"

Cassie nodded. At least she was hungry now. Ever since Keturah had arrived with a swirl of snowy air and a picnic basket.

"Good," Keturah said. "I will leave Ivan with you two, to catch up, and I will go set the food out."

Keturah took off her coat, hung it on a wooden coat tree near the door, carefully lifted her black bonnet off her head and sat it on a side table, and then she went into Michael's kitchen. Cassie heard crockery being placed on the table, and cabinet doors opening and closing.

Michael took it all in stride, as though he was used to having people dropping by, bringing food, and helping themselves to his kitchen.

Ivan hung his black, felt hat on the wooden tree, settled himself comfortably in another armchair, and ran a hand through his sparse hair. She expected him to question her about why she had suddenly appeared here in Michael's house but, instead, he turned the conversation to livestock.

"So, that problem with the horses. It is over?"

"I think so," Michael said.

There was another knock on the door.

"Excuse me," Michael opened it, and this time it was a uniformed police woman whom he ushered into the living room. "Hi Rachel. Let me introduce you to my wife."

After introductions had been made, the policewoman removed her hat and coat, hung them up, and then chose a rocker next to Ivan.

"I stopped by your place, Ivan. Noah, told me you were here," Rachel said. "I'm afraid I have some bad news."

Keturah came to the kitchen door, wiping her hands on a dishcloth. "What bad news?"

"It is about Gertie Maddox," Rachel said. "She and her lawyer have been busy."

"Then let the bad news wait for now so our appetites will not be spoiled." Keturah frowned. "The soup is hot, everything is on the table, and I sat out an extra bowl for you, Rachel, when I heard you at the door. Everyone. Come."

Cassie glanced at Michael. He looked happy.

"While everyone gets settled," Ivan told Michael. "I will go down and check your stove. It does not seem to be putting out much heat yet."

"Thanks," Michael said. "The wood was a little wet and I was in a hurry."

By the time everyone had taken a seat, there was another knock on the door. Everyone paused while Michael answered it.

"Maam and Daett didn't come back," Noah said. "And I was worried about why Rachel was looking for them, and…"

"Come on in," Michael said. "We were just sitting down to supper."

"Run back to the house and bring the rest of the soup, first," Keturah called. "And another loaf of bread."

"I sure will," Noah left to take care of his errand.

By the time Noah got back, they had already engaged in a silent prayer, and Keturah had ladled soup into everyone's bowls. She put the extra that Noah brought into the pot on the stove to warm.

"I brought pound cake, also," Noah said. "And that fruit salad you made yesterday."

"*Danke*, son. That was good thinking," Keturah said. "Rachel, it is your Aunt Lydia's recipe for pound cake that I used."

"One of my favorites," Rachel said.

Cassie was so engaged in processing all the busyness and conversation swirling around her that, for a few blessed moments, she forgot she was sick and the beef vegetable soup was the best she'd ever tasted.

"Now," Ivan said, once everyone had eaten their fill. "We are ready for this bad news you brought us, Rachel. Thank you for not spoiling our supper with it."

"No problem." Rachel blotted her lips with a napkin. "Gertie's lawyer called the police station right before I came over here. He said that, unless I force you to hand over baby Holly to Gertie, he will bring charges against you for kidnapping as well as wrongful death."

"I can understand the kidnapping charges, but wrongful death?" Michael sounded puzzled. "That doesn't make sense. Keturah *saved* a life. She didn't take one."

"Gertie's lawyer is claiming that Lily was not dead when Keturah took the baby; that she caused Lily's death by performing that C-section."

"Based on what?" Michael asked. "Did the autopsy say that Lily was still alive when the baby was born?"

"No, but it didn't say specifically that she wasn't."

Ivan's voice was indignant. "My Keturah would not make such a mistake."

"Of course not," Rachel said. "But there was no one there at the time who can be a witness to that fact."

Keturah said nothing, but pressed the back of her hand against her mouth while the conversation flowed around her. Cassie could tell this was hitting her hard.

"What about the Good Samaritan Law?" Michael said. "Doesn't that protect someone like Keturah? She was only trying to help."

"It's a good law," Rachel said, "but it's not bulletproof."

"They could actually prosecute her then?" Michael asked.

"Anyone can file a lawsuit," Rachel answered. "It doesn't mean they will win."

"I simply do not understand this woman's desperation to get her hands on little Holly," Ivan said. "She is a grandmother, yes, but her actions and words are not those of a *loving* grandmother. We are afraid for the baby."

"I agree. She has shown little grief over her son's death," Rachel said. "And she seems to be hopped up on something all the time. There is a greediness to her demands that bothers me. She seems to want the baby just because she wants the baby."

"Excuse me, but Michael told me about this today on the way here," Cassie said. "I was already wondering if a wrongful death suit might be their main focus. Now, I'm certain of it. Getting guardianship of the baby would be a means to an end."

"My wife is a lawyer," Michael explained to Rachel. "She knows stuff."

"I do not understand any of this," Ivan said. "What end?"

"In the eyes of the law," Cassie said, "it is Lily's child who will suffer by her mother's death. If a wrongful death suit were to stand up in court, any monetary award would go to the baby. But, being as she is just a baby, the money would be handled by her guardian, of course. In this case, her grandmother. Without that grandchild, Gertie has no personal connection to Lily, or to whatever money might come from the lawsuit. She can only proceed with a wrongful death suit if she does so on behalf of the infant."

"What money?" Ivan said. "We don't have a lot of money."

"Are you saying that Keturah opened herself up to this lawsuit by simply saving the baby's life?" Michael asked.

"Yes."

"I often do not understand Englisch ways," Ivan shook his head. "This thinking seems upside down to me."

"And yet it makes sense of Gertie's behavior," Rachel said. "Mabel told me that Gertie lives on money she's received from various lawsuits. Slip-and-fall, whiplash, etc."

"But Keturah didn't do anything *wrong*," Ivan protested. "How can they sue for a wrongful death when my wife did nothing wrong?"

"To some people," Cassie said. "Lawsuits are just a different version of playing the lottery. Do it enough times, they figure, and they might get lucky. I'm afraid that Keturah's actions on that backroad early Christmas morning made her a perfect target for a lawsuit."

Chapter Fifty-One

Suddenly, Cassie felt herself fading. "I'm sorry, but I think I need to lie down."

"You've been up too long," Michael said. "Do you need another pain pill?"

"Please," Cassie said.

For a few minutes, there was a scramble to make sure she was comfortable, finding the pill, and a glass of water with which to take it.

"Thank you." She handed the glass back to Michael and leaned back against the couch pillows.

"You are ill," Keturah said, kindly. "What is wrong?"

"My wife had surgery recently," Michael said, cautiously as though he didn't know how much Cassie wanted told.

"It is good that you are here then, where I can help take care of you," Keturah patted her hand. "You must rest now. I will clean the kitchen before we leave. Ivan? Noah? Please help me so we can gather things up and go quickly."

In moments, Cassie heard the sound of cabinets opening and closing, and water splashing into the sink.

"It's been good to meet you, Cassie," Rachel said, as she gathered her things. "Thank you for your insight."

"I wish I could be more help," Cassie said. "Before you go, do you happen to know anything about the lawyer who is representing Gertie?"

"Some guy by the name of Adrian Stevenson. Mabel told me that Gertie ran into him at a flea market. He had a booth there with his law degree nailed up behind him. He was having formal consultations right there. Making out wills on the spot for people. That sort of thing. Had a computer and printer set up on a card table."

"That sounds like something Adrian would do." Cassie smiled. "I know him. Interesting character. We went to law school together."

"What's he like?" Rachel asked.

"Lousy social skills. Apparently he had some sort of a prejudice against deodorant. Always wore cheap suits that looked like he'd slept in them. No law firm wanted to hire him after he graduated. At least not after the first interview. People tended to underestimate him. I graduated at the top of our class, but it took everything I had to beat him. I never cared for him as a person, but he is very sharp and his law degree is bona fide. If Keturah ever has to take the stand, and Adrian is questioning her, my guess is that he'll have her so confused and turned around that she'll confess to anything."

"It would be terrible for Keturah to have to testify in court," Michael said.

"I agree," Cassie said. "What's the timeline, Rachel?"

"I don't know yet, but they are pushing hard," Rachel said. "I can't bear to put that baby girl into what I believe to be a dangerous situation, but I also don't want to have to arrest Keturah for kidnapping. It might come to that unless something happens and soon."

"Then stall," Cassie said.

"How?"

"Has there been a DNA test yet to make certain Tony is Holly's father?"

"No," Rachel said. "Nobody's even questioned it. Lily lived with Tony for the past three years. Tony had her under a very tight control. It never occurred to me that he might not be the father."

"I have no doubt you are right," Cassie said. "But Adrian would consider you asking to run a DNA test before handing the baby over as a reasonable request. So would the court. If it were me, I would tell the lab to take their own sweet time with the samples. Tell them there's no rush."

"They would love that," Rachel said.

"In the meantime, concentrate on finding out more background on Gertie if you can. As the grandmother, she has a firm standing with the court unless we can find a good reason for a judge to throw out her claim. Winning a slip-and-fall judgment doesn't qualify."

"I'll work on that," Rachel said.

"Now, Michael, what Ivan said about not having any money… is that true?"

"They have a modest income from their dairy herd, crops, and what Keturah makes. It's enough, but it isn't a lot."

"Right," Cassie said. "But how much *land* do they own?"

"Nearly two hundred acres. It belonged to his grandfather."

"How much does an acre go for around here?" she asked.

"Depends on what kind of land and where it is," Michael said. "Property in this area has skyrocketed in recent years. Ten… maybe twelve thousand if it is undeveloped."

"So, if you factor in the house and barns, Ivan is sitting on a couple million dollars if he sold his farm?"

"I guess so, but he would never sell," Michael said. "We call some of the farmers around here 'paper millionaires.' They might be worth a fortune on paper, but they often struggle to buy groceries and pay the taxes on their place. Do you really think Gertie and her lawyer would actually take an Amish farmer's land?"

"Adrian will take anything he can legally get for himself and his client," Cassie said. "He probably already knows Ivan's net worth down to the quarters in his sock drawer, and yes—depending on the judge and the jury and a myriad of other details—a successful wrongful death suit could potentially cost Keturah and Ivan their home."

Chapter Fifty-Two

The next morning, Rachel stopped by the office to tell Ed about her meeting with the Hochstetlers and Cassie's advice to insist on a DNA match.

"Good idea," Ed said. "I received a visit from Bishop Sam Yost about an hour ago. Gertie and her lawyer have come up with another brilliant plan to squeeze money out of Lily's death."

"How?"

"They contacted Bishop Yost and said that, if their church does not find and deliver the baby within the week, they will sue the church for negligent homicide."

"Whoa!" Rachel was astonished. "How can they bring the church into it? No one from the church was even there."

"You are vastly underestimating Gertie and her lawyer," Ed said. "Where did she come up with this guy again?"

"Flea market," Rachel said.

"Flea market?"

"Wouldn't be the first place I would look for a lawyer, but apparently its working for Gertie."

"So far," Rachel said.

"Anyway," Ed continued. "Their basis for threatening to bring a suit against Sam's church is because Keturah did not have a cell phone on her person. They maintain that if the church did not have a rule against their people owning cell phones, Keturah could have called for help, and

Lily's life might have been saved."

"They have a point," Rachel said. "I don't know if it will stand up in court, but it is a valid argument."

"I know." Ed drummed his fingers on his desk. "I guess this is one of those cases where we could honestly say that no good deed goes unpunished."

"Looks that way," Rachel said.

"Have you gotten the DNA samples yet?"

"Working on it."

"Any idea yet who killed Tony?"

"I haven't heard a word."

***

It was important to keep the integrity of the custody line of the DNA samples intact. Rachel wasn't sure if her personal involvement in the case would eventually cause an issue, so she asked Kim to go take the sample directly from Holly. Keturah allowed her access to the baby, and Kim returned with a tiny lock of the baby's hair.

"How is Holly doing?" Rachel asked.

"Rosy cheeks, healthy, and as hungry as a little piglet," Kim said. "Makes me want to have a baby."

Getting Tony's DNA wasn't difficult. It just involved a call to her friend, Bill Sherman.

"I'll talk to our lab," Bill said. "They'll take care of it."

"Any progress on finding out who killed Tony?" she asked.

"Yeah," he said. "We think we know who, but we aren't sure why, or where he is. One of the guys who always hung out around Tony has gone missing. The other gang members are up in arms about it, of course. I don't expect him to survive if the others find him before we do."

"Anyone I know?"

"You hang out at Tony's much?"

"Never."

"Then I doubt it," he said. "The guy's name is Dane Richardson. He and Tony grew up together. He had a clean enough record that Tony made him join the military when he turned eighteen."

"Made him join the military?" Rachel said. "That doesn't make sense."

"Actually, it's happening more and more. If a kid in a street gang miraculously turns eighteen without having a record, the godfather sends him into the military for training. Hand-to-hand combat, weapons instruction; it can be very useful in today's gang wars. They come back. Train others. And the taxpayers pay for all of it."

"I don't understand why they would come back. I mean, after a few years in the military, I'd think they would mature out of the lifestyle. They aren't street kids anymore. They would even have work skills."

"Some of them do get out. Some are too loyal to the group. Some don't have a choice."

"What do you mean, no choice?"

"Just what I said. If you're part of one of the bigger gangs, it's hard to hide from them. Plus, if you got family, and the gang knows where they are, they are in danger if you try to leave."

"So how did you find out who did it?"

"DNA. Tony didn't go down easy. There was a lot of blood on the scene as well as fingerprints. Dane's in the system."

"Any idea why this Dane guy killed him?"

"None," Bill said. "At least not yet. Working on it."

"Can you give me any information on Tony's mother?" Rachel said.

"You mean the crazy lady that was yelling at us when you came to look at Lily's bedroom?" Bill said.

"That's the one," Rachel said. "The Amish are risking jail by hiding that baby from her while I try to figure out what to do."

"I'll look into it," Bill said. "I'd hate to see her take in anyone's kid after the way she was acting. Even after you left, she was trying to get into the house. She didn't realize our officer and dogs had already sniffed out pretty much everything that Tony was hiding. Once we let her in—with supervision—and she looked in all the places she wanted to look, she lost interest."

"I'll see what I can find out and get back to you," Bill said. "Hey, I gotta go. My gorgeous lunch date just showed up and I don't want her to change her mind."

Rachel could hear the love in his voice. "Is it Lori?"

"Yep. Everyone in the station is jealous of me. It's a hard life trying to beat the men away every time my wife shows up."

"Tell her I said hello." Rachel clicked off.

She called the lab, giving them a heads up about the samples they would be receiving. When they asked her how soon she needed it, she hesitated. Telling them to take their sweet time, as Cassie had suggested, did not feel right, nor was it professional. Instead, she simply told the truth.

"We are in no hurry for the results this time," she said.

Which was true. She was most definitely not in a hurry for the results.

Her next phone call was one she had been particularly dreading. She called Adrian Stevenson and gave him the news that they would not be moving forward with the transference of the baby to Gertie's care until they got the DNA results back from the lab.

To her surprise, he accepted her information with calm. Then he asked for the name of the lab to which she would be sending the samples. Her guess was that he had anticipated her move, and had already decided it would be wise to counterbalance it with a request of his own for speed.

There was nothing she could do about it, but she hoped Cassie started feeling better fast. She couldn't imagine what lawyer tricks Cassie might have up her sleeve. Michael's wife might be the only hope little Holly had of being raised by a loving, normal, family instead of Gertie Maddox.

Chapter Fifty-Three

....

"I'll be fine," Cassie said, the morning after Michael had brought her back to his house in Sugarcreek. "Please go to work. There is no reason for you to stay."

"What will you do while I'm gone?" he asked.

"Do you have Wi-Fi?"

"Of course. Why?"

"I plan to do some work on the situation with the Hochstetlers. I have to be back at the James Cancer hospital next week," she said. "So I want to get as much research done as I can before I go back."

"Do your incisions hurt?"

"Some," she said. "But I'm going to try not to take any pain meds today if I can help it. I need for my mind to be sharp."

"Tylenol," he said. "You can at least take some Tylenol."

"Of course," she said. "I'll take some Tylenol. Now, go take care of all your four-legged patients."

There was love in her voice as she said that. Her husband had unpacked for her, placing her things in an empty bureau in his bedroom. His bed was not large, and he was still afraid of accidentally bumping into her in the night, so he'd brought in a fold-out cot and slept beside the bed. If she so much as got up to go to the bathroom, he was there to help.

In the past, that much solicitousness would have annoyed her. Now, having tried to tough it out on her own, she was unbearably grateful.

"I'll be home at lunchtime," he said. "I'll call first and bring something from Joe's Home Plate for you if you want. That's Rachel's husband's restaurant. I usually eat there at least once a week. They have great burgers and baked beans and potato salad. Pies too, if you're lucky. Does that sound good?"

"It does," Cassie said. "Now, give me your password so I can log in."

And still, he fussed. He made a thermos of tea for her. Laced it with honey like he knew she preferred, then stood looking at her all worried-eyed before he left.

"Seriously, Michael," she said. "Am I going to have to threaten to go back to Columbus so you'll leave for work?"

He looked as though she had slapped him.

"That was a joke, Michael," she said. "I'm sorry."

"I'll be back at lunch," he said, and then left.

"Note to self." She could hear his truck starting up. "Don't try to joke, Cassie. You aren't good at it."

She had barely gotten logged onto Michael's Wi-Fi when there was a quick knock on the door, then the door opened and Keturah stuck her head in.

"I saw Michael leave," Keturah said. "I thought maybe you'd like some company while he is gone."

For a moment, the old Cassie almost came back. Her first instinct was to tell Keturah that she was busy. That she had work to do. That she did not need any company today.

Instead, she shoved the old Cassie, the woman she had grown to dislike, into the background, stepped outside her comfort zone, and met Keturah's bright smile with one of her own. "I'd absolutely love some company today."

"Oh good! I have a surprise for you."

Keturah opened the door all the way, and there stood Agnes, with a baby in her arm, three older children, and another woman also holding a baby whom Keturah introduced as her other daughter-in-law, Betty.

"Well, hello," Cassie said, bemused by being inundated with company again. This was the most entertaining she'd done in years, and was apparently going to be doing it whether she wanted to or not. "Please, make yourself at home. Have a seat."

"Oh, we didn't come to sit." Keturah was, yet again, holding the picnic basket. "We wanted to keep you company on Old Christmas while we made candy for the children."

"Old Christmas?"

"January sixth," Agnes said. "Today."

"I don't think I've ever heard of an Old Christmas."

"Not every Amish family observe it, but some of us still celebrate the old ways," Keturah said. "It's supposed to be the day that the magi brought gifts to the baby Jesus. We fast for the first part of the day, but we break our fast at noon. After a nice meal, we give the children homemade candy. I sometimes tell my grandchildren about the gold, frankincense and myrrh that the magi brought Jesus. It's also a day for visiting—so we decided to bring Old Christmas to you."

"And unless you object, we're going to make the candy right here, you lucky girl, you!" Betty laughed. "Agnes and I weren't sure you would welcome us coming in on you like this, but Maam insisted."

Cassie's mind was whirling. All these children and women would be here all day? Making candy? When would she have any time to do any work?

"We should go," Agnes saw her hesitation. "I don't think Cassie is feeling up to all this commotion today."

The old Cassie would have agreed and seen them out the door with pretend regrets. The old Cassie would have been appalled at the idea of spending the day with women she barely knew, and children running all over the house.

The new Cassie, the woman who had experienced such loneliness that she thought she would suffocate from it, decided that today was going to be a good day to be surrounded by new friends.

"It will be nice to hear other people's voices today. I've never made candy of any kind whatsoever. It sounds fascinating. I'll enjoy learning."

Keturah bustled into the kitchen. "Come on in, children. Wash your hands. We will be needing your help."

Later, when Michael called about lunch, she told him not to bother, that she was well cared for. When he came home from work in the late afternoon, she had a plate of various chocolates, hard candies, and caramels—all homemade. Plus a roast in the oven that Keturah had discovered in the freezer and put in a Dutch oven for her and Michael's supper.

She was still terribly sore from the surgery and glassy-eyed from consuming too much sugar, but she was also content in ways that she had never experienced before. Today, in spite of everything, had been truly lovely. Betty was such fun. She couldn't remember laughing so much in pretty much forever.

By the time they had eaten the roast, and Michael had sampled the candy, she realized that her strength had finally, once again, completely given out. Michael tucked her back onto the old green couch and she dozed while he straightened the kitchen.

It had been an amazing gift of a day.

Chapter Fifty-Four

Ivan was meeting with the bishop, ministers, and deacon of his church early in the morning, before services started. He had come without Keturah so that he could talk privately with these men. He had asked for the meeting, and it was going to be a hard one. Never had he dreamed that he would have to do such a thing.

It was Bishop Samuel Yost's family who were hosting church this Sunday morning. Samuel's home was large. Its high-ceilinged basement was well able to accommodate the thirty-seven families who made up their church fellowship. For privacy, however, since Samuel's wife was busy getting things ready for the meal that would follow, the men met in the barn.

"And what is this worry you have," Bishop Yost said, when the six solemn men were assembled. "Is it about your Noah becoming interested in Beth Yoder? If so, I share your concern."

Samuel's words surprised Ivan. Noah had not mentioned the Yoder girl to him since the night the Christmas baby was born. Ivan had hoped that the relationship had blown over. Apparently, not if others had noticed. He had been remiss in not keeping Noah in the forefront of his prayers. Too many other things had crowded that concern out.

"It is not about my Noah," Ivan said. "Not yet, anyway. The reason I asked to talk with you is because I have been told there are those who are threatening to name our church along with my wife in a wrongful death suit because of our ban against cell phones. Although my wife acted righteously in saving that baby's life, it is because of her actions that we might have to deal with the Englisch court system. I am told that she might have to testify, and that the lawyer is full of tricks."

"It is indeed a hard situation," Bishop Sam Yost said. "We already knew, and have been in prayer about it, as I'm sure you have also. Has the Lord given you any wisdom?"

"I cannot honestly say that God has spoken to my heart, and yet I know what I must do. I cannot allow my church to suffer because of what has befallen us. I will soon become too old to continue working the land my father gave me. My son, Reuben, has a daadi haus he has offered for his mother and me. I want the church to know that, if these people continue to push and demand, I will sell my farm if I must—for money to satisfy their greed so that they will go away and leave our church alone."

"But is greed ever satisfied?" Bishop Yost asked.

"He makes a good point," Adam Miller, one of their older ministers spoke up. "From what I have seen, greed is like a fire. Feeding it only makes it grow. I think if these Englisch people who want to sue you are successful, they will come back even stronger and demand more."

"I had not thought of that," Ivan said.

"We appreciate you trying to protect our church, but it is not your place to protect us, Ivan. It is God's," Bishop Yost said. "It is maybe a little *hochmut* for you to think that selling your farm will solve so many problems. You believe this sacrifice will protect Keturah from having to testify, as well as protecting us from being sued for our ban on cell phones. You are placing too much importance on your own abilities and possessions."

"You are right, Bishop." Ivan had not realized that his actions could be seen in this light. He accepted Samuel's mild criticism with humility.

"I appreciate your instruction."

"You have lived long enough to see that there is wisdom in waiting, and that is what I am counseling now. Wait and pray for the Lord to provide a way of escape for you and for our church. Do not begin the process of selling your farm. Your son, Noah, may have great need of it before long. I have seen signs that the Yoder girl is putting away some of her rebellious ways. Perhaps it is that your son is having a godly influence on her?"

"That would be a welcome thing, indeed," Ivan said.

"Keturah is a good woman," Bishop Yost said. "She has done much good in her lifetime. You have been a wise husband to allow her the freedom to care for our young mothers. We need faith that somehow the Lord will find a way to turn all of this around. That neither you nor we will be forced to go into the Englisch courts, and that the Christmas baby will be given to the family who will care for it best."

When church was finished, Ivan went home feeling lighter than he had since this whole business with the lawsuit had started. No one could ever blame him for not having been willing to sacrifice his home for the church. He would heed the bishop's advice and wait for the Lord to sort things out.

Chapter Fifty-Five

....

"Rachel?" Joe said. "Can you stop by your aunts? Darren went over to pick up some pies over an hour ago and he's still not back. It's a ten-minute trip. He's not answering his phone and, not only are we completely out of Lydia's pie, I need Darren's help with the prep work this afternoon to get ready for the supper crowd."

"Will do." Rachel turned off her computer. Two girls on the missing person's list had looked promising but, on a closer examination, there had been a butterfly tattoo on one, and a birthmark on the other. Lily had no birthmarks or tattoos. Later, she intended to make another trip to Cleveland to see if she could pry more information out of Mabel about Gertie.

The Amish school beside the Sugar Haus Inn was in full swing as she drove into her aunts' graveled driveway. The older girls were playing Duck, Duck, Goose in the snow with the younger children. The boys had built two snow forts, amassed a cache of snowballs, and were having fun pelting each other with snowballs.

Unlike the Englisch schools, Amish children did not take a Christmas break. Instead, they got out of school much earlier in the spring than non-Amish children.

It was a pretty sight, the different ages, everyone outdoors playing, including the young teacher who was also involved in the Duck, Duck, Goose game.

Darren's car was still there in the driveway, which worried her. What could have prevented him from taking the pies back? Perhaps they were not quite done when he arrived?

The sight that greeted her when she entered the kitchen was upsetting. Lydia was sitting in her rocker, not rocking, not talking, just staring. Bertha was peeling apples at the table and scowling. Anna was sitting in a corner, looking afraid. Darren was standing at the table in an apron, trying to roll out pie crusts.

"What on earth?" Rachel exclaimed as she came through the door. "What's happened?"

"Your husband, and that restaurant, and that famous chef telling everyone about Lydia's pies, has broken my sister—that's what's happened!" Bertha said.

Rachel went and knelt down in front of Lydia.

"Do you need to go to bed, Lydia?" she asked. "Are you feeling unwell?"

"Got to make more pies," Lydia mumbled.

"What happened?" Rachel asked Bertha. "What can I do?"

"I think she's had a nervous breakdown," Bertha said. "She just keeps sitting there talking about having to make more pies."

"Should we take her to the hospital?" Rachel asked.

"And spend all the money she's saved up from making all those pies?" Bertha shook her head. "I don't think so. The only thing I can think to do is actually make the pies. I've got her recipe here. I think, once we get them finished, maybe she'll go to bed then. And Joe needs to find a local bakery to make his pies from now on. Lydia's had it and so have I."

Rachel looked at Bertha, trying to peel nearly a bushel of apples by herself. Anna, looking frightened. And Darren, flour all over himself and the floor, awkwardly trying to roll out pie crusts. She made a decision.

"This is enough," she said. "This has to stop, and it has to stop now. I'll be right back."

She marched next door to the school house, and had a short conversation with Naomi, the schoolteacher, who was also one of Rachel's oldest friends. When Rachel returned, she had four eighth-grade girls with her.

The cavalry, in the form of four young Amish girls, had landed.

They entered the door, and the girls, all of them fourteen-years-old, and well-trained in domestic work by their mothers, made quick work of removing their coats and black bonnets.

"I brought reinforcements," Rachel told Darren and Bertha. "Darren, you need to go back to the restaurant and help Joe with the prep work for the supper crowd. Flora," she turned to the nearest girl, "grab a knife and start peeling apples. June," she pointed to another, "you start mixing more pie crust together. The lard is in that tin bucket. Flour is in the twenty-pound sack sitting on the chair. You other two, help clean and then do whatever else Lydia here tells you to do."

"Is this the recipe?" June asked, holding up a small sheet of paper with careful handwriting on it.

"It is," Bertha said, relinquishing her best paring knife to Flora.

June peeked into the red canister sitting on the table. "How many pies are we making? Looks like we might need to get more sugar."

"I'll take care of that," Rachel said, grabbing her keys. "Anything else?"

"Cinnamon," Lydia said, coming out of her trance. "We need more cinnamon."

Rachel and Bertha glanced at her, surprised.

"Are you feeling better, Aunt Lydia?" Rachel asked.

"You know what?" Lydia stood up. "I believe I am. When you go get the cinnamon, bring back a dozen lemons. And a couple oranges. I always put a little orange zest in with the sugar."

"What sort of a design do you put in the crust?" June asked. "My mom makes one that looks like a wheat stalk."

"I do too," Lydia said. "But make sure you brush some melted butter onto the crust to help it brown. If one of you girls will help, I think it might be good to make four more chocolate pies as well. There's a lot of stirring that goes into a chocolate pie."

The competence of these girls would have been surprising to most Englisch people, but each one had been working beside their mothers since they were toddlers. Each one was capable of creating a good meal for a large family with little or no help. Rachel thought that maybe, if today went well, she would talk to Naomi about the possibility of having a section of home economics—taught by Aunt Lydia—each afternoon after school, for which the girls would get paid.

"We need more firewood," a girl named Violet said. She sailed out the back door, came back in with a small armload, and expertly stacked inside the firebox.

Amish teenagers. Some of the most competent people on earth. It was the perfect answer. Rachel could kick herself for not thinking of it earlier.

"Butter," Lydia instructed. "Make sure each apple pie has one half cup of butter sliced into the apple slices. No more no less. Nice apple slices, Flora. Thin but not too thin. Just right. Rachel, go get that sugar and cinnamon. Some more baker's chocolate too. I think maybe Joe won't run out of pies tonight after all."

Anna stood up from the stool where she'd been watching, wide-eyed in the corner.

"Can I come with you, Rachel?"

"Of course," Rachel said.

"Me, too," Bertha said. "I could use a cold soda pop right now. Never did care much for cooking."

Going to Cleveland was not going to be an option today, but today had been an emergency. Worse things had happened in their family than Lydia falling apart from too much baking, but there hadn't been many.

Chapter Fifty-Six

....

Ed was leaning back in his chair, drumming on his desk with his fingers again as Rachel came in. He did that when he was in deep thought, especially when the thought was not a good one. One could almost tell what kind of a mood Ed was in by how fast his fingers drummed. This time, he was drumming very slowly, which meant that he was troubled and trying to work something out in his head.

"We got the DNA results back," he said.

"That was awfully fast," Rachel said. "Gertie's lawyer must have really lit a fire under them. Cassie was hoping that asking for the DNA test would buy her a little more time to research and prepare."

"I don't think we're going to need Mike's wife for this," Ed said.

"What are you talking about?"

"Tony is not the father of Lily's baby," Ed said.

This news was so unexpected, it felt as though a bomb had gone off in the room.

"But... that means Gertie can't sue us anymore. She has no connection to the baby whatsoever." Rachel's mind spun with the ramifications of what Ed had just revealed. "No lawsuits. No more threats over custody. Gertie is not going to be happy about this, but what a relief for Keturah and Ivan!"

Ed wasn't smiling. Something was wrong.

"So, who is Holly's father, Ed?"

"A gang member by the name of Dane Richardson."

"Dane..." she sorted through her mind. Where had she heard that name before?

Then she remembered and her heart plummeted.

"Dane is Tony's killer."

"Yes."

"Let me guess. Now *Dane* wants the baby? Or maybe he has some horrible relative waiting in the wings to take her?"

"I have no idea what Dane wants," Ed said. "They haven't found him yet."

"So what do we do now?"

"It's a long shot," Ed said, "but I called a reporter I know. He's doing a quick human interest piece on this. It should be on the six o'clock news tonight. If Dane is in the area, he might see it."

"What's this going to accomplish?" Rachel said.

"I'm gambling that it'll shake something loose. Maybe someone knows something. Maybe someone will turn Dane in. Maybe nothing. Your guess is as good as mine."

***

Rachel called Adrian Stephenson, Gertie's lawyer and gave him the news about the DNA. He took it well, but seemed unhappy about having to be the one who would have to break it to Gertie. He suggested she keep his contact information in case she was ever in need of a good lawyer.

Then she stopped by the Hochstetlers and informed them that they could bring Holly out of hiding because the DNA had shown that Tony's mother no longer had any claim on the baby. They promised to go over to Michael's and let him and Cassie know.

She watched the six o'clock news. The reporter got most of the story right.

Joe brought home supper—leftovers from the restaurant. They listened to Bobby chatter about school while they ate, then Joe put Bobby to bed. Once Bobby was asleep, they had some ice cream while they discussed Darren's latest plan to build a small, bare-bones pie-baking building in the back of the Sugar Haus Inn. He wanted to employ Amish girls for a couple hours after school each day to make pies under Lydia's supervision.

They went to bed, but she could not sleep.

Then her cell phone rang.

"This is Rachel," she said.

"Did I wake you?" She recognized Mabel's voice.

"Unfortunately, no."

"Good. I think you'd better come up here," Mabel said.

"Why?"

"I don't want to explain on the phone," Mabel said. "Just come."

"I'll be getting there in the middle of the night," Rachel said.

"I know." The old woman's voice quavered. "Please, Rachel. Please just come."

"Okay, Mabel. Calm down. I'm leaving now."

"What's going on, babe?" Joe mumbled, from his side of the bed.

"Police stuff," she said, sliding out of bed. "You go back to sleep."

He already had. Running a restaurant was not easy. Joe slept like a rock most nights.

She put on her uniform, slipped her Glock into her shoulder holster, a small Smith & Wesson Airweight .38 into her ankle holster, and slid a knife into her pocket. If she was going to Mabel's in the middle of the night, she felt it was best to go armed.

There was so little traffic on the road at this time of night that she made it to Mabel's in record time.

Once she pulled into Mabel's driveway, she checked in all directions, and then slid warily out of the car. She didn't know what to expect but, in this neighborhood, bad things could happen. Especially after dark.

She went to the front door. Knocked. Waited for the telltale lifting of the blinds, which didn't happen. Instead, Mabel came straight to the door and unlocked it.

"I'm glad you came, Rachel." Instead of wary, the old woman seemed worried and agitated. "Someone here needs to talk to you."

When Rachel followed Mabel into the small living room, a young man stood up. He pretty much filled the space, dwarfing the furniture with his size. Muscular. Built like a refrigerator...

"I'm Dane Richardson," the man said. "I was Tony's bodyguard."

"I remember you," she said. "I remembering wondering why Tony needed a bodyguard."

"When you move as much product as Tony, you need a bodyguard."

"Product as in...?"

"Tony didn't care what he did as long as he made money."

"Like his mother then."

"I guess so. In a way." He kept shifting his weight from foot to foot, as though trying to decide whether to stay or flee.

"What can I do for you, Dane?"

"You have my little girl?"

"Baby Holly? No. She's with some people who are taking good care of her."

"I didn't know she was mine until tonight. Me and Lily... we weren't together much."

"Okay." She evaluated his size and strength, and was grateful she had come armed. She would be no match for this man otherwise. "Look, Dane. I have to ask you something. You were in the military. I looked up your records this afternoon. You were a model soldier. You had job skills. You didn't have to come back here after you served your time. So, why did you?"

"My brother and Tony grew up together. Tough guys. Both of them. I was just the kid brother hanging out with them. Then my brother got shot and Tony kinda stepped in and became my family after that. A kid needs a family. You grow up like me and my brother, you make a family out of anything you got, even if it's just a bunch of other kids like you. Except there was something wrong with Tony. He could do something good for you, then turn around and be scary mean. No predicting."

"But you weren't a kid anymore. You could have gone anywhere."

"Once a Ghost, always a Ghost. If you weren't loyal to the gang, Tony got mad. Besides, me and Lily fell in love. We didn't mean to. I knew she was Tony's. Had to be careful so no one knew. We wanted to leave but Tony would have killed us both, or had someone else do it. But I had to stay. To watch over Lily. Make sure Tony didn't hurt her."

His eyes looked strangely haunted in an otherwise strong face.

"What happened the night she ran away?"

"Tony was crazy angry that night," Dane said. "He thought he'd been double-crossed by one of our soldiers and was taking it out on everyone. I told her to get out of there and I would stay behind. I figured if I stuck close to Tony, didn't leave his side, it would give her time to get out, get away, and have her baby in peace. If he went after her, I would be there to keep him from it."

"You would make two of Tony," Rachel said.

"I do now," Dane said. "But when you grow up scared of someone, you tend to stay scared of them. Size didn't protect you from Tony."

"So, why did Lily come to Sugarcreek?"

"It was that newspaper story Mabel says you found. Lily must have read it a hundred times. She liked the part about how you went after the kidnappers when they took your little boy. I think she thought you might be the kind of person who could help her if she could just get to you. I think, when she ran, it was the only place she thought it would be safe to go."

"Did she have any family?"

"No one she ever wanted to see again."

"Do you know who or where her family is?"

"She wouldn't tell even me."

"The Cleveland cops say you killed Tony. Your DNA was found at the scene."

"Tony didn't give me much of a choice."

"How's that?"

"After Lily died, I didn't want to be part of the gang no more. I figured I'd done enough. I was sick of it. I went to Tony and told him I wanted out. He didn't like that. He went off on me."

"Off?"

"He came at me with a knife. Said there was only one way to leave the Ghosts and that was to become a real one. Tony was always good with a knife."

"What happened?"

"I was better."

"All that, just because you wanted to leave the group?"

"Yeah, but that wasn't the only thing we had been arguing about. I was worried about Lily's baby. I wanted Tony to sign those papers you talked about so she could get adopted by some nice family. He didn't want to."

"Why?" Rachel said. "He seemed almost ready to when we were at the morgue."

"That was before his mom got hold of him. After Gertie found out about the baby and learned what had happened, she got all excited. Said she thought she knew a way to make money off the kid. You'd have to know her. Gertie stays awake nights trying to figure out how to get money out of people."

"The couple times I saw her, she seemed high on something."

"Pills. Tony used to complain that she eats them like candy."

"You're wanted for murder, Dane," Rachel said. "You know that, right?"

"Yeah."

"I'm a cop. You know I have to arrest you… if I can."

"You probably can't." His voice was matter-of-fact. "I'd have to let you, but you need to let that wait for now. This thing with Tony isn't why I needed to talk to you."

"Okay," Rachel said. "I'm listening."

"I'm that baby's girl's daddy, right? For sure?"

"DNA lab said so."

"Remember when you thought Tony was the father, you told him he could sign papers that would give her to someone else? Right? Make it legal?"

"Yes," Rachel said. "I remember."

"I'm her daddy, but I can't take care of her good. Not now, probably not ever. Me and my brother, we bounced around in foster care until we aged out. I don't want my little girl to go through that. I want her to have a real family."

Rachel was impressed. "I'll call the social worker. There are lists of people hoping for a baby. You could probably have some say in choosing…"

She stopped. Dane seemed to be getting agitated.

"What?" she said.

"That newspaper story said you nearly died trying to protect your husband's son. Is that right?"

"He's also *my* son," Rachel corrected him.

"Right," Dane said. "I been thinking. I figure if you can love a step-kid so much that you would protect him with your life, you could feel the same way about another kid—like an adopted daughter."

It took a moment for her to realize what he was saying. The realization made her dizzy.

"I—I need to sit down," Rachel knees went weak, and she felt for the armchair beside her and sank into it.

Mabel hobbled into the kitchen to get her a glass of water.

"Here," Mabel said. "You've had a shock."

If Dane had had any sense, he would have run right then and she would have been unable to catch him. In fact, she wasn't certain she could even stand up unassisted right now.

"Let me get this straight," she said, as the dizziness passed. "Are you offering to allow me to adopt your daughter?"

"I think Lily would really like that," Dane said. "A lot. I like it too. The thing of it is, I need to get this taken care of before I go to jail. The Ghosts are everywhere and I'm not bulletproof. When you come up the way me and my brother did, you don't expect to live past twenty. I've made it to twenty-six. That's, like, pretty good."

And Rachel thought that the Amish were fatalistic. This sort of mindset broke her heart.

"You came back here, knowing you'd have to give yourself up and put yourself at risk—just to make sure your baby would be taken care of?"

The big man shrugged his massive shoulders. "She's my daughter," as though that answered everything.

She was still trying to wrap her head around what was happening. She and Joe were going to have a daughter? Bobby was going to have a little sister?"

"I want her to be safe," Dane said. "I don't know nobody else I can give her to who will keep her safe and raise her right. Nobody."

A baby. She was going to have a baby.

She glanced up. There were tears streaming down Mabel's cheeks, but Dane was looking confused.

"Did I do something wrong?" Dane asked.

She had never hugged a fugitive before, but she did now. She stood up, walked over to him, and hugged him as tight as she could, even though her arms only went halfway around him.

"I'm going to love your little girl so much," she said. "And my husband, Joe… he's a really good man. He'll be so kind to her. And our Bobby has been begging for a little brother or sister. He has such a tender heart. She'll have a wonderful big brother, I have three aunts who are going to be so happy to have another child in the family, and…"

"It's going to be okay then," he said, patting her shoulder. "I'm doing the right thing. My little girl will have a real family."

"I'll do the best I can to protect you too, Dane," she said.

He smiled down at her and shook his head sadly, as though he knew the reality too well.

"So—do you know how to do this?" he asked. "Make it all legal and everything?"

"I know someone who does," she said. "Just give me a second."

She pulled out her cell phone, and her finger hovered over the numbers as she got ready to call Cassie… who was sick. Cassie who would have to get dressed first—always painful right after surgery. Cassie who would have to make the long trip up here.

She changed her mind. Maybe, instead, she would call the second-best attorney to graduate from OSU law school the year that Cassie graduated. Adrian Stevenson had said to call if she ever had need of a good lawyer. Her guess was that he had more knowledge about guardianship, or adoption, than Cassie. He might even have the papers already. Plus, he lived close. It was in the middle of the night, but any lawyer who was hungry enough to hire themselves out at a flea market wouldn't let a little thing like being called in the middle of the night to stop him from getting work.

Adrian picked up on the first ring.

"This is Rachel," she said. "Remember when you said to call you if I ever needed a good lawyer? Well, something extraordinary has just happened..."

Chapter Fifty-Seven

It was a Saturday night, and Keturah and Ivan were doing something rather rare for them. They were sitting side by side, holding hands, doing absolutely nothing, and they were completely alone. Keturah had washed her hair for church services in the morning, and it was drying, unbound, loose and flowing down her back.

Their *ordnung* specified that women should not cut their hair, but Keturah suffered with headaches when her hair grew too long. Since Ivan was the only one who ever saw her with it loose, he gave her his husbandly permission to cut it off halfway down her back, although he had a strong suspicion that she would have done it with or without his permission. His father had once told him that sometimes it was wise to give one's wife permission to do the thing she would do anyway.

She kept it just long enough to pin up beneath her kapp. He cut it for her with her sewing scissors whenever she asked. It was their secret that he did this.

It was good for a husband and wife to have a few secrets, he thought. She knew where he put their extra money when there *was* any extra. He knew she always kept a package of miniature candy bars hidden away in her top drawer. Keturah was a disciplined woman but, sometimes at night, she would lay abed for a while and read and, sometimes while doing so, she would allow herself to have a small treat. He did not tease her about this, nor did she tease him about his need to keep a mason jar of money buried in the barn.

Another secret between them was that she loved to have her head rubbed when her hair was down. Tonight, he patted his lap. "Come, sit here. Lean against me and let me rub your head."

She had always been a tiny woman. He often wondered how she had done all the heavy work she had accomplished over the years, let alone giving birth to three big boys. Already in her nightgown, she easily moved onto his lap and lay her head against his chest.

They had been young when they married. She had been seventeen. He had been eighteen. They had seen no issue with this at the time. He had inherited land and knew how to farm. She had been well-trained by her mother in domestic chores and knew how to run a house. She often came out to the fields with him to help harvest or plant. If company was coming, he knew how to sweep the floor and help ready the house. They helped each other and it had worked.

Their love for each other had deepened so much over the years, he hardly knew where he stopped and where she began, so close were they in spirit and mind.

He began to gently massage her head and neck. She leaned into it, making small groaning noises as he expertly found the knots that formed when she had been under too much stress for too long.

Nearly fifty years they had lived together, in lean times and in plenty, and yet he could count on one hand the arguments they'd had. His other two sons had married women with as much character and faith as their mother. Noah—well, he wasn't sure about Noah. He hoped the bishop was right about Beth beginning to turn away from her rebellious ways.

He wasn't surprised when Keturah said something that made him see that her mind was going in much the same direction.

"Would you have stayed Amish, had I not?" she asked.

He gave this some thought as he moved his hand down to work

between her shoulder blades, another spot that often bothered her.

"I would not have left the church, but I would not have been as content with anyone else."

"That's what I thought. Michael's wife was asking me today to tell her the secret of our long marriage."

"Oh? It's good that she is asking. What did you say?"

"I told her that, from what I'd seen, one of the main ingredients to most strong marriages was kindness. I said that so many divorces and troubles could be avoided if people could just manage to be kind to each other."

"Wise words." He finished the massage and pulled her close, kissing the top of her head. "I would agree with that."

"Is Rachel enjoying her new baby?"

"Oh, yes. Agnes and I went over there today. Little Clara was missing her 'doll baby.' Agnes and I had a good, long talk with Rachel about how to care for an infant. She had many questions."

"Was Agnes missing Holly as well?"

"A little, but I think she is also relieved. It is hard caring for two infants at once."

"And soon, we will have Betty and Reuben's little one to hold. Our family is growing, Keturah." He kissed her neck. She smelled clean and sweet from the lavender oil she always put in her bath. His heart swelled with love for her, and with gratitude for his family. "God is good."

"He is," Keturah said. "Even during the times when it seems like He has forgotten."

***

Cassie was napping on the couch when Michael came home late. "Did I wake you?" Michael pulled off his boots inside the door. "I'm sorry. I had a last-minute surgery. Jeff Furman's dog got hit by a car. The poor thing had a punctured lung."

"Were you able to save him?"

"Yes. He'll be okay. Sweet dog. Licked my hand even though he was in pain."

He sat down at the end of the couch and pulled her feet onto his lap.

"How are you?" he asked. "How has your day gone?"

"I'm continuing to feel stronger, but today wore me out a little."

"What happened?"

"Rachel came by and brought Bobby and the baby with her."

"How did that go?"

"Great. You never saw a woman so happy about a child. She was positively glowing. Bobby was adorable, trying to help his mother change the baby's diapers. He was also practically bouncing off the walls before they left. That child has a *lot* of energy. Just watching him about wore me out, but Rachel and I had a good visit."

"I'm glad," he said. "It feels a little chilly in here, would you like for me to start a fire in the fireplace? It's been awhile since we got to just sit together and watch a fire."

"That would be nice," she said. "I'll go make you a sandwich while you bring the wood in."

"Do you feel up to doing that?"

"A sandwich? Yes. Besides, it will make me feel better to do something for *you*, for a change."

By the time she got the sandwich made, and took it and a glass of milk into the living room, Michael had prepared the fire. He had put some of the contents of his paper shredder in the middle, had placed the kindling on top of it, and had a couple of logs ready to lay on it once he got it started.

She placed his sandwich and milk on the mantel and stooped to pick up a couple shreds of thick parchment paper he had dropped on the floor. It looked vaguely familiar. She looked closer and saw just enough words that she could identify what it was.

"You shredded the divorce papers?" she asked.

"Yes." He struck a match.

"When?"

"Before I went to Columbus to see you."

"Before you knew I was sick?"

"Yes."

"Why?"

He blew on the flame until it consumed the nest of paper and began to lick at the kindling. Then he placed the two logs on top. When he was satisfied with the fire, he stood up and said, "I destroyed the papers because I had no intention of signing them. I went to Columbus to let you know that I did not intend to lose you without a fight."

"And now?" she asked. "How do you feel now?"

He brushed his hands off on his pants. "I still don't intend to lose you without a fight."

"Even after my surgery?" she said. "A lot of men would run. A lot of men *do* run."

"I have no desire to run from you," Michael said. "And I never will. I won't lose you again, Cassie."

She did not realize she was holding her breath, but she was. It was not so much in the words he had said—anyone could say words—it was the total acceptance she heard in his voice and saw in his face. Michael was no actor. What you saw was what you got, and the only thing she saw in his face was love.

Then he ruined it.

"By the way, Ohio State University called today. I contacted them awhile back. They're offering me a position of instructor in their veterinarian college."

"You turned it down, right?"

"No, I told them I would take it."

Cassie was stunned. "You can't teach there and work here."

"I called Doc Peggy today—that veterinarian over at Millersburg. Remember how I mentioned that her daughter graduated from vet school recently. Peggy jumped at my offer."

"Your offer?"

"To take over Doc Taylor's practice."

"I'm confused," Cassie said. "You love your job. Why would they need to do that?"

"The months we spent apart just about killed me, Cassie. I enjoy living here and working here, but it isn't worth it if you are unhappy. I've also made arrangements to list the house. The sale of the farm will keep us afloat for a long time, you won't have to work again until you're completely well."

"Let me see if I understand," Cassie said, flatly. "You've accepted a position at Ohio State University, made arrangements to sell your practice, and listed this wonderful old house without bothering to mention any of this to me?"

"Yes." He looked at her quizzically, as though puzzled by her tone of voice. "I thought it would make you happy."

"You insufferable jerk!" Cassie was surprised at how angry she felt. "How dare you make such decisions without consulting me?"

"Now I'm the one confused," Michael said. "Why are you so mad? This is *exactly* what you said you wanted a few months ago. You were even willing to divorce me when I refused to go along with it."

"Things have changed."

"How?"

"I've been making my own plans," Cassie said. "I was going to live here with you, and get to know Ivan and Keturah and her daughters-in-law better. Agnes and Betty are so nice and they know things I want to learn. I thought I would look into retooling my law degree and maybe start using it to advocate for children. And I was going to study Pinterest and go to antique stores and flea markets and redecorate this house into something really stunning. Once I beat this disease—and I *will* beat it—I wanted to live. Really live. I was going to be happy, Michael. And now you're going to spoil it all."

Michael looked at her with wide eyes while she ranted. When she stopped, he stared at her for a moment, then he began to chuckle and, the next thing she knew, he was lying back against the couch holding his stomach and laughing so hard he was crying.

She was still indignant. "What's so funny?"

"*You* are, Cassie. For such an educated woman, sometimes you are a hoot!"

"Don't laugh at me."

"I can't help it." He sobered up and wiped his eyes. "I guess I'll have to call Ohio State back, decline that teaching job, tell Peggy that my offer is no longer valid, and start... I don't know... living my life here with you. It takes me awhile, but eventually I do figure things out."

***

It was three in the morning and baby Holly would not stop crying. Rachel had fed her, and diapered her, and rocked her. Joe had seen that his wife was nearly dead from exhaustion, had sent her to bed, and took over.

Joe had the baby in his arms now, walking the floor. His new daughter did not have a fever, and she was much too young to be cutting teeth. Nothing seemed to be wrong except apparently it was her time to cry. He remembered Bobby being much the same at that age.

Bobby. That child was so funny. He had peeked outside his bedroom door, squinting like an old man and begged him to please make the baby stop crying. When Joe said he was trying and not succeeding, Bobby marched out in his Spiderman underwear, grabbed a pair of headphones, put them on, then marched back into his bedroom and slammed the door.

Bobby didn't mind waking Joe and Rachel at the crack of dawn, but apparently he didn't like having his own sleep disrupted.

Slowly, as Joe walked back and forth across the floor, the baby calmed down. Finally, when she had been silent for several minutes and he was fairly certain she was asleep, he sat down with her in his arms and simply admired his new daughter.

Their household was in complete chaos, Rachel was worn to a frazzle, Bobby was having to make some major adjustments, and Joe would probably be nodding off at work tomorrow—all because of this tiny scrap of humanity.

She was worth it all.

Too soon, she would be out of the baby stage. She would start crawling, then talking and walking. He would have the honor of getting to teach her and love her through her little girlhood and through her teens. Eventually, he would get to walk her down the aisle at her wedding. She was going to be such a bright strand woven into the fabric of their lives.

Apparently, he had spent entirely too much time around Rachel's Amish relatives and neighbors. Here he was with a growing family that he wasn't even sure if he could adequately support—but he had never been happier.

He had a daughter, and a son, and a wife he loved more than himself. He had a thriving restaurant, more good friends than he could count, and his rift with his brother had been healed.

It was amazing to think that all these good things had happened solely because his truck broke down three years ago in this remarkable place called Sugarcreek.

Author's Note

....

My son, Caleb, once worked as an English teacher in the Ohio juvenile justice system. He was taught many things, including how to defend a student against another student's attack, how to disarm a boy coming at him with a homemade knife, and how to teach without using many of the aids most teachers take for granted—like pencils—because they could be used as weapons.

The only thing he could not learn was how to keep his heart from being broken as he helped individual boys study for their GED exams and listened as they privately told him about their fear of the gangs' young "godfathers" and the possible repercussions if they did not do everything their godfather said to do. He learned that these street gangs, in spite of their ruthlessness, often filled the need for family in a boy's life.

As he told me about what he was learning of street gang culture, I could not help but compare it to the Amish and their family-centric view on life. The Amish are a flawed people, but there is never a vacuum of family in an Amish person's life. Next to God and the church, taking care of one's family is the most important element in the Amish culture. Few decisions are made by individuals or leaders of the church without first evaluating how it will affect their families.

I thought it would be interesting to create a story in which Rachel would have to work within both cultures in order to save a child. As always, I thoroughly enjoyed giving my heroine a happy ending.

-Serena

About the Author

Serena B. Miller decided to get serious about writing fiction while she was working as a court reporter in Detroit and found herself developing an overwhelming desire to compose a happy ending for every transcript she typed. She and her minister-carpenter husband live in a southern Ohio farming community, in an 1830s log cabin that has been in her family for five generations. Serena was delighted when an Amish community formed not far from her home, and she has enjoyed getting to know these hard-working people. When she isn't canning tomatoes, splitting firewood, shooing deer out of the blueberry bushes, or feeding grown sons who drop by daily to see if she's cooked anything good, she helps out at her church and sings at the drop of a hat. She also falls in love with all her characters and writes as many happy endings for them as she can.

www.serenabmiller.com

More books by
Serena B. Miller

LOVE'S JOURNEY IN SUGARCREEK:

Love's Journey in Sugarcreek: The Sugar Haus Inn - Bk I

Love's Journey in Sugarcreek: Rachel's Rescue - Bk II

Love's Journey in Sugarcreek: Love Rekindled - Bk III

LOVE'S JOURNEY ON MANITOULIN ISLAND:

Love's Journey on Manitoulin Island: Moriah's Lighthouse - Bk I

Love's Journey on Manitoulin Island: Moriah's Fortress - Bk II

Love's Journey on Manitoulin Island: Moriah's Stronghold - Bk III

THE UNCOMMON GRACE SERIES (AMISH):

An Uncommon Grace - Bk I

Hidden Mercies - Bk II

Fearless Hope - Bk III

MICHIGAN NORTHWOODS SERIES (HISTORICAL):

The Measure of Katie Calloway - Bk I

Under a Blackberry Moon - Bk II

A Promise to Love - Bk III

SUSPENSE:

A Way of Escape

COZY MYSTERY:

The Accidental Adventures of Doreen Sizemore

NON-FICTION:

More Than Happy: The Wisdom of Amish Parenting

VISIT **SERENABMILLER.COM** TO SIGN UP FOR
SERENA'S NEWSLETTER AND TO CONNECT WITH SERENA.

Made in the USA
Coppell, TX
08 March 2020